"Dance with ...... **d hi**.........

Falcon led her out onto the floor, pulled her closer than was proper, his hand at her back guiding her firmly. She caught her breath in surprise, but couldn't find the will to draw away from him.

"No one else held me this close," she said breathlessly.

"Good." His green eyes glittered darkly. "Make sure no one else does. I'd hate to have to kill a man over you." His voice had hoarsened, but there was something almost careless in his tone despite his savage words, as if killing a man over her was something he wouldn't hesitate to do.

Victoria lifted her chin, her confusion lending her a flash of spirit. "You don't own me."

"Don't I?"

"No!" she snapped.

Falcon smiled slowly, and when he spoke, his voice was low. "I will, Victoria. I'll brand you so completely mine that other men will see it from ten feet away. . . ."

THE DELANEYS, THE UNTAMED YEARS

Golden Flames

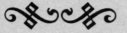

Kay Hooper

BANTAM BOOKS

TORONTO · NEW YORK · LONDON · SYDNEY · AUCKLAND

GOLDEN FLAMES
A Bantam Book / May 1988

ISBN 0-553-21899-9

Published simultaneously in the United States and Canada

Bantam Books are published by Bantam Books, a division of
Bantam Doubleday Dell Publishing Group, Inc. Its trademark,
consisting of the words "Bantam Books" and the portrayal of a
rooster, is Registered in U.S. Patent and Trademark Office and in
other countries. Marca Registrada. Bantam Books, 666 Fifth
Avenue, New York, New York 10103.

PRINTED IN THE UNITED STATES OF AMERICA

O   0 9 8 7 6 5 4 3 2 1

To my friends, Iris and Fayrene. Thanks.

I

1

Falcon Delaney drew his glass toward him and, with the other hand, reached for the gold coins lying on the bar. As soon as the coins lay in his palm he went still, staring at his drink. The loud noise around him in the dingy waterfront barroom faded, and he felt his breath quicken as excitement stirred in his veins.

Christ, he thought then, *this thing is beginning to affect me the way a beautiful woman would!*

Some would have called it obsession. Falcon called it duty.

Ignoring the fight going on in one corner and the loud beginnings of another nearby, he slid his gaze to his hand and slowly opened the long fingers. And his eyes focused, as if on a lodestar, on a single, dully gleaming coin.

A three-dollar gold piece.

After a moment, his expression betraying no undue interest, he picked the three-dollar piece from his palm and placed it on the bar. Then he dropped the remaining coins into his pocket and fished out a five-dollar gold piece, placing it on the bar also.

"Sam," he said quietly.

The bartender, five feet away in a very noisy room, heard the summons instantly, and responded by moving quickly to stand across the bar. Busily wiping the stained wood with an equally stained cloth, he stole a glance at the lean, powerful man who had called him. "Yes, sir?" Not many rated a "sir" in Sam's establishment, but he bestowed it on this stranger automatically.

One long finger tapped a coin gently. "Do you recall who paid with this coin, Sam?"

Sam looked at the coin, then darted another glance at the stranger's face. "Well, sir—"

The stranger's free hand pushed a five-dollar gold piece across the bar. "Think hard, friend," he invited gently in his soft voice.

Sam was tough enough to have survived a good many years on the waterfront. He was also smart enough to know what was necessary in order to spend a few more years there. "Yes, sir, I remember." He kept his voice low, even though no one was near the stranger.

"Do you know him?"

"No, sir, not really. He's been in here once or twice. He's here now."

Falcon removed his hand from the five-dollar gold piece and pocketed the other. "Describe him. And tell me where he's sitting now."

"He's sitting by the front window, alone. Mean-looking bastard. Black eye patch and a scar down the other cheek."

"No one has asked about the coin or him tonight, have they, Sam?"

Sam met the mild, green eyes steadily. "No, sir. No one at all. I never saw that coin."

Falcon drew out a thin cigar and became wholly absorbed in lighting it. "Thank you, Sam," he murmured.

Sam swept the five-dollar gold piece neatly off the bar and moved away, expressionless.

Drawing strongly on the cigar, Falcon allowed smoke to veil his eyes and half-turned to glance casually around the room. He spotted the man instantly—sitting alone by the window, powerful shoulders hunched as he stared moodily down at his drink.

Falcon watched him without appearing to, his mind speculating. One coin. Hardly basis enough for an arrest. But the man was about the right age, and, God knew, any leads at all had been few and far between.

He was marking time tonight, or had been until he saw the coin. Word had come from another agent that the list had finally been assembled, so that, finally, they would know the men who had composed the circle of power out of Charleston. But Falcon had grown bored with waiting, and had spent the afternoon down at the waterfront. There would be no harm, he decided now, in keeping an eye on this man.

Falcon thought of the long years, the fruitless search for a million dollars in gold. He thought of trails ending in nothing. He thought of the years he had spent in Texas as a Ranger, searching, always searching for some hint of a gold shipment stolen by rebels years before.

Almost ten years of his life spent searching.

Unconsciously, his jaw hardened, and something inside him hardened too. This was the first time he had stumbled across one of the specially minted coins, the first time he might be able to question a man who'd possessed one. Keep an eye on him? Hell, no. This time, he meant to take full advantage of the kiss of luck. This time, he meant to get some answers.

Falcon finished his drink and cigar leisurely, watching the man unobtrusively. And he speculated. Why, he wondered for the thousandth time, had so few of those coins found their way into circulation? And why had this one turned up after so many years?

Even in the turmoil of war, it had been relatively simple to determine that almost none of the stolen shipment had been used in payment for anything; after April of '63 there had been no evidence that the Confederacy had been in possession of the money. In fact, after that time, the gold had disappeared. There had been only a few of the specially minted coins changing hands during the war . . . and then nothing.

They had heard rumors from their spies in the South, rumors of a falling-out among the thieves. Rumors of treachery. But none of the spies had been able to get anywhere near the secretive group believed responsible for the theft. It was only now, after years, that they had been able to piece together certain facts.

And now . . . this lone coin. None knew better than Falcon how unwise it was to trust in coincidence, and he was bothered by the coin turning up. It had been years since any of the coins had come to light—and then it had been only a handful, un-traceable.

Was he assuming too much? Did he believe this coin was a valuable piece of evidence only because he *wanted* it to be?

He had heard other, older agents talking from time to time about the "hellish cases". Those assignments that dragged on, year after year, with no progress, and the plodding work that continued with no end in sight. That kind of thing destroyed good men. Face a man with a gun, Falcon knew, and it would all be over quickly—one way or another. But a case such as this one—obscure, clouded by the chaos of wartime, the trails going colder by the year—yes, it could wear a man down.

Out of the dozens of agents who had begun this search, only a handful remained.

Pushing the speculation from his mind, Falcon's eyes narrowed as he watched the man by the window check his watch and then rise and purpose-fully leave the barroom.

Instantly, Falcon slid away from the bar and made his way through the crowded room, hardly noticing that hardened waterfront denizens gave way before him as though by instinct.

Sam noticed. On the whole, he was glad he had answered the stranger's questions.

The waterfront was alive with noise and dark-ness; Falcon ignored the noise, and the darkness was an old friend. He moved easily and silently from one patch of gloom to the next, his eyes never leaving the man striding along some distance ahead.

Would he discover just another hand that had

innocently touched the gold? Would this man tell him he had received the coin in payment, or in change, or that he couldn't remember and what the hell difference did it make?

Another dead-end trail?

Falcon unbuttoned his coat and loosened the gun he wore stuck inside his belt. Out of deference to the city he was visiting, he had chosen not to wear a gun openly; the loose cut of his coat hid this one admirably. He had worn a gun since he was old enough to lift the weight, and not even a "civilized" city could persuade him to abandon the habit.

And no man in his right mind went unarmed at the waterfront.

Intent on his quarry, Falcon almost swore in surprise when the man went into a lighted shop with dusty books displayed in the front window. It was hardly a destination Falcon would have suspected this man to have as his goal, but it wasn't that surprising either. Falcon had known weathered saddletramps who cherished the few books they'd been able to beg or borrow.

So why had his hackles risen like a dog's with the scent of a cougar in the air?

Frowning a little, Falcon hesitated in the shadows of a nearby deserted building. Then, loosening his gun a bit more, he strode quickly to the door of the shop and went inside.

He saw no one for a moment, just shelves and shelves of books. He smelled them, dry and dusty, and—from somewhere outside this room—dampness and mildew. And then he smelled something else; a whiff of lavender, as unexpected and intoxicating as a single flower found blooming in the desert.

She moved into his view, intent on the shelf of books one gloved finger glided along slowly. Her hat was precisely angled, her calico dress neat, her kid boots only a little dusty. Wheat-gold hair was arranged simply, with delicate ringlets lending even more fragility to her exquisite face. She moved with a grace that was totally unconscious and utterly riveting.

And Falcon discovered then that, whatever his obsession with the gold shipment, his reaction to a beautiful woman was quite definitely a thing apart after all. It might have been the sheer unexpectedness of her presence, or perhaps even his heightened senses—but whatever the cause, Falcon had never felt such an instant and total attraction in his life.

For one of the very few times in his adult life, he allowed his emotions to distract him. He couldn't question the man *here*, not with her in the shop, not the kind of questioning he meant to do. He could wait outside . . . but if there was a back entrance? . . . Cursing his own indecision, he finally stepped forward, toward the woman, intending to move on to the rear of the shop and find out if there was another door.

She glanced up, meeting his unconsciously fixed gaze with the greenest eyes he had ever seen. Then those eyes flickered beyond him, widening, and emotion flashed in the depths like sudden, green fire.

And something hard struck him a solid blow just beneath his right ear. He felt the instant wave of sickness as he fell forward, the blinding pain and shock. And he was already losing consciousness as he hit the floor, hearing only dimly a sharp, feminine cry of alarm and the sudden scuffle and thudding of booted footsteps.

Victoria Fontaine picked herself up from the hard floor, aching all over, and reached instantly into the little hidden pocket of her skirt for matches. She struck one and cautiously looked around. A damp cellar. She stood beside a rickety wooden table with a sooty lamp on it. To her relief, she saw there was plenty of oil inside it and lighted the lamp.

The big man lay sprawled at the foot of the steps, just where he had been left, and she carried the lamp over and quickly knelt at his side. A touch assured her that his pulse was strong, and there didn't seem to be any blood. A gentle search of his head with expert fingers located the swollen area beneath his right ear, and experience with the results of such injuries told her he would be unconscious for some time yet. She bit her lip in hesitation for a moment, then left the lamp on the floor beside him and moved lightly up the flight of stairs.

The door at the top was locked, of course. Too thick and stoutly made to be easily dislodged, especially since the stairs were steep and there was no way to find the necessary leverage to force through it. She pressed an ear to the thick wood and listened intently.

"You botched it, you stupid bastard." A low voice, cold and hard. And—familiar?

Victoria frowned. Where had she heard—?

"What was I supposed to do?" another male voice whined. "He followed you from Sam's, and he was goin' to—"

"He followed me?"

"Slid out the minute you left, Read. And he was goin' huntin'—I saw 'im check his gun."

"I took his gun." A third voice—more cultured, but not much. And she knew this voice; she had taken him to be the owner of the shop when she had spoken to him earlier. "He came in, looking around; he didn't see me. But he saw the woman. Looked at her like a starving man at a church picnic. Couldn't take his eyes off her."

After a moment, the cold, hard voice spoke again, thoughtfully this time. "I don't know who he is, but I can't take the chance he knows something. We'd better move out tonight."

"What about the woman?" asked the whiny voice that made Victoria's skin crawl.

"We don't need her."

"Maybe you don't, but I—"

"Shut up."

"She was bustin' out of that dress, Read, and her legs was really somethin'! When her skirts flew up like that, I got a look all the way up her legs. I'd like to crawl between 'em and—"

There was a sharp sound, like the crack of a pistol.

"Aw, Jesus, Read, did you have to—"

"I said, shut up." The hard voice was very soft now. "Buy your whores in whorehouses and leave ladies alone. Try to act like a man. Now, move out. Whoever owns this place can let them out in the

morning. I got the address from the hotel, so we can
go directly to . . ."

Victoria strained to hear the rest, but the footsteps moved away, a door closed loudly, and then
there was silence.

She stood there on the top step for a moment,
considering what she had heard. It was all very
puzzling. She had the odd feeling that she was
more than an innocent bystander in all this, even
though the men had seemed most concerned with
the big man they had knocked out.

The big man . . .

She went back down the stairs, glancing around
once before kneeling beside him again. There were
mildewed books piled here and there, but little else
that she could see. The lamp threw off scant light,
leaving the corners and lower walls in darkness.
She couldn't see so much as a scrap of canvas to
provide a cushion against the cold hardness of the
floor, there were no windows, and there was nothing at all to use in battering against the door at the
top of the stairs.

She checked his pulse again, hesitated, then
sighed and began arranging herself on the floor.
The bottom step, she thought, would have been
much better, but she could hardly drag what she
estimated to be two hundred pounds of unconscious man to the steps and then raise his head and
shoulders. As it was, she found it difficult to raise
him enough for her to wriggle her legs beneath him
and cushion his bruised head in her lap.

The floor was wretchedly cold and hard, but she
managed to fold as much of her dress as possible
underneath her hips, and that helped a bit.

As comfortable as she could be under the circumstances, she absently chose one of Morgan's favorite oaths and murmured, "Bloody hell." Her own voice sounded unnaturally loud in the silence of the cellar, and she sighed again as she looked down at her unwitting companion.

A big man, certainly. Well over six feet, with broad shoulders tapering to a narrow waist and hips, he looked both powerful and fierce in a contained way. He was also, she thought, strikingly handsome, only a curving scar on his left cheekbone marring the good looks. He was dressed casually, all in black; he was clean-shaven, and had thick, black hair. A man who looked to be somewhere in his thirties, and who was handsome in a dark and brooding way. A man who was quite likely dangerous, who had moved like a cat, and whose vivid eyes had—

"Looked at her like a starving man at a church picnic."

Victoria became suddenly conscious of the warm, heavy weight of his head in her lap, and she recalled that moment upstairs when her eyes had met his. She had felt a peculiar sensation—hot and cold and taut. Something in his eyes, something so intense she had felt overwhelmed by it. Something naked.

She realized that her index finger was slowly tracing the crescent scar high on his cheekbone, and hastily moved her hand away. But there was no place she could rest her hands except beside her on the cold floor—or on him. Her left hand came lightly to a stop on his chest. Her right hand hovered uncertainly for a moment until her gloved fingers found the shining thickness of his coal-black hair. She brushed a lock back from his high forehead, and saw that her fingers trembled.

He was a stranger: why did she feel drawn to him, affected by him? Unlike many of the men she had encountered here in the city who were sweetly perfumed, he smelled of horses and tobacco, of sunlight and dusty winds, like the rough western land she had grown to love. He had worn a Peacemaker Colt tucked inside his belt, and the men upstairs who'd taken it off him had been almost instinctively wary of him, she thought shrewdly.

She felt, gazing down upon him, that his voice would be soft and unusually cultured, that he would be polite and well-mannered. He would be a man to whom servants would instantly respond with respect, a man to whom other men would look for leadership in a crisis.

Victoria frowned a little, disturbed. Not since her first meeting with Morgan so many years before had she felt such instant certainty about a man. She looked at the powerful length of him stretched out on the floor, his strength apparent, the danger of him shocking in the small, dark cellar, and her heart gave a peculiar flutter inside her breast.

Falcon, with so many years of danger behind him, didn't awake with a groan of lingering pain or a shiver at the coldness of the floor; even his subconscious guarded him from any sound or action that could prove deadly should an enemy be nearby. Instead, he became slowly aware of the pain and the cold floor, and that something warm and firm cushioned his aching head.

His eyes opened fractionally and, through his lashes, he saw calico material and strands of thread where there should have been buttons, the strained fabric at the top of the gown revealing a hint of golden skin. He became fascinated by the rise and fall of breasts beneath the calico. His eyes opened more, and he saw that the woman was gazing across the room, her face wearing a faint, troubled frown.

From his position, he could see the vulnerable flesh of her neck, the clean line of her jaw, and a bottom lip worried by small white teeth. He took a deep breath, quite unconsciously, aware then that one small hand rested on his chest while the other stroked his hair.

She looked down, green eyes startled as she saw he was conscious, and removed her hands hastily, a wave of lovely color sweeping up her cheeks. Her cheeks . . .

Falcon sat up slowly, fighting dizziness, half-turning to stare at her face. "One of them hit you." His voice, low and raspy, sounded as if it belonged to someone else.

Her eyes followed his hand as it lifted to touch the faint bruise on her cheek just below her eye, but she didn't flinch or try to move away. Instinct told her this man meant her no harm, but experience told her any man's intentions could change in an instant. There was something very male in his eyes, in the tilt of his head, that both attracted her and made her wary. Her gaze returned to his face, and she smiled. "He wasn't pleased when I fought him," she murmured. "And it will be gone by morning."

Realizing that his fingers were brushing over her

satiny skin again and again in a steady rhythm, Falcon forced his hand away from her. Gingerly probing the lump beneath his ear, he asked, "How many were there?"

"Three. One hit you, the second grabbed me. I never saw the third, but I heard him talking later." Partly because she was curious about why he had apparently been following that man, and partly because something in his eyes compelled her, she reported exactly what she had heard—except the last of the conversation upstairs, which had concerned only carnal appetites.

Falcon listened in silence, watching her lovely, serene face and hearing the soft, faintly accented voice. For a lady dumped unceremoniously into a dank cellar with a total stranger, she was extraordinarily calm, he observed. And still. He couldn't remember ever encountering a woman so utterly still. She didn't fidget, her expression remained serene, and the gloved hands folded in her lap might have been carved from marble.

It was obvious that their attackers had treated her roughly. In addition to the bruise on her cheek and the buttons ripped from the bodice of her dress, her hat was gone, and the wheat-gold hair was disarranged so that a single, long braid fell over one shoulder to lie on her breast.

She was incredibly beautiful.

Falcon concentrated on other things. "You say you never saw one of them; can you describe the other two?" he asked finally.

She nodded almost imperceptibly. "The man who hit you was of medium height, slight build, dark-haired. He had a thin face and eyes set close together. Dressed roughly in dirty clothing. The other man was one I took to be the owner of the shop when I came in. He was tall, thin, neatly dressed. Brown hair and eyes."

She was observant, he noted, and realized that the man he had followed from Sam's, the man with the eye patch, must be the third man, the one the other had called Read.

Looking intently at her, he tried to keep his mind on that man and the gold, and had little success. "I'm Falcon Delaney," he said abruptly.

"Victoria Fontaine."

"I'm sorry you were dragged into this, Miss Fontaine." He got to his feet slowly, stretching cramped and aching muscles, literally willing the dizziness he felt to pass.

She started to correct his assumption that she was unmarried, but something kept her silent; her gloved hands hid the gold wedding ring. She didn't tell him she was married. And that frightened her. She felt no disloyalty to Morgan; he would be the last man to condemn her for failing to disclose their relationship.

In any case, it could hardly matter, she told herself. Falcon Delaney would have no further place in her life after they were freed from this cellar. And why should she explain the understanding between her and her husband to this stranger?

But why didn't she just tell him she was married?

After a moment, she said, "It appears the situation was beyond your control, Mr. Delaney. There was nothing you could have done to change the results."

Falcon didn't agree with that. He should have

been more alert, less . . . bewitched . . . by her presence. But he didn't say so, of course. He looked down at her, frowning a little, then looked up toward the top of the stairs.

"It's a solid door," she murmured. "And there's no room at all to get any leverage."

He had the distinct impression that she was right, but climbed the stairs anyway and tested the door. Two minutes convinced him that forcing the door would be impossible. He came back down the stairs. "It looks as if we're trapped here, at least until morning," he said.

Victoria gazed up at him, starkly aware of his size and sheer presence in the small room. And she didn't know whether to be relieved or disturbed to find that her impressions as he lay unconscious had been uncannily accurate. His voice *was* soft and deep, innately polite, and he seemed well-mannered. And though he had no accent, there was a curious cadence to his voice that she found very pleasing. Delaney. Was he Irish?

"I'm sorry, Miss Fontaine," he said again. "Your family will be worried by your absence."

She hesitated. "I'm visiting New York."

"Alone?"

Victoria heard no censure or disapproval in his deep voice, but felt compelled to explain nevertheless. "I'm staying in a very respectable hotel, and there are acquaintances to escort me if I so choose. None of them, however, will expect to see me until tomorrow night."

He frowned, but, after a moment, merely extended his hands to her. "You can't be comfortable," he said.

She found that she was reaching up to accept his help, and rose to her feet feeling a little confused. She couldn't seem to breathe except in shallow gasps, and her heart thudded against her ribs. He was so *big*, so curiously intense. She could sense that in him, feel it as if every nerve in her body had come stingingly alive and aware. He made her think of something wild, some creature wearing composure as a cloak to hide its danger.

What was *wrong* with her?

He didn't release her hands immediately, but stood staring down at her. And his eyes were abruptly shuttered, his face hard.

Like his voice.

"You chose to have no escort while visiting a shop in the worst part of the city? Why, Miss Fontaine? Why did you come to the waterfront tonight?"

2

T here was no reason for his sudden suspicion, except her presence in a part of the city she should never have come to accompanied, far less alone. But in the instant when he had helped her to rise, he had seen something in her eyes, something alien to his impression of a serene lady. He couldn't even put a name to it, but all his instincts told him he had never encountered a woman such as her—and that anything was possible where she was concerned.

And she was *here* tonight. What could a lady such as she want in a shabby waterfront bookshop? It didn't make sense, and Falcon had learned to be wary of events that didn't make sense.

She was looking up at him now, frowning a little, drawing her hands slowly from his grasp. "I was looking for a book," she said. "A particular book."

"At the waterfront?" He could hear his own incredulity. "Without an escort?"

Almost imperceptibly, she stiffened. "I was told I might find the book at this shop, Mr. Delaney. As for the location, I am unfamiliar with the city, and had no idea it was a waterfront address. However, when

20

I arrived here, I chose to go ahead with my search for the book." Her voice remained soft, but there was a chill to it now. "Do you mind telling me what *you* hoped to find here? Those men seemed under the impression that you had followed one of them."

He looked down at her for a long moment. It was absurd, of course. She couldn't possibly be involved. *Involved in what? You're not even sure . . .*

"I did," he said finally, and the hardness had left his voice. "I wanted to question him about—about something that happened a few years ago."

"Something?"

"Something that was stolen. I'm a Texas Ranger." Not *just* a Ranger, of course, but she didn't need to know that.

Her face came alive with curiosity. "I see. Did you follow him all the way to New York?"

"No. Someone pointed him out to me tonight, and even though I'm not officially on duty, I decided to question him." It was enough; he didn't intend to explain himself fully. "And so we were both thrown into a cellar." He smiled suddenly.

Victoria was rather astonished at the effect of his smile. It softened his lean, hard face remarkably, leaving it unnervingly handsome and charming; and it made her legs feel suddenly weak, her skin hot. She looked away hastily, forgetting that she had intended to ask more questions. "Yes, we were," she said in a voice that sounded unusually breathless to her own ears. "Until morning, apparently."

He glanced around, his smile fading but not disappearing entirely. "Not a very comfortable cell."

"No," she agreed, linking her gloved fingers together and gazing down at them, saying no more because she couldn't seem to control the absurd tremor in her throat.

Falcon looked at her downbent head. Since he had dismissed from his mind the man called "Read," and the gold, because there was nothing he could do about either at the moment, his thoughts instantly returned to this woman and the effect she was having on him. He thought inanely that he would feel much more detached about the situation if only she were still wearing her hat. That hat, he thought, had marked her in some obscure way as a lady, and with it gone, and her hair down and her dress torn, only the prim gloves on her small hands were left to remind him she *was* a lady.

He cleared his throat. "Why don't you sit on the steps? It's better than the floor, and I'll try and find something to make us a little more comfortable until morning."

Silently, she followed his advice, going over to the stairs and sitting on the third step. One of her hands went to her bodice and tugged a bit to pull the gaping material together, as if she had only then realized.

Falcon, watching, felt his mouth go dry. He caught a glimpse of the curve of one creamy, golden breast, and turned away quickly to begin exploring their cell. With the feeble glow of the lamp, there was more darkness than light, but he welcomed the gloom, since it hid his body's reaction to her.

For God's sake! What was wrong with him? How many times had he sat in saloons and watched disinterestedly while girls moved all around him with their breasts bared to the nipples? And how many times over the years had he left a bedmate sprawled out naked on tumbled sheets? It wasn't as if the female body held any secrets he hadn't long ago explored.

So why, now, did he feel like some stripling aware of helpless desire for the first time in his life? His body was hot, tensed, throbbing. Sweat beaded his brow despite the chill of the cellar. His mouth was dry, and his heart beat heavily against his ribs. A single, fleeting glimpse of a golden curve framed in calico, and he could scarcely think!

It had been many years since Falcon had been at the mercy of his senses and emotions. Many long years. Rummaging among the stacks of mildewed books, he frowned in concentration, shifting his mind until it focused on this disturbing lapse of his self-control.

And thinking of that led him to think of the struggle to develop control, and why he had made that deliberate decision. Led him to think of home. Surprising himself then, Falcon felt an abrupt stab of longing for Killara—for home. He had seen his home only rarely these last years, in brief visits that had allowed little time to feel the pull of the baked Arizona earth that was a tug at the heart-strings.

It came to Falcon with yet another shock that he was thirty-four years old . . . and that his father was seventy-one. The old man, he realized, *was* an old man. A very old man. And yet, Falcon had never known a man with more life than Shamus. More fire.

It was, Falcon thought, one of the reasons he had

left home so young to make his own way. All the
Delaneys had that fire, and Falcon had felt it
strongly, almost uncontrollably, in himself. He had
known very young that to remain at home was to
invite a confrontation between himself and his
father; they were too alike in temper and too
different in ambition.

Shamus was bent on building an empire, on
forging a family dynasty that would last a hundred
years and more. He was shrewd and tough and not
above manipulating those around him, in the "best
interests" of the family. And though Falcon loved
his family and Killara, he strongly disliked being
forced to do anything by anyone, a dislike that had
made his childhood a battleground between himself and his father.

So Falcon had left at sixteen to scout for the
army, riding away in the night to avoid his father's
anger, and had learned painfully to subjugate his
temper through self-discipline. He could meet his
father—now—with no impulse to disagree or ar-
gue. He could accept Shamus's paternal commands
equably—whether he obeyed them or not. And it
was still, after all these years, more often not. He
could observe with rueful affection the frequently
ruthless methods his father chose to employ in
getting what he wanted. If pressed, Falcon quietly
returned to his solitary life, and so avoided trouble-
some argument.

Falcon felt no guilt at this abandonment of his
family; four of his eight brothers survived—Joshua,
older than Falcon, Dominic, Court, and Sean, the
youngest. He also had sisters-in-law and nephews

and nieces who, with his brothers and parents, made for a large family to people Killara.

Yet, it said something of Shamus that he had shouted after Falcon at the end of his last visit that he wanted more grandchildren, and that it was Falcon's duty to his father to get busy producing some—lawfully, if he didn't mind.

Falcon smiled a little, remembering. To his knowledge, he had produced no children whatsoever. His thoughts returned to Victoria Fontaine, and his smile faded.

Damn. The most powerful love of his life was for home and family, and yet not even that could distract him—except momentarily—from thoughts of her.

He banged his shin violently against a wooden keg with an unwary step, and swallowed a curse.

"Are you all right?" she called softly.

"Fine." He realized he had snapped the response, and tried to relax. But it was impossible. And he railed at himself silently, struggling to damp the violence of his reaction to her. *She's a lady, fool! Not some tart, eager to lay with you in the back room of a saloon. Not a bedmate bought for a single night to ease the ache in your loins. If she's even been kissed, it was by some gent in a decorous moment at a garden party!*

His hands were shaking when he located a rusted iron cot propped against the wall behind some books and drew it into the center of the room. Shaking, for God's sake!

"What's that?"

He set the cot on its legs and carefully probed the straw-filled mattress strapped to it. "A cot. And it hasn't been down here very long, I'd say." He was relieved that his voice emerged calm and casual. "The mattress is fairly clean and dry. More comfortable than the steps or floor, at any rate." He caught the scent of lavender, and knew she had left the stairs to join him.

"I'll get the lamp," he muttered, and turned away to lift it from the floor and set it on the rickety table beside the cot. He saw that she was still standing, and was about to gesture for her to sit down when a rustle and faint squeak near the far wall caught his attention.

It caught hers too.

Victoria didn't start or cry out, but she stiffened.

"Of course there would have to be rats," he said. "The lamp should keep them away from us."

She obeyed his gesture to sit on the cot, but her back remained stiff and her hands were clasped tightly in her lap. Falcon, discovering that his standing position made the view of golden flesh at her bodice all too visible, decided that, for his own peace of mind, he'd better sit as well. "I'm afraid I can't do anything about the chill," he said.

She half-turned her head to look at him, a fleeting look that caught the light of the lamp and made her eyes gleam. "I didn't expect you to, Mr. Delaney. Some things are beyond mortal man."

"Falcon." He smiled. "Improper, but the entire situation is improper. If you had male relatives in the city, I could expect to be called to account for compromising you."

"It was hardly your intention to do so," she pointed out. "And no one will know, in any case, except a shopkeeper who's a stranger."

He had tilted his head a little—watching her, listening to her soft, faintly accented voice. "You're a Southerner?"

She nodded. "I was born in Charleston. But the war . . . I live in New Mexico now."

"Unusual," he commented, "for a Southern lady to live in the territories."

"Not so unusual, I think. The war changed a great many lives."

"I would wager it certainly changed yours."

"You were there?"

"In the South? Afterward."

"Then you were a Union soldier?"

He heard neither resentment nor dislike in her voice, only curiosity. "Yes."

She sighed. "I was too young to understand why the war ever happened. I only wonder how long it will take for those wounds to heal."

"A century or two." He smiled faintly. "We're still a country divided in many ways. And will be, I think, for a long time."

It was something Morgan had said more than once, and Victoria believed it. She shivered, and felt his warmth as he leaned nearer.

"You're cold, Miss Fontaine." He started to remove his coat, but she stopped him with a light touch on his arm.

"No, I'm fine. It was just . . . ghosts out of the past. And my name is Victoria. As you said, it is an improper situation."

He nodded, wondering if she had any idea at all just how bewitching her smile was. Abruptly conscious that his time in the city was limited, and no longer deceiving himself about his interest in this woman, he said slowly, "If we had met at a ball, I might have been stealing a kiss about now."

Her eyes widened, not shocked so much as aware, and she felt the same hot tingle of that first glance upstairs; his eyes were sleepy, darkly green, and something intensely hungry lurked in their depths. In a voice that was breathless, she murmured, "Behind a marble column or in a dark garden?" And she felt shock then, because she had not instantly rebuked him for the familiarity. They were too alone here, too intimate to allow a light flirtation. Yet somehow . . .

"In a dark garden, I think," he said, his voice low and husky, eyes intent. "With the scent of flowers all around us. Do you use lavender soap, Victoria? I smelled the lavender before I saw you, and thought of flowers."

Victoria had never felt so aware, so—trapped. She was caught in his eyes, spellbound, and couldn't breathe. Nothing like this had ever happened to her before, and this man was a *stranger*. All the assurance gained through her years as the wife of a wealthy and cultured man deserted her in a rush, and she felt achingly raw and vulnerable. "I . . . that is, you shouldn't—"

"I know I shouldn't. It doesn't help, knowing I shouldn't. Have men told you how green your eyes are, Victoria? How lovely you are? Of course they have. You've heard all the pretty words since you put up your hair and let down your skirts."

She swallowed hard, and when his gaze dropped slowly, she realized that her torn bodice was gaping again over breasts that felt strangely tender. Instinctively, she reached up a hand to draw the edges together, and when his hand stopped the gesture, they both caught their breath. Holding her gloved hand, his knuckles were pressed against the inner curve of her breast, and his thumb moved slowly to stroke the smooth skin of her breastbone.

"Don't," she whispered, unable to draw away. Aware that his hand trembled. That hers trembled.

He leaned toward her very slowly, bracing himself on the hand lying on the cot just behind her buttocks. The warmth and soft, womanly scent of her was going to his head like old wine, and he felt the swollen throb of his loins even as his lips touched hers. Her fingers tightened almost convulsively around the hand at her breast, and he felt her heart pounding.

Her lips were cool, trembling. His tongue parted them gently, and he felt her start of surprise as he went deeper to explore the wet warmth of her mouth. Not wine, he thought dimly, but a raw, sweet brandy, its taste so sharp and clean that nothing else could ever compare. He felt the tremor that shook her, knowing his own body had answered with a shudder of hot desire, and he fought to remember that she *was* a lady, that he couldn't take her with the careless need of lust. But was it that? Only that?

Victoria had never felt so confused in her life. One moment they had sat calmly talking about the war, and the next moment he was kissing her with intense desire. It was wrong, she knew it was wrong—and yet she couldn't stop it. Waves of heat, each more potent than the last, swept through her body, and she was drowning in the searing pleasure. His knuckles were pressed to her breast, she was *holding* them there, and the sinuous caress of his tongue had ignited a curl of fire deep in her belly.

Her entire body tautened until her breasts hurt and her stomach muscles knotted, and there was an aching heat between her thighs that she had never felt before. And she almost cried out in disappointment when his mouth lifted slowly from hers.

Gazing into her dazed, heavy-lidded eyes, he said hoarsely, "I'm a blunt man, Victoria. I want you."

"No." But the word was only a wisp of sound, no anger or sharp denial pushing it.

"Yes." He kissed her again, lightly this time, and his smile was slow. He had learned patience over the years, and intended to use that patience now in getting her into his bed. He didn't think beyond that. "I'll bow to the dictates of convention—as far as I'm able. I'll try my damnedest to court you like a gentleman. But I can't promise that, Victoria. I want you too much to be very patient for long."

Victoria bit her bottom lip, feeling another wave of heat when his gaze followed the little gesture. She wanted to tell him about herself, to explain Morgan. She had to explain about her marriage to Morgan. But the words wouldn't come. For the first time, she realized that explanations could hardly be as blithely offered as she had supposed.

Would he believe that hers was a marriage of convenience, that Morgan had promised to set her free when another man entered her life? How could she explain? She couldn't, not now. She had to think. . . .

And then she forgot to think, because his hand released hers and slid inside her bodice to surround her breast. She gasped, staring at him, feeling her entire body react feverishly to that bold caress as her nipple rose tautly into his palm.

Falcon's eyes were half-closed, his breathing rough and uneven as he watched her face and felt her breast come alive beneath his touch. His long fingers squeezed gently, just once, and then he slowly withdrew his hand, feeling the tightness of her nipple as his fingers glided over it. He wasn't at all sure he could keep his hands off her for the remainder of the night, but, though her response to him had been immediate, he was all too aware of the innocence in her.

She was no saloon girl who would hike her skirts at the first gleam of a coin, nor was she one of the "ladies" he had encountered from time to time who behaved decorously in public but who were known to bed any man in private.

No, Victoria was different. Young and a lady born, she was confused by her own awakening senses, and unless he handled her carefully, she would shy away from him in fear. He meant to handle her carefully. He hadn't wanted a woman so much in his life.

"I don't know you," she whispered.

"You will," he promised. He rose from the cot, looking down at her. "You should lie down and try to sleep. I'll sit on the steps." He wanted to lie on the cot close to her, to sweep away the material of her bodice and feast on the tempting mounds revealed to his hungry eyes. He wanted to strip her naked and pleasure her until she was writhing in passion, until she eagerly accepted his swollen shaft with her wet heat. And what he wanted gleamed in the vivid depths of his eyes.

Victoria had once watched a rabbit frozen, mesmerized, by the hawk swooping toward it. *Was it like that, then?* she wondered dimly, staring up at him. Staring up at a man so intensely overpowering that she knew she would find no defense against him and the desire he evoked.

"Lie down," he repeated softly, and went over to sit on the steps.

After a moment she did lie down, still trembling and confused by the heat in her body. It had been a long time since there had been a woman in her life to advise her, and she had to wonder if what she was feeling now was something every woman felt. Closing her eyes and feigning sleep, she thought about that, trying to find some answer to the bewildering array of questions that her powerful reactions to this man evoked.

There had been occasions in the past when people had gathered at one of the ranches and socialized, and she remembered now that the wives had talked freely around her, with no suspicion that she and Morgan had never been lovers. As curious as any virginal young woman, Victoria had listened, only smiling shyly when her own opinions had been sought.

Some of the wives, she remembered, had talked darkly of their men's appetites, and of "a woman's duty." But there had also been some who seemed perfectly content with their marital relations. There had been no mention, however, of feelings so violent they left a woman breathless and hot, no mention of the sheer pleasure of an intimate kiss or a warm, rough hand surrounding an aching breast. . . .

Eyes closed, starkly aware that he was only a few feet away and that they were utterly alone, Victoria tried to make sense of it all. He wanted her. He had said that he would court her—but what did he mean by that? Not, she thought, marriage. He didn't have the look of a man who would plan on settling down contentedly with a wife and children. No. He had the look of a lusty man of strong appetites, a wanderer whose relationships with women were quite deliberately brief. He wanted her—in his bed.

And she? What did she want?

Morgan had taught her so much since he had taken her away from Regret, her family's plantation near Charleston. He had been father, friend, and brother, but never lover. That was a part of her life into which he had never ventured, not even to warn her how it would feel. And she realized now that he had deliberately sent her to New York, primarily because every man who met her in New Mexico as Morgan's wife quite logically assumed she was unavailable, and in New York, she could choose whom to meet as an available woman.

Had he realized, she wondered now, that it was time for her to acknowledge her own womanhood? Had he sent her away from the ranch in the hope that she would find a man who made her feel this incredible sense of wonder and excitement? She thought that perhaps he had, for Morgan had always been amazingly perceptive where she was concerned.

But you didn't warn me, Morgan. You didn't warn

*me that I could feel this with a man who wants my
body but not my heart.*

She knew what she should do, of course. In the
morning, when they were released from their pris-
on, she should very briskly and firmly part company with Falcon Delaney and refuse to see him
again. That was what she should do, what any lady
would do. Any decent lady.

Victoria woke with a start, conscious that hours
had passed. She felt stiff and sore from her tumble
into the cellar, and the damp chill of the small
room was making itself felt as well. She sat up
slowly, swinging her feet to the floor, and started in
surprise when he was almost instantly beside her
on the cot; she hadn't even heard him move.

"I'm glad you were able to rest."

Victoria started to respond, but a sudden scurry-
ing noise and the brush of something furry over her
ankle made her turn toward him quickly with a
gasp. "I don't like rats," she said breathlessly, only
then realizing that her hand had reached out to
him, and that she was grasping his upper thigh. His
hand came down over hers before she could move,
holding it strongly against him, and she forgot all
about rats in the stark awareness of hard muscles.
Her gaze lifted quickly to his face, finding it taut
suddenly, his eyes blazing.

"That's one rat I should thank," he said in a
thickened voice.

Victoria tried to pull her hand away, but he held
it easily, and she went still when she realized how
aroused he was. "What—what time is it?" she
asked unsteadily.

"Morning. The shopkeeper should arrive soon." He pulled her hand slightly toward his inner thigh. "Touch me, Victoria. I promise I won't forget you're a lady. The gloves remind me."

"No. I—"

"I watched you sleep." His voice was low, husky. "I sat on those damned steps for hours, watching you. Wanting you. A dozen times I almost woke you."

"Falcon, don't—"

Something flared in his eyes. "I've been wondering how my name would sound on your lips." He didn't attempt to move her hand any farther, but refused to release it, and his thigh was taut and hard beneath her touch. "I like the sound of it, Victoria." In the heat of his own response, it was difficult to gauge her reaction, but Falcon concentrated on that. He would push her as far as he dared, because he knew only too well that, unless he made her fully aware of the desire between them, she would send him firmly on his way once they were freed from the cellar.

She licked her lips nervously. "Please release my hand."

"Why? So you can fold them primly in your lap again? So you can hide the fire in you with stillness and a ladylike serenity? That's only a mask, Victoria, and we both know it now. Did they teach you that a lady never feels passion? They were wrong. You have a body made for a man. My body knows. Do you want to feel how much my body wants you?"

She pulled her hand away, folding both in her lap.

Falcon wasn't disturbed by the retreat. She was confused, he saw, but not angry or offended by his bluntness. He chuckled softly. "Not proper? No, but I did say I'd *try* to court you like a gentleman. And to reassure your mind on that point, I have a nice, gentlemanly invitation for you. A friend of mine is having a party tonight. A ball, really. The cream of New York society will be there. I want you to come with me."

Victoria was carefully not looking at him. "My friends expect me for a theater party," she said softly.

He reached out to touch her face, forcing her gently to look at him. Without a word, he leaned toward her and covered her startled lips with his. He didn't give her a chance to protest or resist; his mouth was hot, demanding. Unlike the earlier sensuous exploration of her mouth, this time he possessed her with a stark, irresistible power. And this time she did not start in surprise when his tongue delved deeply; this time she swayed toward him, her cool lips heating in a burst of fire.

Falcon stroked the side of her graceful neck slowly while the kiss grew hotter, deeper. He could feel the tiny heartbeat in her throat fluttering wildly like a caged bird, and when his hand dropped to brush lightly across her full breast, he felt her jerk, felt the instant response of that straining flesh.

He lifted his head reluctantly and gazed down into clouded green eyes. And it was an effort to say anything at all, an effort that told him his control was stretched to its limits. "Tell your friends something came up," he murmured hoarsely. "Come with me tonight."

Victoria found herself nodding helplessly, and far back in her mind was the painful, bewildering knowledge that there would be little she could deny this man. Perhaps . . . perhaps nothing at all. And though that knowledge was frightening, it was also undeniably exciting.

Falcon smiled in triumph, but whatever he would have said was stayed by the sound of footsteps in the shop above them. He kissed her again lightly, and then got up and went to climb the stairs and alert a bewildered shopkeeper to their presence.

Victoria sat where she was for a few moments, deciding to let him deal with puzzled shopkeepers. Automatically, her hands went to her hair and the torn dress, and she acknowledged dimly that no one looking at her would have any doubt she was well on her way to being a fallen woman.

To call Victoria's return to the safe bosom of her "respectable" hotel an anticlimax would have been stating the matter rather accurately. They had found her purse and hat in the shop, and the *very* respectful shopkeeper had lent the aid of a few dress pins with which to repair the ravages to her clothing. Falcon escorted her back to her hotel with the smooth manners of a gentleman born; so precisely proper were his attentions that Victoria stole an incredulous glance at him while they were in the cab—and discovered a devilish twinkle in his lazy green eyes.

He left her in the lobby at her firm request, but

reminded her cheerfully that he'd be back, and when, and politely requested that she "wear something pink" for the ball.

Moments later in her room, she sat rather limply in a chair and wondered what on earth had happened to her. She sat there for a long time, her thoughts vague and confused, and then slowly drew off her gloves to stare at the thin gold band adorning her left hand.

She removed her wedding ring finally and placed it in her jewelry case. Out of sight. But not out of mind. She tried not to feel guilty over the action, knowing full well that Morgan would have applauded it. The knowledge did not help her. She felt she was betraying her husband. Even more, she felt she was somehow betraying the man she would meet within a matter of hours. He thought she was free.

She scolded herself sharply later over breakfast, reminding herself that Falcon Delaney was clearly uninterested in a permanent relationship. He wanted her, but she strongly doubted marriage had crossed his mind. Men like Falcon Delaney didn't marry, she thought, startled at the strength of her dismay. No, they didn't marry. They sampled every flower that enticed them with its scent or color and then went on, alone.

And what, she wondered in shame, did that make her? What kind of woman would let such a man kiss her, touch her? Her marriage to Morgan was one in name only—but that fact made her willingness to see Falcon again all the more damning. In the old South of her childhood, just being seen alone with him in a closed carriage would have

been enough to ruin her, and spending the night
locked in a cellar with him would have resulted in a
marriage swiftly arranged—at gunpoint if necessary—by her family.

But she had no family except Morgan, and this
was hardly the old South. Morgan would have been
the first to remind her of that, and the first, she
thought, to remind her she was free to do as she
liked.

She could not help wondering, however, if Morgan had realized the problems their marriage could
entail. It had been a solution, then—but now? How
could a married woman ever explain to another
man that, in reality, she was free? How could she
explain a husband who was both more and less
than a husband?

And what did it matter, really? Believing she was
innocent, Falcon Delaney would hardly be surprised to find a virgin in his bed. *In his bed* . . .

Victoria paced her room far into the afternoon,
struggling to come to terms with her confusion. It
was a new world, she reminded herself, with less
stringent social rules. The carefully structured life
of her childhood had been destroyed by the war,
and there was less now that was absolute. And she
had spent the last eight years in a raw new land,
with its blunt men and practical women, a land
where prosaic ranch life had rendered the niceties
of behavior something less than vitally important.

But there were still things an innocent young
lady—or even a young married woman—could
hardly do and still keep her good name and self-
respect. Lying with a man who wanted only her
body was certainly one of them.

"Life is too short and uncertain to allow you always to play by the rules, Victoria. Remember that. Sometimes you just hold your head high, step boldly forward—and damn the consequences."

Morgan's advice echoed in her mind, and she felt an unfamiliar recklessness grip her. No matter what he wanted of her, she was undeniably drawn to Falcon Delaney, and if she sent him away now she knew she would forever regret it. Her body felt alive and aware, as if all her senses strained to burst from her skin like overripe fruit, and it was a glorious feeling. A breathless, exciting, seductive feeling. Could that be so wrong? She was strong enough, wasn't she, to step boldly forward?

And damn the consequences!

She moved slowly to the wardrobe and opened it, taking out a gown of the finest taffeta. Pink, he had said? This gown was a light, ethereal pink, glowing like an expensive pearl. It was low-cut, so much so that she had never yet worn it, despite its beauty. It left her shoulders bare and her breasts revealed almost to their rosy tips, and it made her waist tiny. And in her jewel case was the set of diamonds Morgan had given her on her last birthday.

Victoria put the dress on her bed, absently smoothing the glimmering, silky material. Then she turned and went to the bell rope. A bath first, and she wanted to wash her hair and brush it until it gleamed.

She wanted to smell of lavender.

Falcon Delaney moved through the quiet, almost deserted morning streets of New York until he reached his hotel. It was not the Royal, but neither

was it a tumbledown shanty catering to desper-
adoes. It was a clean, neat place, its customers
affluent men in the city on business—and men
passing through the city, of whom none dared to
inquire their business.

He got his key from a disinterested clerk and
went up to the second floor. In his room, he
automatically locked the door, checked the windows, and made certain his bags were undisturbed.
Finding no sign of unwanted visitors, he removed a
small, leather-bound book from a bag beneath the
bed and sat down.

The journal held neatly written but cryptic entries, and he merely glanced over the last entry
before making another. It, too, was coded, but he
knew the code so well that he wrote swiftly and
without hesitation. Though someone looking over
his shoulder would never have realized it, he was
succinctly detailing the events of the previous
night. And puzzling those events were.

There had been a message given to him along
with his key, stating that the list he had expected to
arrive soon would be delayed for a few days, and
possibly longer. Reluctant to focus his mind on
business—and startled by that unusual lapse—he
nonetheless considered the matter thoughtfully.

The events of the night before were puzzling,
more puzzling, in fact, the longer he thought about
them. The man with the eye patch, Read, and his
henchmen certainly had not acted in the manner of
innocent men. Falcon had been knocked out because, apparently, he had been spotted following
Read and was known to be armed. Victoria had
been thrown into the cellar with him presumably

because she had seen what had happened. But none of that explained what the three men had been doing at the shop in the first place, or what the plan was that Falcon's arrival had "botched."

The elderly, gentlemanly shopkeeper, bewildered, had professed to have no knowledge at all of why strange men should have carefully broken into his shop the night before, pretending to keep it open for business. Falcon believed him. Nothing had been missing from the shop, not even the small amount of money left in the till overnight. Nothing had been disturbed, unless one counted the shelves disarranged when Victoria had struggled with one of the men.

So why had Read and his men broken into the shop with no apparent intent to loot or destroy?

Falcon stretched out on his bed, closed his eyes, and considered carefully, repeating to himself what Victoria had heard from the men.

They couldn't take the chance that he—Falcon—knew something. They had gotten an address, and so could go directly to their destination, wherever that was. Something had been botched by the henchman, something ruined because Falcon had been knocked out? Botched. What could have been botched? What plan had been changed by his arrival?

Falcon swore absently as he realized he had not thought to ask Victoria one vital question about what she had heard. He hadn't thought to ask, and she wouldn't have noticed, probably, because of where she'd been born. He hadn't thought to ask if the men she had heard spoke with Southern accents.

Still . . . it could hardly be connected, could it? Read had paid for drinks with a specially minted gold coin stolen years before in a daring robbery, and Falcon had been knocked on the head because he had turned up unexpectedly. He hadn't been knocked out because of who or what he was, apparently, but simply because a strange man had blundered in by chance, and his mere presence had ruined some plan of theirs.

It couldn't be connected. But Falcon's instincts were prodding him relentlessly, and he realized that, because of experience or because he had seen or heard something he was not yet fully aware of, he believed it *was* connected. There was a piece missing, something he didn't know and couldn't guess, a vital link that prevented him from seeing what had actually happened last night.

What was it?

He couldn't believe Victoria was involved, despite his initial suspicion. Yet she had been there. She had been the only person in the shop other than those men. Had their "plan" involved her in some way? And, if so, why had his arrival caused them to abandon the plan? Falcon was convinced Victoria knew nothing of what was going on, so how could she be involved?

He pushed the questions to the back of his mind. The answers, if they existed, would come to him in time.

After a while, Falcon rose and shaved, then dug out his spare gun and loaded it, and went to have breakfast before returning to the waterfront. It was early, but he was hardly concerned about the sleeping habits of others. He rousted a reluctant

Sam out of bed and questioned him about Read, but the barkeep had nothing significant to say.

"I don't know his name, sir, or where he's staying. He didn't come back last night at all."

"Did he speak with an accent? A Southern accent?"

"I'm sorry, sir, but I didn't notice."

Taking a chance, Falcon questioned a few more waterfront denizens. All he got for his trouble was a feeling that Read had been new to the waterfront, because no one seemed to know anything about him.

His intent questioning had kept his mind off Victoria and what had happened between them, and he was quietly furious now that this new and promising trail had gone cold so quickly. Still, it wasn't the first time, and he finally returned to his hotel, disappointed and annoyed but unsurprised.

He'd have to wait for the list. Wait until there was something more to go on than his nebulous instincts. And, in the meantime, there was Victoria.

Falcon made arrangements for a private carriage for that evening before going up to his room, smiling a little as he thought of the long drive out to Leon Hamilton's palatial estate. It was a *very* long drive, and he meant to instruct the driver to take his time about it.

He felt a brief twinge of compunction at the realization that Victoria Fontaine was unprotected in the city, but reminded himself that she had agreed to accompany him tonight. *After you kissed her senseless!* There was no escaping the fact that he had indeed set out to weaken her resistance to him, but he consoled himself with the thought that he certainly wasn't planning on rape. He had never in his life forced himself on a woman, and didn't intend to start with Victoria.

No, he intended to be very sure that she wanted him as much as he wanted her. There would doubtless be limitless opportunities tonight, he thought dryly, wondering if Victoria could possibly know that the "cream of New York society" was a lusty and forthright bunch with few illusions left. He had been to parties at the Hamilton estate several times these last years, and there were always a few highborn ladies and gentlemen who came in from "strolls" in the garden with the rumpled, gleaming-eyed look of satisfying sex in the bushes.

He had himself, once or twice.

Leon Hamilton, though devoted to his Mary, had been a bachelor of some note for a number of years, and his lush garden, if not precisely planned for dalliance, at least made the pursuit of such occupations immensely gratifying. And the people he called friends certainly took advantage of his hospitality. There were always numerous bedrooms thoughtfully prepared beforehand for unplanned activity, and if Mary would sigh in regret to know that the rooms were lustily shared by couples not wedded to each other, at least she understood and accepted as well as Leon the failings of humanity.

Falcon wondered what Victoria would make of his friends. The glittering New York society of 1871 was a far cry from both the genteel South and the rough Southwest. With manners and—some maintained—morals challenged brutally by war, society had learned just how fleeting its pretty customs

could be. It would have been too much to say that a
"live for today" attitude prevailed, but not too
much to say that there were few moral strictures in
the postwar North.

Falcon ordered hot water for his bath, looking
forward to tonight with a great deal of anticipation.

3

She was waiting for him in the lobby of her hotel, and Falcon paused for a moment just inside the doors to gaze at her before she saw him. The black velvet cloak she wore hid a part of her gown from him, but he saw with a feeling of triumph that she had indeed worn pink. The gown was obviously taffeta, and its delicate pink color, along with the black cloak, set off her fair beauty strikingly. Her hair was up in an intricate style made curiously fragile by a black satin ribbon woven in among the gleaming strands. She had fastened the cloak at her throat, which prevented him from seeing if the diamonds dangling from the small lobes of her shelllike ears were matched by a necklace lending icy fire to her creamy breasts; fortunately, his imagination where she was concerned was vivid.

He approached her on cat feet. "Beautiful. Just beautiful."

She looked up at him, startled by his silent approach, and a faint color swept up her cheeks. But there was something new in her eyes, something half-shy and half-excited, and he knew his seductive efforts in the cellar had borne fruit. He offered his arm with a slight bow, and amusement rose in him when she accepted the arm with a sidelong glance that held a rueful appreciation of his gentlemanly manners.

The lady was no fool; plainly, she found his publicly donned courtesy quite definitely suspect.

"Why do I feel I'm being led into the lion's den?" she murmured as he guided her out to the waiting carriage.

Falcon laughed softly with real amusement. "I can't imagine. Are you afraid of me, Victoria?"

She didn't answer until they were inside the closed carriage and moving. "Afraid of you?" She seemed to consider the matter, gazing at him in the shadowed interior. "I think it would be unwise of me to pretend you aren't a dangerous man."

"Not dangerous to you, surely."

Her green eyes were serious. "Western men are a peculiar breed, a law unto themselves. Sometimes their gallant manners would make a European nobleman cringe in shame at his own lack, and at other times they're as rough and raw as the land that bred them. Dangerous to me? To any woman, I should think."

After a moment, he smiled. "I was born in Ireland."

"Were you? But you're a western man nonetheless. A Texas Ranger, didn't you say?"

"Yes, for several years."

"And a Union soldier before that." Her tone was thoughtful. "And before that—a scout, perhaps? An Indian fighter?"

"Both," he confessed, oddly pleased by her perception.

"And the scar?"

He lifted a hand to finger the crescent scar on his cheekbone. "This? When I was a boy, my brothers and I often rode through Apache camps near our ranch, borrowing the Indian custom of counting coup."

"Trying to touch as many braves as possible? I've heard of it. Is that how you were hurt?"

He smiled. "In a way. My half-broke mustang took exception to a raid one night and threw me. I landed on a sharp stone. A battle scar, of sorts."

She smiled in return, thinking of a young boy cursing his temperamental mount.

"Did I tell you how beautiful you are?" he said suddenly, huskily.

Her smile faded slightly, leaving only the curve of delicate lips. "Yes. Yes, you did. Thank you."

Falcon reached out to touch her cheek gently, and then his hand dropped to toy with the fastening of her cloak. "Is this to keep out a chill? Or me?"

Her gloved fingers tightened around each other in her lap, and Victoria felt her breath grow short. "The dictates of fashion," she said finally.

He unfastened the cloak slowly, holding her gaze with his, very aware that her breath, like his, was shallow and quick. And some distant part of him marveled at these incredible feelings. She felt it too, this aching fire, and he was delighted by her swift response to him. "Fashion can go to hell," he murmured.

Victoria made no move to stop him, and though she knew she should be ashamed of her wanton desire to have him see her, touch her, kiss her, what she felt was excitement.

He opened the cloak completely, pushing it back over her shoulders, and his breath caught at what he saw. The gown was low-cut, baring her luscious breasts almost to the nipples, and against the creamy flesh a diamond necklace gleamed. The lanterns hung outside the carriage sent a part of their light into the shadowed interior, playing over her exposed flesh with the loving glow of pale gold. Her breasts rose and fell quickly, each motion lending to the enticing illusion that the gown couldn't possibly hold the full mounds captive a moment longer.

If it was an illusion . . .

"God, you're so beautiful," he muttered hoarsely, and his hands were on her bare shoulders, turning her toward him; he was inflamed even more by her instantly pliant response.

Victoria didn't even try to resist him. She had invited this, she realized dimly, invited this by agreeing to accompany him tonight, by wearing the provocative gown. And why couldn't she feel ashamed of that? Why did she feel only achingly, vibrantly alive and incredibly excited? Why did she want to feel his hands on her, his lips . . .

One of his hands slid down her back to her waist and pulled her as close as possible, given the crinolines beneath the voluminous skirt of her gown; his other arm surrounded her shoulders and crushed her upper body against him. He could feel the firm mounds of her breasts pressed to his chest, feel as well as hear her soft gasp, and an urgent sound escaped him just before his lips captured hers.

She was prepared for the shocking possession of

his tongue this time, as well as she could be prepared for a sensation so devastating, and her body responded feverishly. Against his hard chest, her breasts swelled and ached, and her arms slid up around his neck of their own volition. He was easing her back into the corner, and she could feel his arousal against her hip, bold and demanding.

When he released her lips at last she could only moan, and her head fell back instinctively as he plundered the soft, vulnerable flesh of her throat. Her fingers twined in his thick, silky hair, and she wanted suddenly to remove her gloves so that she could feel his hair, his skin. And then his lips moved lower to brush hotly against her straining breasts, and she forgot everything except sheer pleasure.

"So sweet," he muttered thickly, cupping a breast while his mouth caressed it, gazing fixedly at the edging of lace that just barely hid a hardening bud from his eyes. He brushed his thumb over that hidden delight, and felt it thrust outward impudently in an instant response. He nuzzled his lips along the rich, lustrous material guarding her treasures, barely aware of the scratching of lace, his tongue flicking the rosy skin and her low moan sorely testing his control. "Victoria . . ."

She had never known such pleasure existed, and the only rational thought in her mind was the desire to feel more. She was hot, cold, shaking—her body a prisoner of the sensations sweeping over it with the relentless rhythm of an ocean's waves. The hot, wet caress of his tongue seared her skin, and his hand gently squeezed her breast until she thought she'd go out of her mind. She cried out softly when it responded to his attentions by

swelling even more, until the stiffened nipple
thrust free of confining silk and his mouth closed
hotly around it.

All her senses were centered there, drawn by his
pleasuring mouth, and they burned with a hunger
she had never known. Something inside her, some
dimly perceived barrier, melted in the heat of his
caress, and she couldn't even find the breath to cry
out her astonished delight.

She was hardly aware of his hand sliding down
over her quivering belly, but a sudden touch at the
vulnerable apex of her thighs jerked an instinctive,
shocked protest from her lips. "No! Falcon, don't!"

"Shhh," he murmured against her breast, his
hand rubbing gently through the layers of cloth
while his mind vividly imagined the soft, damp
warmth too much material hid from him. He
wanted to draw her skirt up, find his way through
the delicate feminine underthings until he could
touch that heat, caress the womanly core of her. His
entire body ached with the need to feel her naked
and passionate against him. His tongue teased her
nipple delicately with tiny, fiery licks that were
fiercely hungry. "Don't stop me, sweet. So sweet.
You taste so good."

Victoria wanted to protest again, but the heat at
her breast had sent a part of its fire lower, deeper in
her body, and the aching inside her became a
hollow, bittersweet need. "Falcon . . . you
shouldn't . . . I can't . . ."

He lifted his head slowly from her breast, his
darkened eyes intent on her flushed face. She
looked thoroughly kissed, heartbreakingly beautiful in her innocent awareness. Her lips were red

and swollen, her eyes sleepy with desire, dimly shocked. He slid his hand back up over her belly, cupping her breast gently and briefly before easing the silk upward until she was decently covered again. Then he surrounded her flushed face softly in one large hand and kissed her, vaguely surprised at the surge of tenderness he felt.

He brought them both upright, drawing the cloak back over her shoulders as she slowly lowered her arms, fastening it again. And when she was sitting demurely, gazing at him with huge eyes, he leaned back into his own corner and sighed. "No one at the party will doubt that I want you," he said softly. "A man can never hide what a woman does to him."

Her eyes flicked downward to the straining evidence of his arousal, and then skittered hastily back to his face in confusion. Between the plantation of her childhood and Morgan's thriving ranch, she could hardly have avoided learning of the physical evidence of male sexuality, but his soft, bold reference to his body's response to her was both shocking and—in some part of herself she didn't want to acknowledge—exciting.

He chuckled softly. "Making love in a carriage is an awkward business," he offered. "If there had been a bed nearby, sweet, a loaded gun wouldn't have stopped me."

Victoria strove to think clearly, but it was almost impossible to do so with his gaze on her. What was the man *doing* to her? And why did he talk about love when she knew all too well that wasn't what he wanted from her at all. "I—I suppose you'd know

. . . about carriages." She felt a stab of jealousy so sharp it bewildered her even more.

He chuckled again, a low, husky sound. "I'm thirty-four, sweet. There have been a few carriages. Does that disturb you?"

"Of course not," she said stoutly. Then, driven, she said, "Are there—is there someone here? In New York?"

"A woman? Only you, sweet."

"Stop calling me that," she managed to object somewhat weakly.

"But you are sweet. I can still taste your sweet skin in my mouth, on my tongue. As sweet as honey."

Victoria tried not to think of her still-burning body, her aching need for something beyond her experience. But it was so difficult when he insisted on talking that way! She concentrated on the rhythmic hoofbeats of the horses drawing their carriage. "Where is this party? We've gone a long way already."

"Almost there. The home of Leon Hamilton."

She had wondered if their destination would be the home of someone who knew her and Morgan, and was relieved to find that this was not the case. And it was unlikely, she had decided, that the "cream of New York society" would contain anyone she had met; Morgan cared little for society, and his friends here were primarily businessmen and their families. Still, she was half-consciously braced to encounter someone who knew she was married.

"Leon Hamilton? *Sir* Leon Hamilton?"

"He abandoned the title when he left England,"

Falcon told her lazily. "It was a terrible blow to his wife Mary. She had a fancy to be called Lady Hamilton."

Both curious and determined to divert her mind from other confusing emotions, she asked, "How did you meet them?"

"During the war. Leon held a post in Washington, and I was often there." He didn't tell her that Leon had been, and still was, a very high official, and Falcon's boss; that was something very few people knew.

Victoria wanted to question him further, but she became aware suddenly that the carriage was slowing, aware of bright lights and gay music and the hum of many voices. And when she looked out the carriage window, she was daunted to see a huge mansion, sprawling with the indolent air of immense wealth.

She had been born in a mansion, and Morgan's home was hardly a hovel, but wealth of this rare type was utterly beyond her experience. She felt suddenly awkward, wretchedly inexperienced, and somehow inferior. And he saw.

As the carriage stopped and a footman opened the door with a flourish, he stepped out and took her hand to help her. And his smile was gentle. "You will undoubtedly be beseiged by amorous admirers in just a few moments, but I refuse to give you up even to our host." He tucked her hand in the crook of his arm and led her up the wide, shallow steps, and Victoria felt inexpressibly more confident.

*   *   *

"I don't know where Falcon found you," Mary Hamilton said cheerfully a few hours later, "but I must say it's doing him a great deal of good to realize he has to fight to *keep* you!"

Victoria smiled at the merry brunette as they both sat, partially sheltered, behind a screen of plants in the vast ballroom. Her confidence had grown even more, for Falcon's prediction had been uncannily accurate. He had given her up to a succession of dance partners, however, because Leon Hamilton had quite literally dragged him from the ballroom almost instantly after the first dance. "Some kind of business, I suppose," Mary had explained wryly.

"Why is that?" Victoria lightly asked her hostess now.

Mary laughed. "Haven't you noticed that since he and Leon have come back into the ballroom that Falcon has looked exceedingly disgruntled because he finds you claimed for dances with other men? It's a new thing for him, I promise you. Women tend to desert other men to fall at his charming feet."

"So I've noticed," Victoria murmured, stealing a glance at the dance floor, where Falcon's partner for the last two dances had been a vibrant redhead with predatory eyes.

Mary noted the glance and sighed. "Yes, Cassie does cling somewhat. Not that she has any right," she added hastily. "But Cassie was born with the conviction that every man just *has* to succumb to her charms, and she's been working on Falcon for a good, long while now." She didn't add that her own impression was that Falcon had quite likely succumbed, to the extent of enjoying those charms at least once out in the secluded garden during a previous party; knowing Cassie, Mary felt that hardly counted as a conquest.

"What are you ladies doing hiding behind the plants?" Leon Hamilton demanded severely as he joined them. "Gossiping, no doubt." He was a distinguished man with silver hair and shrewd, kind eyes, and reminded Victoria of Morgan.

Mary lifted a haughty brow at her husband. "We've both been trundled around the floor, trod upon, leered at, and sweet-talked until we're fairly sick of the sight of you exhausting males. We're fragile flowers, you know, and, without rest, prone to fainting spells."

"You've never fainted in your life," Leon told his wife lovingly. "When Brian was born, *I* was the one who fainted."

Victoria was a little startled, but Mary giggled and told her, "He did too. Facedown on the floor. He almost broke his nose."

"I was better with James," Leon told Victoria in a cheerful tone. "I only *thought* about fainting."

"Miss Fontaine?" One of her previous partners, a somewhat inebriated scion of a wealthy importer, stood before them with a hangdog expression of loverlike pleading. "Dance? You promised me another."

"I'd love to, Mr. Nash," Victoria said promptly, rising to accept his arm. And she had the satisfaction of seeing a dark scowl on a particular face in the crowd; Falcon had begun to make his way toward her, and now turned toward the punch bowl instead with an expression just short of savage.

Victoria kept half her mind on the rather stumbling conversation and feet of her partner, while the rest of her thoughts were concerned with the ball in general and Falcon in particular. He hadn't partnered her since that first dance, but she had felt his brooding gaze on her even as each of them had danced with others. The redheaded Cassie, with all her ripe charms, had been unable to hold his attention.

"Oh, pardon me, Miss Fontaine!"

"Quite all right, Mr. Nash," she acknowledged automatically, shoring him up with a strong arm and attempting to keep her feet out of his lethal path. She choked back a giggle as she glanced around at other couples, and she was fascinated by what she saw.

There were probably a hundred people filling the ballroom, dancing and laughing, people dressed in brilliant colors and with the flush of exertion and enjoyment on their faces. It was hardly the decorous scene she dimly remembered from balls in her childhood, but there was something immensely appealing in the robustness of it all. There were no overt improprieties, although Victoria had seen more than one couple disappear out into the garden with glazed, intent expressions, and her partners so far had shown a tendency toward flowery compliments.

". . . like emeralds!"

She blinked up at the flushed and handsome face of her partner. "I beg your pardon, Mr. Nash?"

Steering her with a heavy tread around a couple

dancing more slowly, he said doggedly, "I said, you have eyes like emeralds."

"Oh." She cleared her throat. "Thank you." Accustomed to her protected status as Morgan's wife, she had found the most difficulty in responding to these wretched compliments with an appearance of ease; it was hardly something she was used to hearing.

"Marry me!"

"No, thank you," she answered absently, stealing a glance toward the punch bowl, where Falcon watched her broodingly and a redheaded Cassie stroked his lapel with one of her talons.

"Miss Fontaine!"

"Oh, hush," she murmured, frowning up at Nash. "People stare when you wail like that! What is it?"

"I asked you to marry me," he told her in an aggrieved, but lower, tone of voice.

Victoria managed to compose her expression into one of reluctant denial, but only because she'd had practice; this was the third proposal in an hour. "I'm very sorry, Mr. Nash, but that isn't possible." Gravely, she added, "You see, I've lost my heart to a riverboat gambler." By this time, she could almost have described that mythical gentleman.

The music ended with a flourish, and the damp hands of Nash unwillingly released her. "Oh, hell," he said.

Victoria curtsied, keeping her face grave, and turned away from his disheartened self. Instantly, she found her hand tucked into another masculine arm, and Falcon was leading her toward the punch bowl.

"If you aren't thirsty," he told her very politely,

"you should be. How many times did he step on your foot?"

"Only once," Victoria replied serenely.

Falcon laughed, a bit shortly. "Do you always let your dancing partners hold you so close?"

She turned to face him at the table, accepting the glass he held out, elated by his tone. But she kept that elation out of her expression. "I don't know what you mean."

"Yes, you do." He stared down at her. "Half the men in this room have had their hands on you in the past hour. It's that damned dress." His gaze dropped to her lavishly displayed bosom, still presenting its enticing illusions, and a nerve throbbed at the corner of his hard-held mouth. "They can't take their eyes off you, they've been drooling over you since we arrived."

"They?" she said very softly.

His gaze lifted swiftly to her face, and there was a flash of reluctant, wry humor in the depths of his eyes before they were shuttered again. "They. Me. I'm just like the rest of these poor besotted bastards, caught in your web."

Victoria felt a strange, hot shiver at the leashed savagery in his deep voice, and she realized for the first time the danger of taunting a man like Falcon. Beneath the civilized, polite manners he maintained in public, she was all too aware of something not quite tame. Wildness. Her free hand reached out to touch his forearm lightly, and she could feel it tense even through the material separating his flesh from hers. "Dance with me," she invited quietly.

He set his glass aside slowly, took hers and

placed it also on the table, and then grasped her hand and led her out onto the floor. The musicians were playing a waltz, and he pulled her far closer than was proper, the hand at her back guiding her firmly. She caught her breath in surprise, very conscious of his body brushing hers with every step, but couldn't find the will to draw away from him.

"No one held me this close," she managed breathlessly.

"Good." His eyes were darkened, heavy-lidded. His gaze dropped to her bosom for a moment, then lifted to her face again, and the green eyes glittered darkly. "Make sure no one else does. I'd hate to have to kill a man over you." His voice had hoarsened, but there was something almost careless in the tone, despite his savage words, as if killing a man over her was something he wouldn't hesitate to do.

Victoria lifted her chin, her confusion about this man lending her a flash of spirit. "You don't own me."

"Don't I?"

"No!" she snapped.

He smiled slowly, and when he spoke, he kept his voice low. "I will, Victoria. I'll brand you so completely mine that other men will see it from ten feet away." He watched her absorb that, saw confusion warring with the anger in her eyes; she was showing her spirit for the first time, and he was fascinated by her.

"I won't belong to you."

"You will."

The interlude in the carriage had shown her that

the pleasure to be found in his arms was wildly
overpowering, and she had not allowed herself to
consider the enormity of that. But now, hearing the
implacable note in his calm voice, she felt a surge
of sheer, blind panic. It was no longer a matter of
whether she behaved with ladylike morals or saved
her good name; in that instant, she realized that
something vital to her very being was at stake in
this dangerous game. He threatened more than her
reputation. He could destroy far more than society's opinion of her, far more than she had believed
possible.

He could destroy her.

With a muffled cry, she wrenched free of him,
fighting her way past several startled couples until
she escaped the ballroom through the French doors
leading out onto the veranda.

"Falcon!"

He paused at the doors, turning reluctantly to
face Leon Hamilton. "What is it, Leon? I've already
made my report." He kept his voice low, but it was
impatient. "I have to—"

"She won't go anywhere," Leon told him dryly.
"The garden is enclosed, remember? Come into my
study. I've just received a message." He turned
away.

Falcon hesitated for an instant, then muttered,
"Goddammit," and followed his host . . . and
boss.

Leon was pouring brandy into a glass when
Falcon entered the book-lined study. He handed it
to the younger man. "You look like you need

something stronger than that doctored punch out there."

"Thanks." Falcon drained the glass and set it aside with the businesslike air of a man who wants to get on to other more important things. "The message?"

"I don't suppose you'd care to sit down?"

"No."

Leon smiled. "I didn't think so." He cleared his throat. "The message. Marcus Tyrone's back in the city. You know he gave us the slip a few weeks ago in that little ship of his? He was heading south, but we lost him. Well, he's home."

Falcon frowned. "When?"

"Couple of days ago, I believe, although I just got the message. Does it matter?"

Falcon didn't answer for a long moment. Did it matter?

Marcus Tyrone. The blockade-running captain was now a successful businessman, and Falcon had made a point of showing himself to the man each time he visited New York. Theirs was an odd relationship, balanced carefully between surface cordiality and animosity, between knowledge and suspicion. They had met formally after the war, and though Falcon had not accused Tyrone of having transported the gold to the rebels, each had heard the silent accusation as the hunter had cordially faced the hunted. There was nothing to be done about Tyrone's involvement now, Falcon was aware, unless he was caught with the gold in his hands.

And since Falcon was not in the habit of deceiving himself, he admitted at least inwardly that he would have disliked it very much if he had been forced to openly accuse Tyrone, or have him arrested. He felt, perhaps oddly, that the other man could have been a friend under different circumstances.

He acknowledged that and thought about it. Perhaps it came from a feeling of empathy, he decided. Tyrone, like himself, was a lone wolf; even in a crowd he stood apart, observing . . . usually cynically.

"'Lord, what fools these mortals be,'" Falcon murmured aloud, then laughed shortly.

"What?" Leon asked.

Falcon looked at him. "Nothing. Does it matter that Tyrone arrived in New York a couple of days ago? I don't know, Leon. I just don't know." He drew a deep breath, conscious once again of jangling instincts he couldn't label or sort. "But I have the feeling that things are happening, things we don't know about yet. Someone's put a match to a trail of gunpowder, and I don't know where the hell it'll lead."

Leon's brows lifted, but in surprise rather than doubt. "I've never heard you sound so sure of anything."

"I'm only sure something's happening. Not what it is. We'll see." He sighed. "Until we have the list, there's nothing we can do."

"Agreed."

"Then I'll go back to the party."

"Yes," Leon murmured. "I thought you would."

* * *

She engulfed him in a wave of perfume at the bottom of the veranda steps, her breathy voice urgent.

"Oh, Falcon, I knew you'd come looking for me! I've been waiting, waiting so long. Here, darling, this way—"

"If I were a gentleman," Falcon said dryly, allowing himself to be led down a path, "I'd certainly accept your flattering offer, Cassie. But since I'm a right bastard, I'll admit that you aren't the lady I came looking for."

Her laugh was a tinkling sound, unoffended, even disbelieving. "That washed-out blond bitch? Oh, forget her, darling. She couldn't warm a man with a blazing torch in her hand, and probably wouldn't know what to do with this lovely thing." Her hand was stroking the front of his trousers passionately. She had pulled him behind a bush and tugged down the low-cut neckline of her gown to rub her generous breasts against his chest.

"You have a filthy mouth, Cassie," Falcon said pleasantly, his tone hiding the distaste he felt as he looked down at her and wondered why her ripe breasts and expert hand left him completely unmoved. He hadn't had a woman in weeks, and the interludes with Victoria had left him achingly aware of the lack; why wasn't he responding to this very attractive and willing woman now?

She stood on tiptoe, her free arm wreathing around his neck, and her lips were hot and avid. "A skilled mouth, darling," she reminded, fumbling with buttons, taking him into her warm hand eagerly.

He was aware of her mouth and her fingers, and a

detached part of his mind remembered a very enjoyable hour or so spent in this garden with her some time back. She was an accomplished lover, completely abandoned, and Falcon knew well that half the men at tonight's party had sampled her generous charms. Born poor, she undoubtedly would have become a whore; born wealthy enough to do as she pleased, and with the "protection" of an older, wealthy husband—willfully blind to her activities—she was merely one of the ladies whose silks, satins, and fine public manners disguised the soul of a slut.

"A skilled mouth, darling," she repeated, her voice a panting, breathless sound now. "Let me—" She started to drop to her knees, uncaring of the damp ground and her silken gown.

He felt a sudden revulsion, directed at himself as much as her. It was the wrong time, the wrong place, the wrong woman. "Stop it, Cassie." He held her shoulders hard, pushing her back and away from him, automatically straightening his clothing.

"You want me," she stated, her eyes glistening in the moonlight. "You went wild between my legs!" Her hands went to her full, naked breasts, and she held them toward him as offerings.

"Once," he said coolly, unmoved by the display and distantly bothered by that unusual reaction. He had never been a man to ignore a willing woman, particularly one as beautiful and skilled as Cassie. "Men are like that, you know. Show us a scented garden and a scented, willing woman, and even the best of us go a little wild." He was surprised by his own words, puzzled by the self-contempt and distaste he felt. "But not again, Cassie. Go back into the ballroom and hunt fresh game."

From arrogant certainty she descended abruptly into whining need. "But I want you!" She released her swollen breasts and began pulling up her skirts hastily, revealing a total lack of undergarments and pale flesh with a dark-furred mound that gleamed in the moonlight. "I'm wet with wanting you. I can make you feel so good, I can—"

"Cassie, for Christ's sake!"

She stood staring at him—her skirt held bunched around her waist, mortified tears filling her eyes— realizing in shock that he really didn't want her. There had been disgust in his voice. *He didn't want her!* He had taken her once in this very garden, as lusty as she was herself, giving her unbelievable pleasure—and now he didn't want her.

It was that blond bitch, that washed-out, whey-faced blond bitch with her cat's eyes. "You're panting after the wrong bitch, Falcon." She laughed harshly, dropping her skirt, reckless in her indignation. "It's all over the ballroom that she's lost her heart to some riverboat gambler! She probably spread her legs for him too. She's the kind who only does it for *love*—" Cassie broke off and stepped back abruptly, her eyes widening and the fine hairs on the nape of her neck stirring, shocked by an abrupt coldness in the air. It was menace, and it came off Falcon in icy waves.

"Get out of my sight, Cassie, before I break your neck," he said softly.

Fearful, pulling the neckline of her gown up over naked, bouncing breasts, she ran.

*   *   *

He found her at the very bottom of the garden, leaning against a tree and absently hugging herself for warmth in the evening chill. Victoria looked at him, eyes huge with hard-won calm. He came to her, slowly. She could see him in the gleaming light from the decorative lanterns hung along the garden paths, his face shadowed, hard.

"Victoria."

She felt a hot shiver, just as in the ballroom when she had sensed the threatening strength in him, the untamed part of him that was so alarming. She felt now as if something primitive growled at her in the darkness of a dangerous place, crouched, ready to spring for her throat. . . . Her struggle to come to terms with the threat of him was just a fragile leaf now, blown by a cold, relentless wind.

"Falcon?" She didn't even know why she questioned, except that he wasn't *Falcon*, somehow it wasn't him. "It's cold. We should go back in."

"Not just yet." He moved even closer, a hand on either side of her and on the tree at her back, preventing her from moving. "We have to finish the conversation we began inside, don't we, Victoria?"

She was very still. "It's finished."

"No. You belong to me, Victoria. I'll hear you admit it now, or I'll make it a fact." His voice was so soft and casual it was chilling. "I'll make it a fact that neither you nor anyone else will ever be able to deny. Right here, right now."

It was too much, suddenly too much. She didn't know what she was feeling, didn't understand his implacable savagery, and she had never felt so lost in her life, not even when her home and everything she had known had died in a war that made no sense to her young mind. Tears spilled from her eyes, and a sob caught in the back of her throat as she looked up at him in mute bewilderment.

He was stiff for a moment, silent, and then a harsh sound escaped him and he pulled her into his arms. His embrace was gentle, and his voice shaken. "Don't do that, dammit. Don't. I didn't mean to frighten you, sweet. I just went a little mad when I heard— Shhh. It's all right. I won't hurt you. I promise I'll never hurt you."

Victoria's arms crept around his waist, and she burrowed closer into his warm, hard body instinctively. Promises? Promises from him? "You looked as if you almost hated me," she whispered. "As if you wanted to hurt me."

"No," he soothed, brushing his lips over her forehead, baffled by his own tenderness. "I was just half out of my mind because—" He hesitated, then finished roughly, "I heard you'd lost your heart to some damned riverboat gambler."

She lifted her head, staring up at him in astonishment. "What?" Absurdly, a giggle fought to escape her throat. "But I just made him up, invented him! Because they *would* keep proposing, and I didn't know what else to say!"

After a moment, a laugh shook him. "Your amorous dancing partners? I ought to wring Cassie's neck!"

Victoria stiffened and pulled back a little. "Cassie? She said . . . And you believed—"

He bent his head to kiss her swiftly. "I think we're both jealous fools," he said in a husky voice, pleased by her reaction to the other woman. "I wouldn't have Cassie if she offered—come to think of it, she *did* offer. Rather blatantly, in fact. And I sent her away, sweet."

"Noble of you!" she snapped, but softly.

"She wasn't the woman I wanted," Falcon murmured, concentrating on exploring the silky flesh of her throat.

Victoria hadn't even been conscious of tilting her head back, and felt dizzy. "We . . . we should go back to the house," she whispered unsteadily.

"It's so much nicer here. Lord, you're so warm and sweet!" He shifted against her subtly, the movement somehow widening her legs so that he stood between them. Then he moved again.

Victoria gasped, her legs going weak as she felt the starkly intimate pressure of his bold arousal against her. Her arms tightened around him convulsively as heat swept over her. "Falcon!"

"I know," he said in a taut, raspy voice. "It hurts, doesn't it, sweet? Wanting hurts. It feels as if I've wanted you forever, hungered for you." His mouth captured hers fiercely.

Victoria was hardly aware of the soft, hungry sound, like anguish, that tangled in the back of her throat, hardly aware that her arms had shifted, going up around his neck with a will all their own. His mouth was possessing her, branding her, and the subtle thrusting movements his body made against hers had ignited a fire that was burning her alive, melting her. She didn't feel the rough bark of the tree scratch her bare back, she only felt him— his body against her, his mouth on hers passionately, his hands cupping her breasts.

"No," she murmured when his mouth lifted from

hers at last, and she wasn't sure if she protested his touch or the ending of that fiery kiss.

Falcon seemed sure. He chuckled softly, a rough sound, and his teeth nipped lightly at her bottom lip. It was an incredibly sensual caress, drawing a gasp from her. And his voice was dark, liquid, heated.

"You enjoy my kisses, don't you, sweet? They make you burn, just as I burn." His hands moved suddenly, grasping the laced edging of her neckline, and she caught her breath again as the material was pulled down to free her breasts. His hands surrounded the full mounds, squeezing gently. "And when I touch your lovely breasts, you burn even more." His head lowered briefly, and a scalding tongue brushed in a tormenting caress across both breasts.

Victoria stared up at him, dazed, mesmerized by his voice, his words, his caresses. Her hands were clasped on his shoulders, her lower body molded pliantly to his, and beneath his hands her naked breasts ached, the nipples tight and hard, throbbing. Yet, still, there was that part of Victoria that had been schooled in a gentler age, an age of pretty manners and ironclad strictures, of circumspection. And it was that part of her that denied what was happening to her, desperately denied these overpowering feelings he evoked with the ease of a magician.

"No," she whispered, and it was that girl who spoke. That gentle, mannered girl who had managed to continue her gentle existence, despite war and violence and the death of so many in her young life, because of the iron will and obsessive determination of one man who had fought to see his tattered dream alive in her.

And Falcon, staring down at her face, understood a part of what he was seeing. It moved him unutterably, what he saw in her eyes, in her lovely face. He saw the last fragile, gallant tendrils of a way of life gone forever, of an innocence no amount of brutality could destroy. He didn't know, couldn't begin to guess, what kind of strength it had taken for her to hold on to and protect that inner fragility, that gentle core of herself, during the horrors she must have experienced in the war; he knew only that he would not harm it, no matter what the cost to himself.

Very slowly and gently, he pulled her gown back up, smoothing the material with a touch that was tender rather than passionate. He bent his head, kissing her very softly, then drew her arms down and took her hand. He led her down one of the paths until they came to a secluded gazebo that was small and delicate and contained a single padded seat constructed for two.

They sat for a moment in silence, hearing the distant rhythm of the music and the closer, soft sounds of the garden as a cool breeze stirred the plants.

"Tell me about your family," he said finally, quietly. "Parents, brothers, sisters?"

The seat was curved and she was half-facing him, her eyes fixed on him. She didn't know why he had stopped, but, although her body felt hot and restless, she was glad he had. It was all happening too fast; she needed time to think. "My family?" Her voice was low, husky.

"Yes. Tell me about them."

She drew a shuddering breath, fighting not to remember too much. "They died in the war. My mother and father, my brothers."

He was gazing at her with a new, searching intensity. "And left you alone? What did you do?"

I killed a man. The memory came out of nowhere—jarring, agonizing, buried and unexamined in all the years since Morgan had taken her away from Regret. She caught her breath, feeling the color drain from her face, feeling cold.

Falcon frowned and reached to take her hand, surprised and unsettled by her sudden pallor, her stricken eyes. God in heaven, what could she have gone through to cause this reaction after so many years? And then he remembered the South in the last days of the war, the brutality and confusion, the chaos. He felt an icy dread grip him as he thought of the soldiers who had roamed across a bloody, defeated land, looting and burning out of hatred and rage. Taking out their revenge for a brutal war on the defeated enemy.

"How old were you, sweet?"

"Fifteen." The response was automatic.

"Victoria." He kept his voice calm. "Were you —hurt? Did someone hurt you?"

She looked at him blindly. "Hurt me?" Her voice was toneless. "He . . . he tried. But I killed him. He killed Papa and old Sam, and then he caught me. And I killed him." The detached voice was curiously childlike.

"How did you kill him?" Falcon asked quietly.

"With a knife. Jesse gave it to me. Jesse is—was my brother. He told me what to do if anyone tried to hurt me. And I did it." She looked down at her gown, a puzzled frown creasing her brow. "There was so much blood. It was all over my dress, my hands, and it was warm and sticky. So much blood." Her free hand smoothed the material of her gown, as if she would have wiped a stain away.

Falcon waited quietly, hurting inside for what had happened to her. It could have been worse, in many ways; she could have been raped, badly hurt, even killed. Instead, she had killed. A fifteen-year-old girl raised to be gentle and kind had thrust a knife into the body of her attacker and survived. No wonder, Falcon realized, she had protected that gentle core of herself for so long; when she had killed to defend herself, everything inside her must have gone into shock. The only surprising thing was that she had managed to keep that part of herself alive, even if deeply buried.

She looked at him, finally, saw him. "I—I'd forgotten. I never told anyone about that."

"I know."

Puzzled, she said, "Why did I tell you?"

After a moment, lightly, he said, "Because I asked, sweet."

Looking at him, Victoria had the sudden feeling that there was something between them now, something he had put there. His eyes were unreadable, his faint smile unrevealing. She was bewildered, hurt suddenly.

If Falcon saw, he didn't respond to the hurt. Instead, still in a light tone, he said, "Why don't we go back inside? It's getting cold out here."

It was, indeed, cold.

*   *   *

The carriage ride back to her hotel a couple of hours later was silent. Falcon stepped out of the carriage to offer her an impersonal hand, and when she said coolly that he didn't have to come in with her, he bowed to a perfectly impersonal depth and held the door for her, wishing her good-night in an easy, impersonal tone.

Victoria held onto her composure while she got her key from a sleepy desk clerk and went upstairs. She undressed and put on her nightgown, unpinned and brushed her long hair, and gazed into the round mirror with blank eyes.

I killed a man.

Had that been it? Had Falcon's ardor cooled instantly upon hearing that the virtuous lady he was bent on seducing had blood on her delicate hands? Was he one of those rough, hard men who possessed an idealized vision of women, a vision easily and often shattered by reality? She wouldn't have thought so.

But something had changed him. So passionate in the garden, so tender. And then, abruptly, so formal. Polite and smiling, but with shuttered, unreadable eyes.

Victoria went to bed, blowing out the lamp, pulling the covers up over her shivering body. She lay on her back, staring up at a dark ceiling, and felt hot tears trickle from the corners of her eyes.

And she knew, then, what he had done to her.

Falcon ordered the coachman to return to the Hamilton estate, knowing the party would go on for hours yet. His mind was deliberately blank, his posture in the carriage careless and relaxed as he lounged back. He gazed out the window at darkness, and when the carriage arrived, he got out, told the driver to wait, and went inside the huge house.

He found Cassie near the punch bowl, her face sulky and bored as she stared at the dancers. She looked up as he approached, and the first flash of pleasure was replaced by wariness. "I thought you'd gone," she said.

"I came back." He took her hand and began leading her toward the door to the entrance hall. She didn't resist, but once they were in the deserted hall, Cassie hissed a question.

"Where do you think you're taking me?"

He paused with a foot on the bottom step, looking at her with hard, hot eyes. "That's up to you. I can take you upstairs or take you in the garden."

Cassie understood him immediately, and felt a sudden, hot wetness between her legs. The earlier insult forgotten, she thought only of the pleasure he had shown her once before. "Upstairs," she murmured. "But not a bedroom. I know a place."

He allowed her to lead the way, his mind still blank. She drew him into an alcove in a darkened part of the second floor hallway and immediately slid her arms up around his neck. "Against the wall," she breathed.

He pushed her back against the wall, taking her mouth savagely, crushing her body against his with one hand while the other yanked up her skirts and probed roughly between her legs. She moaned into his mouth, writhing, her legs parting widely. "Take me," she whispered. "Now, Falcon. Right now!"

He waited for desire to fog his senses and swell his body, waited for the pounding, driving need to bury himself in the willing female body. But his body refused to respond to this female body, and suddenly his mind wasn't blank anymore.

He was furious at himself, and self-contempt and guilt washed over him. Not Cassie's fault, of course, and rejecting her coldly now was something he couldn't bring himself to do. She wasn't an animal with no feelings, and she didn't deserve what he was doing to her. No one deserved to be used as he had wanted mindlessly to use her.

Some distant part of him realized that he was caressing her expertly, guiding her toward the release she so desperately needed. And he waited until she was shuddering and half-sobbing, her body limp, before he pulled away slightly and smoothed her skirt back down over her thighs.

"Falcon?" Her voice was breathless, bewildered. "Is something wrong? You didn't—"

He managed a laugh, never more grateful than now for the control built up over a lifetime. "I'm sorry, Cassie. I must be more tired than I realized. Forgive me?"

Her laugh was throaty. "Oh, *I've* nothing to complain about! But we could stay the night, and—"

"No." He stepped back, smiling. "I have to return to the city. But there'll be other parties." There wouldn't be, he knew. Not another party like the one this night.

Cassie accepted his arm, politely offered. She was smiling, feeling as satisfied as she had ever felt. But she wondered, as he escorted her courteously downstairs, why his eyes had changed. They had been hard and hot at first; now they were dark and quiet, almost as if he were hurting inside. . . .

4

New Mexico

Read Talbot peered into the distance, narrowing his good eye. "Helluva ranch," he grunted. "I see my dear old friend has done well for himself."

"*He hasn't spent the gold!*" Sonny's voice was a desperate whine, and grated on Read's nerves.

"Shut up, you fool!" Read snapped quietly. "This range is crawling with Fontaine's men. Bring them down on us and we'll never see the gold."

"But he hasn't spent it all?" Sonny whispered.

The third man lying prone at the top of the hill spoke coolly. "He didn't need any of it—then or now." Gus Rawlins exchanged a glance with Read. "You know what I found out in England. Fontaine made his fortune with a fleet of pirate ships thirty years ago, then bought himself respectability. He wouldn't have been received at all in Charleston if that had gotten out."

"Pity we didn't know then," Read agreed.

"But the gold . . ." Sonny murmured.

Read exchanged another glance with Gus, both aware that Sonny was lost in gold fever. He had been a fairly dependable, if stupid, man until they had discovered Morgan Fontaine's young wife enjoying herself in New York; with the scent of gold in his nose, Sonny had fallen into feverish desperation. His panicked attack on the stranger in New York had ruined their plan to snatch Victoria Fontaine after they had lured her there with a false message, and to use her to force the knowledge of the gold's whereabouts from her certainly doting husband. Read had been unwilling to take the chance that the stranger knew her and would realize she had been kidnapped.

Men such as that one, Read reflected now, had an annoying habit of butting in where they had no business, and he wanted no dangerous stranger on his back trail. Particularly one who had apparently followed him to the bookshop for some unknown reason. Still, that man was back in New York, and Read knew of many methods to force information from an unwilling man without resorting to the screams of a lovely young wife.

And he wanted her for himself. He had recognized her, of course, the moment he saw her. Eight years older and a woman now, he had nonetheless recognized the terrified girl who had so nearly killed him. But that didn't matter, that she had nearly killed him. She was Morgan's woman, and he meant to have her. He meant to take everything of Morgan's, everything he had claimed and built and stolen. Everything.

The plan would have worked, it would have *worked*—if Morgan hadn't stolen the gold. They could have seen the South rise triumphant. But now it was dead, and Morgan had to be punished for killing it. He would lose everything, just as Read had lost everything that mattered to him, everything that was important, everything he loved.

"I still don't understand," Gus said, "how he managed to stay hidden for eight years. We never knew—"

"Of course we didn't," Read said. "Because not one of us knew who he was. When he came to Charleston, he never said where he was from. And, since he knew so much about ships, we all figured that was his line of business. None of us was likely to come way the hell out here, and he knew it. We were looking up north for him, not out here. He just kept quiet."

"If it hadn't been for spotting his wife," Gus agreed, "we might never have found him."

"Read . . ." Sonny whined.

"Shut up," Read said, his voice a low growl, and turned his eyes back to the sprawling ranch below. "He rode out yesterday. We'll wait and see if he rides out today."

New York

For two days, Falcon wrestled with himself. He haunted the waterfront, asking hard questions of hard men as he tried to keep his mind on business. But each night he returned to his hotel room and lay on the bed, staring at the ceiling, and business, only a surface occupation at best, vanished from his thoughts. Like ore to a magnet, his mind returned to Victoria.

He wanted her. With every hour that passed, he was more aware of his need, his restless desire to

return to her hotel and hold her, and explain away
the hurt he had seen in her eyes. And it was *that*
desire that stopped him, baffled him—that desire
to take away the hurt. Stopped him because he
didn't understand his own motives where she was
concerned.

It had happened in the garden. She had told him
tonelessly about killing a man in self-defense, and
something inside him had turned over painfully.
He had shied from the feeling instinctively, unwilling to examine himself, and had deliberately put a
distance between them.

Lying on his bed on the third night, Falcon's lips
twisted in a grimace as he remembered the results
of that. He had gone to Cassie, thinking, if he
thought at all, only of wiping out the unfamiliar
emotions in the willing embrace of another woman. And the realization that he couldn't do it, that
his mind and body refused that simple solution,
had kept him away from Victoria since.

What *was* it about her? She was beautiful, yes,
and innocent; God knew both could tie a man in
knots. She was usually serene, her green eyes vivid,
and yet intelligent, calm, tolerant. The fires of
passion and temper lurked just beneath the serenity, which was intriguing as hell, he acknowledged.
And with that deep well of passion tapped, she was
vibrantly alive, aware, responsive; a man could go
mad, he admitted to himself, knowing he could
evoke that response from her.

And underneath it all, in some carefully preserved part of her, was a fifteen-year-old girl, and a
gentler time when fragility had been cherished and

respected and her world had been unmarred by war.

Falcon fumbled for a thin cigar and lighted it, frowning up at the ceiling. And so? She wasn't the first woman who had fought for her life and won. Christ knew she wasn't the only survivor of the war, however brutal the cost to her. And it had been years ago. So why did she have the subtle trick of inspiring a new and bewildering tenderness in him? Why did he feel the overpowering urge to stand between her and anything that could hurt her?

She was just different, he thought, from any woman he had ever known. He knew strong women; there were many in his family, including his mother. He had known serene women, women wounded by war or hardship, women who were gentle, women who were passionate, women with green eyes.

He swore and watched expelled smoke shape the harsh words. She was just a woman. Once he had taken her, he could forget her, as easily as he had always forgotten. *If* he could ignore that look in her eyes, that look of a fragile, gentle, desperate girl preserved in a simpler time.

Falcon set his teeth and decided he could ignore it. He had to ignore it. Or change it. All he had to do was show her, as painlessly as possible, that her girlhood was a thing of the past, consigned there by time rather than a war. She was a woman now, and this world was not the one of her childhood. She would see that, and the look in her eyes would be gone. And then he could take her to his bed and pleasure them both.

She was willing, after all; she couldn't hide that from him. And if he didn't get her out of his mind soon, he wouldn't be worth shooting. He had to take her to his bed. He'd please her, he was sure, and he had never yet known a woman to regret *that*.

He jabbed out his cigar and reached for the light, feeling relieved, back on balance. He just wanted her, of course. There was nothing more to it, nothing at all.

Victoria came out of her hotel, drawing on her gloves; when she saw him waiting for her, she stopped as though she had run into a wall. Automatically, she smoothed the material over her fingers, staring at him, helplessly aware that her feelings were showing on her face, in her eyes.

The sight of him fed a hunger that had grown hour by hour, and she knew that hunger was obvious. But she had been so afraid she would never see him again, so afraid. There was no shuttered look in his eyes now, no formal smile. His eyes were intense with that familiar desire that even in her memory turned her bones to liquid and heated her flesh, and his half-smile was lazy with promise. A distinctly improper look to give her, she realized vaguely, especially in broad daylight on a public sidewalk, and she could have laughed aloud.

He stepped forward and took her arm, leading her in the direction she had turned after leaving the hotel. "Where to, sweet?" he asked softly.

"I was—just a walk," she murmured. She sent him a glance, puzzled and wary despite her relief at seeing him again. "I didn't expect to see you."

He was holding her hand in the crook of his arm, and smiled down at her indolently as they walked slowly. "No? Why is that, sweet?"

With a flash of temper, she said, "You know why."

He chuckled softly. "Yes, I suppose I do. Did it never occur to you, sweet, that if I hadn't drawn away from you a bit, we might well be in that garden still?"

She flushed vividly and fixed her gaze on the sidewalk in front of them. "Oh." Her voice was small. Was it that? Only that? Somehow, she didn't think so, but she didn't want to ask again. Not now.

"I want to take you to a party tonight," he said lightly.

"Another one?"

He chuckled again. "Another one." There was something reckless in his eyes then, a laughing challenge thrown her way. "A special sort of party—very exclusive, very private. It will be at a house here in the city."

She gave him a look that mingled doubt and suspicion. "I don't think I should—"

He pressed her hand, interrupting to say thoughtfully, "I've never seen your hands without gloves, do you realize that?"

Considering what he *had* seen, she thought, flushing again, her hands hardly seemed to matter. "Falcon, I don't think—" she began determinedly, only to be cut off again.

"Small hands. Soft hands? Yes, soft hands. So soft they feel like satin. And long, delicate fingers that touch with the lightness of a butterfly." His thumb slipped underneath the hand on his arm and rubbed the hollow of her palm slowly. "And if I put

my lips here, where it's warm and a little rough
. . . Would you like that, sweet?"

Victoria kept her eyes resolutely downward, feeling hot and shaky and hoping vaguely that none of
the passersby heard or realized that he was, as they
strolled decorously along the sidewalk, seducing
her. Damn him. "Stop," she murmured.

"Only if you say you'll come with me tonight. I'll
stop if you agree, sweet. For now."

"That's blackmail," she managed unsteadily,
very aware of his thumb rubbing her palm in a
slow, tingling rhythm until she couldn't feel anything but that, the promise of that.

"Isn't it?" he agreed politely.

There was a moment of silence, and she sighed.
"All right. I'll go with you." She wasn't at all
certain that, if she refused, he wouldn't resort to a
more blatant seduction right there on the sidewalk.

He chuckled, and his thumb rubbed an instant
longer before he removed it and patted her hand
lightly. "Wise of you. In case you hadn't noticed,
Victoria, I'm rather determined where you're concerned."

She sent him a look. "Is that what it is?" Her
sense of humor came to the fore, rescuing her from
the deep, throbbing demand of passion he had
evoked so swiftly and easily. "No, I didn't notice."

He laughed aloud at her dry tone. "Too determined to accept a denial from you, sweet."

Victoria decided not to pursue that. "What kind
of party is it?" she asked casually.

"A gambling party." He was watching her as he
answered, and was delighted by the series of
expressions that followed one another across her

lovely face. First, interest and curiosity, then, doubt and uncertainty, and, finally, wariness.

"Is that proper?" she asked, an unconscious severity in her tone.

"Not in the least," he answered, his tone cool. "However, you will find many of the highborn ladies of the city in attendance, and gambling as expertly as the gentlemen. And since their reputations are at stake as well, you won't have to fear the loss of your good name."

Victoria glanced at him, feeling a pang that she didn't have to look far to identify. She looked down quickly to hide the realization from him. No gentleman who felt respect for and had serious intentions toward an innocent lady would even think to take her into such a place. But, she reminded herself sternly, she had known what he wanted from her since the beginning; it was a bit late to cavil at it now.

"Would she could make of me a saint, or I of her a sinner."

Congreve, she identified automatically, remembering the dusty book in Morgan's library, and the long hours spent reading beautiful words. And then, realizing that Falcon was looking at her, she said casually, "It sounds interesting." *You're going to make a sinner out of me, and why don't I care?*

"Good." He turned them back toward the hotel, smiling.

Why don't I care?

Falcon straightened away from the wall and moved smoothly and silently down the hallway, slipping through the door before it could be closed. "Hello, Tyrone," he said pleasantly.

Marcus Tyrone, ex-blockade-runner and now a shipping magnate, studied his visitor for a moment with veiled gray eyes, and then moved across the office and settled in his chair behind the desk. "Delaney." His voice was just as pleasant as the other's, and his hard face wore a faint smile. "What brings you here?"

"Curiosity," Falcon answered, stepping over to the visitor's chair in front of the desk and settling in as if for a prolonged stay. "I don't like questions with no answers."

The two men regarded one another across the desk, neither giving away his thoughts. They were both big men, both dark, and both had survived considerable dangers in their varied pasts. Tyrone had come out of the war with a sizable fortune, and had rapidly built a shipping empire; Falcon came from a wealthy family, but had spent his adult life in a career far less lucrative than the other.

In appearance, they might have been brothers. Neither was given to showing his feelings, and both tended toward the cynical while observing their fellow man. In business affairs, each would have unhesitatingly trusted the other. And there was, in fact, a curious sense of empathy between them, unacknowledged by either but felt by both. They might have been friends.

They were, in truth, enemies of a sort.

Tyrone shrugged. "I don't like answers with no questions."

Falcon inclined his head; nothing of his relaxed posture suggested that every sense was alert. "Fair enough. I've often thought," he went on pleasantly, "that the decision to transport the gold south on a blockade-runner was an interesting one."

"It does seem unexpected," Tyrone agreed in a thoughtful tone. "Damned risky, in fact. What gold are we discussing, by the way?"

Falcon played along. "A federal gold shipment, stolen in '63. A rebel plot, presumably to finance the war effort. Funny thing is, precious little of that shipment ever surfaced."

Tyrone lit a thin cigar, frowning a bit. Then he looked at his visitor with clear, calm eyes. "Fancy that. I don't suppose it could have gotten *misplaced* along the way?"

"Somehow, I doubt that," Falcon said, tacitly telling the other man he didn't suspect him of having kept the gold for himself. "I think it was delivered. In Charleston."

"Then, I assume," Tyrone said placidly, "that the men who . . . commissioned the shipment took rightful possession."

"I wonder." Falcon let the silence grow for a few moments. "There were all kinds of wild rumors just about then. Rumors of a group of powerful men in Charleston who were prepared to do just about anything to achieve a victory for the South. I believe I even heard a rumor that they meant to use that gold as payment for an assassin to gun down Lincoln."

"I wouldn't know anything about that," Tyrone said.

"No, of course you wouldn't," Falcon agreed, with no more than a hint of irony in his voice. Abruptly, he added, "It seems to me those men would have been very careful about the captain they chose to transport the gold. Quite a temptation, a million dollars. Unless, of course, he didn't know what he was transporting."

Tyrone smiled.

Falcon tried a slightly different tack. "I think we'll find that at least one of those men knew a certain captain quite well. Well enough, at any rate, to trust him."

"An interesting theory," Tyrone said. "Tell me— do you really expect to find your gold after all these years? It seems a bit unrealistic."

"I'll find it." Falcon smiled slowly. "It's only a matter of time, and I have plenty of that. And patience. I never leave a job half-finished." He rose to his feet. "I'll be around, Tyrone. I'll probably see you again."

Tyrone's smile remained until the door closed behind his visitor, and then faded. He stared at nothing for a long time, then crushed out his cigar in a heavy glass ashtray on his desk. "Damn," he said softly.

The carriage ride that night was brief, and Victoria—cloaked again in black, with a shimmering green gown peeking out from beneath—was grateful for that when Falcon told her. Grateful and—disappointed? But she should have known he wasn't a man to allow any opportunity to slip by unnoticed.

"Take off your gloves, Victoria." He was lounging back in his corner, relaxed, watchful. Smiling lazily.

She looked at him, caught almost instantly by his eyes, his hot, hungry eyes. *Would she could make of me a saint . . . or I of her a sinner.* How easy it was for him. How easily he was making her a sinner. Slowly, she drew off the short gloves and held them in one hand. He reached out and took them from her, tucking them into one of his pockets.

He held out a hand in a silent command, and, very slowly, she put one of hers into it.

"Small and soft," he murmured, then straightened and lifted the hand, palm up, to his lips. She gasped when she felt his tongue, her fingers fluttering against his lean cheek. And then the carriage was halting, and he released her hand, looking at her with eyes that gleamed darkly.

The house was a respectable brownstone in a good neighborhood, and no raucous sounds issued from it to proclaim the activities within. A doorman admitted them, his large size and rather battered face hinting that his duties probably included dealing with the occasional rowdy patron; he murmured a greeting to Falcon in a respectful tone, gave Victoria a faintly surprised glance, and closed the door behind them.

"Why did he look at me like that?" she asked softly as they climbed the stairs to the upper floor.

After a moment, Falcon said, "Max? Surprised to find a real lady inside these walls, no doubt." The words were mocking, but there was something new in his tone, something sharp and grim. As if, she thought, he were suddenly regretting bringing her here.

She glanced at him, puzzled, but had no time to question him. A maid at the top of the stairs took her cloak, and when she turned to face him again, his eyes went over her emerald-green gown with a look that was half pleasure and half pain.

"Dammit," he muttered.

She lifted her chin, the green of her eyes intensified by the gown, and by anger. "I'm sorry you don't like it."

He met her stormy eyes for a moment, his own gaze somber, then studied her gown again. It was low-cut—the neckline displaying as much of her charms as the pink ball gown had done—and trimmed in lace and satin ribbons. He looked back at her face, where the soft veil of her Windsor hat shadowed her features mysteriously. Then he sighed explosively.

"Oh, I like it. So will every other man in the house." He took her hand and tucked it into the crook of his arm, his own hardheaded nature hell-bent to go through with this now that they were here. But she didn't *belong* here, dammit, even Max had known that the moment he'd laid eyes on her; Victoria didn't just *look* like a lady, she *was* a lady— and even an ex-boxer whelped in the gutters of New York could see that!

"I don't understand you," she murmured help-lessly, and he was saved from replying to that when a second ex-boxer-turned-doorman opened a set of double doors at the end of the hall to allow them into the main rooms of the house.

Victoria's hand tightened on his arm as they went in, and she gazed around with wide eyes. Smoke and the mingled scents of perfumes and spirits hung in the air, and the sounds of laughter, swear-ing, and an occasional argument sliced through it. There was a glittering profusion of gowns and jewels, half again as many men as women, and a concentrated attention to the business of gambling that was almost absolute. Except, Victoria noted with startled eyes, a few couples here and there with other matters on their minds, and total disregard for onlookers.

Here and there she saw a face she recognized from the ball a few nights before, and she realized Falcon had not deceived her in saying that the highborn of the city would be present. But what he hadn't said—and what she noticed almost instinctively—was that the patrons of this "private" house were a mixed lot. Among the glittering gowns, jewels, and laughter of the very rich were also the grim, sometimes cruel faces of professional gamblers, the cheap tawdriness and bright smiles of young women who would no doubt accept payment for an hour or so in one of the private rooms, and the rough conversation and manners of workers or tradesmen with the price of a game.

"We don't have to stay," Falcon said to her quietly.

She looked up at him as they paused inside the room, and her smile was half forced and half reckless. He had brought her here, after all—and she even thought she knew why. Not because Falcon didn't regard her as a lady, but because he *did*. She had thought about it carefully this afternoon, remembering several occasions when some reaction of hers had shaken him, defusing his blatant determination to seduce her. He was hardly a man without a conscience, she knew, and it was clear that some part of him was bothered by her innocence.

So he had brought her here, to this place where ladies and gentlemen checked their reputations at the door so that they could enjoy gambling with cards, dice, and each other, as well as with persons they would normally have little or nothing to do with.

Her smile became suddenly natural as she decided it was time Falcon discovered that innocent ladies were often many other things as well. She felt reckless, vividly alive, and strongly aware of Morgan's advice. *Damn the consequences.* "Poker, I think. Will you stake me?"

His eyes narrowed for a moment, and then he nodded. "My pleasure, sweet." He led her to a table where a game was breaking up, beckoning to a dark-suited man with an expressionless face who was standing by with chips.

"Gentlemen, may we join you?" Falcon asked the remaining three men at the table.

As soon as Victoria was seated at the table, she made up her mind to come out of the game a winner. Judging by their clothing, the three men here could well afford the loss, and she wasn't at all concerned about Falcon. She looked at the chips he had placed before her and asked, "How much are these worth?"

"The whites are fifty, the reds a hundred, and the blues five hundred."

She had never played for money before. "Dollars?"

"Don't worry, little lady." The heavyset man on her right grinned, a wolf's grin if she'd ever seen one. "The rest of us are plenty anxious to take Delaney's money; he has the luck of the devil."

Victoria silently marked him as the one to run up the stakes on, and gathered the hand she'd been dealt. So Falcon had been here often before? It didn't really surprise her. She would have been surprised to hear that he was a hardened gambler, sensing instead that he enjoyed playing the odds, but probably wasn't addicted to the game. As the hand began to be played, she realized that three of the men at the table clearly considered her a beginner. The fourth, Falcon, seemed very watchful, his eyes unreadable.

Coolly, she began raising the stakes, and even the man with the wolf's grin started to lose his tolerant smile. One by one, the other players folded, until there was only Victoria and the wolf. He was bluffing, and she knew it. She also knew that Falcon was watching her intently, but that didn't bother her.

Calculating that the pot held something like five thousand dollars, Victoria calmly called the wolf's raise and waited for him to lay down his cards. Not quite bluffing, she noted as she saw his hand. Three aces.

"What have you got, little lady?" he asked, confident.

Victoria fanned out her cards and placed them faceup on the table, smiling gently. A flush, in hearts.

The wolf looked a bit stunned, but pushed the chips across the table to her. "Your trick," he murmured.

Three hands later, Victoria folded and retired from the game, satisfied that she had made her point. She was a winner by several thousand dollars, after having been at no time a loser. She had earned the wary respect of the three men she had soundly defeated, and Falcon's interest had never wavered.

He didn't allow her to stray from his side, even though he continued to play, taking her hand and glancing up at her thoughtfully. Victoria smiled and moved to stand just behind him, and when he lifted her hand to his shoulder, she allowed it to remain there.

She watched the game for a moment, then allowed her gaze to stray, taking in the activities around her now that the game no longer demanded her complete attention. She wondered if this kind of place had existed even in the decorous society she remembered before the war; she thought it probably had.

For the first time, she began to understand that people were merely people, and that vice was old. Public morals and manners might bow to the dictates of convention, but there would always be places like this one. Men and women would always be drawn to one another despite marriage vows and public censure, drawn to drink and gamble, drawn to escape the strictures imposed on them.

She looked down at the raven-black hair of the man seated before her, looked at her hand lying possessively on his black-clad shoulder, and her sigh went unheard in the noisy room. If Falcon had brought her here to make a point, he had certainly been successful. He had proven to her that manners and morals were surface things, easily discarded.

"You're a lady, Victoria—don't ever lose that." Morgan's voice sounded in her mind.

But what did it *mean?* Where was the dividing line between *lady* and *woman?* If not the decorum and morals taught to her almost from birth, then what? Though he had taught her many of the necessities of survival and self-protection—how to hunt and track and handle a gun—Morgan had avoided challenging in any way the first fifteen years of her life, the things she had been taught during her childhood. He had, in fact, subtly but strongly impressed upon her that she should never forget what she had been taught. She could run a plantation or ranch, handle servants, balance household accounts, converse with people across a dinner table or at a ball, dance, ride sidesaddle, fashion her own clothing and hats, and plan or even cook a large meal.

She could track an animal or a man across land that would give an Apache pause, ride a horse for days on end, and shoe it if necessary, handle a pistol or rifle with ease and precision, trap or fish for her meals, find water in a desert and shelter in a storm, in winter or summer. She could remove a bullet from an injured man and treat his wound and fever, deliver a baby, or a foal, or a calf. She could play poker. She had killed a man.

And yet she was a lady. Or was she?

Victoria looked around at the other women in the room, the ladies and the whores, and wondered what made them different. Was it only that the whores were honest, that they made no effort to hide what they were beneath fine manners?

Unconsciously, she shook her head. No. Perhaps for these women, in this place, yes—but not for all women. Then what was it? What made a woman a lady?

Her abstracted gaze sharpened as a white-aproned servant passed with a tray of glasses, and she took a glass of brandy for Falcon, leaning forward to place it at his elbow. She caught her breath as her breasts were pressed briefly to his back, and saw his eyes gleam beneath the thick lashes as he glanced up at her.

"Thank you, sweet." He turned his head to kiss the hand on his shoulder lightly.

She straightened again, a little flushed. *Oh, damn, what was it?* Was it this jumble of emotions Falcon ignited in her? Did a woman's body know something a lady's never could? Born a lady, had she become a woman only when Falcon had held her, kissed her, touched her?

Victoria was confused, angry. No one had *warned* her, no one had told her this would happen. No one had said that a dark, green-eyed Irishman who was untamed beneath his polished surface would make her doubt and question the teachings of her life. First, her mother had told her that she would marry and bear children, that a man would always protect her, that there were things in life she would never have to worry about. Then the war had come, changing all that she knew. And then, Morgan had come into her life and taught her how to protect herself, whether she faced the elements, animals, or a threatening man. But no one had warned her that a man would threaten her with no other weapon than the compelling strength of his passion.

After a moment, she bent just enough to murmur, "Excuse me," to Falcon, and then slipped away into the crowd. Resolutely ignoring an amorous pinch from a drunken gambler she passed, she moved on until she reached the wide doorway leading to another room. It was in her mind to find someplace quiet where she could think, but two steps into the room convinced her this was hardly what she was looking for.

It occurred to her belatedly that she should never have abandoned the relative safety of Falcon's presence.

This room, like the other, held card tables, but where the attention there had been focused more or less on the gambling, in this room, another vice was being explored. The number of women and men was fairly equal, the laughter softer, the caresses bolder—and nobody was playing cards.

Victoria turned hastily back toward the door.

"Hey, honey, how 'bout a drink?" The rough voice emerged from a shadowy corner as a big, heavy man stepped out in front of her.

Victoria kept her voice calm and level, hoping it would penetrate the man's alcoholic fog; few men were desperate enough to molest a lady—even here, she hoped. "Please let me pass, sir." She started to step around him, but the man blocked her.

"Not so fast, honey!" He laughed, a booming sound, and reached out to grip her arm. "I got money. I can pay. Why don't we go have a little drink, an' then—"

"Release me, sir!" Here was one man who didn't think she was a lady; the offer of payment told her that. She started to push his hand away, but he caught hers. Then both his arms were around her, pinning her own at the small of her back, and his hot whiskey-breath was heavy on her face.

"Now, be nice, honey. How 'bout a little kiss?"

Victoria was shaken, growing afraid, but when his stubbled chin scraped across her face and wet lips searched for her own, instinct took over. Her knee jerked up, the impact muffled by her heavy skirts, but still strong enough to take him by surprise and cause a certain amount of pain.

He grunted, his body contracting, and his arms tightened convulsively around her with a force that took her breath away. "Hellion! I'll teach you!" His raspy voice was furious, pained, cruel.

She tried to bring her sharp heel down on his booted toe, struggling violently to escape him; she was hampered by her woman's skirts and defeated at the outset by his strength and fury. He drew back an arm to strike her, his dimly seen face contorted by rage, and Victoria braced herself for the blow she couldn't avoid.

But then the man was jerked away from her as though he weighed nothing, yanked around to face another large figure, and met a blow that knocked him reeling. With a bellow, the drunkard rushed his attacker, blind rage impelling him. But iron fists staggered him with two lightning punches, and a third knocked him backward to measure his length on the floor.

Victoria had been more or less pushed aside by the fight, and she winced when she realized that the fight wasn't going to be confined to the drunken man and Falcon. One man started to rush past her toward Falcon with angry mutters, and she barely caught his more sober companion's urgent warning.

"For Christ's sake, man, don't go after Delaney! He'll kill you!"

After that, the confusion was total, the noise unbelievable, and the enthusiasm complete. It might have begun with Falcon defending her honor, but within minutes no one seemed to know—or care—how it had started. It hardly surprised Victoria, since she had seen a brawl or two in the last years; nor did it surprise her to see a bright look in Falcon's eyes that told her he was enjoying his part in the melee.

The other men were enjoying it too.

The man who had warned his friend about Falcon was standing near Victoria when the fight became a glorious free-for-all, and she caught a pained look from him. He sighed, loosened his tie, murmured, "Excuse me, ma'am," politely to Victoria, and broke a chair over another man's head.

She should have been shocked. Perhaps she should even have found a deserted corner—somewhere—and folded gracefully into a faint in the best tradition of Southern womanhood. The truth, however, was that Victoria wanted to laugh. Her own rebellious anger was still alive in her, and she was annoyed to realize that a man could express his anger in a fight while a woman couldn't. Or, at least, wasn't *supposed* to. So, when someone reeled drunkenly into her and grabbed her waist, possibly for support, she broke a vase over his head.

She looked up as the man crashed to the floor, meeting Falcon's eyes unerringly. He grinned at her suddenly, an infectious grin that was boyish, and she heard his low laugh even through all the crashings and thuds and grunts. Then he became distracted as someone took a wild swing at his jaw, and Victoria lost sight of him.

She was rather busy herself; the brawl had reached the point where the women either had to get involved or hide under some sturdy piece of furniture. Since the furnishings in the room consisted mainly of card tables, there wasn't much to hide under. She lost her hat at some point, and removed one shoe at another point because she'd run out of vases and table legs.

And she almost hit Max with the shoe when he appeared, suddenly, at her side. The doorman was unsurprised to find a lady's shoe waving in his direction, and his rough voice was unfailingly polite when he addressed her.

"Excuse me, ma'am, but you'd best be leavin'. They'll be bringin' the wagon round any time now."

"The wagon?"

"Police, ma'am."

That hadn't occurred to her, but doubtless Max knew what he was talking about. "Oh." She looked toward the melee, where Falcon's height made him visible. "But I can't leave without Falcon—"

"I'll fetch him, ma'am." Max casually backhanded a man making for Victoria with clutching hands, then waded into the brawl toward Falcon.

Giggling despite everything, Victoria tried to brace herself against the wall long enough to get her shoe back on, but there was a great deal of pushing and shoving going on, and she found it impossible. "I wonder where my hat got to?" she said to Falcon as he and Max reached her.

He looked at the shoe in her hand and grinned suddenly. "I can't imagine. Shall we leave?"

"Certainly." As they stepped into the relative quiet of the other room—which was deserted, since all the occupants had either joined the fight or left—she added calmly, "May I borrow your arm?"

He offered it silently, watching with a solemn expression as she held his arm and bent to put her shoe on.

Max was just as grave, waiting until she straightened to say, "The back way'd be better. You'll have to walk to the corner to find a cab."

"I know the way," Falcon murmured.

"I'll fetch the lady's wrap," Max said, and vanished.

Falcon led her out into the upper hallway, and then through a narrow door and into a secondary hallway, where a steep flight of stairs led downwards.

Max reappeared. "Here you are, ma'am."

"Thank you, Max." She allowed him to place the cloak around her shoulders, fastened it herself, then smiled at him. "It's been a pleasure meeting you."

He blushed. "Thank you, ma'am. The same, I'm sure."

Chuckling, Falcon led her down the stairs and out into a narrow alley through an unobtrusive door. The night air held a faint chill, but wasn't really cold, and there was little damp. The alley was deserted, save for themselves.

"Handy thing, a lady's shoe," Falcon murmured, tucking her hand into the crook of his arm.

Looking up at him, she said, "I'd like to know how you managed to escape without so much as a bruise! I was pinched and pummeled and squeezed—"

Interested, he asked, "By the lad you clouted with that vase? Or one of the three you got with the shoe?"

"All of them." She sighed.

He laughed again, a low sound of real amusement. "You surprised me a bit back there, sweet. First, your expertise with cards, and then, your— shall we say, spirited?—self-defense."

"But you still think of me as a lady," she said, realizing that the lightness she had intended was missing; even to herself, her voice sounded dismal.

He turned them left, then, as they came out of the alley, giving her no more than a glimpse of the strident activity going on in front of the house they had left. After a moment, he said, "You are a lady; why should I think anything else?"

Victoria hesitated, then said recklessly, "Wasn't that why you took me to that house? So that you could make a point about the shallow veneer of a lady? I wasn't the only *lady* in that house, Falcon—"

"Yes, you were," he interrupted quietly. "Even Max could tell that. You didn't see him warn anyone else, did you?"

"I thought it was because he was your friend."

"Max? He is. But I've spent a night in jail before, and he knew it," Falcon said in a dry tone. "Despite his blushing back there, he's tough as nails, and doesn't care about anybody. Except you, obviously. *Blushing.*" He shook his head. "Max wasn't worried about me. If you hadn't refused to leave without me, he would have left me to be rounded up with the rest. It was *you* he was concerned for. He knew you didn't belong in that place."

"Why?" Her voice was soft, bewildered. "*Why?* What makes me different from those others? And why does it disturb you, whatever it is?"

Falcon walked beside her in silence for a few

moments. The street was deserted, no cabs or carriages or pedestrians moving in the darkness. His voice was rough when he finally answered. "Why? I'm damned if I know, sweet. It isn't your fine clothing or gentle voice. It isn't even the way you move or hold your head It's . . . something else. In your eyes. Something you were born with." He laughed curtly. "Something not even a missing hat or a lethal shoe can alter."

"You say it as if it's a curse," she murmured.

They were about to turn a corner onto a more traveled street, where the sounds of hoofbeats and the creak of cabs and carriages could be heard, but Falcon stopped and drew her into the shadow of a building. She could feel the hardness of brick against her back and the strength of his hands on her shoulders, and in the shadows, his face was curiously both implacable and indefinite.

"A curse . . . Yes, sweet, it's a curse." His voice was harsh, angry. "I've never yet taken an innocent to my bed, much less a virtuous *lady* with a sweet drawl and a tragic past and a trick of making me feel things I'm better off without. There's no place for a woman in my life, Victoria, no room. I haven't spent more than two weeks at a time under the same roof since I was sixteen years old. My bedmates are bought for the night. Whores. Do you understand? I pay for my pleasures, or else find them in some secluded bedroom or garden with a willing and knowledgeable woman who *might* call herself a lady even if no one else does!"

5

Victoria stood silently, listening unflinchingly to words that were delivered like blows.

"I've spent half my life on the move, and I'm not going to change now. And I've seen what that kind of life does to a wife, Victoria. If she goes with her man, she finds a brutal life, facing the dangers, perhaps left alone in the middle of nowhere; and after a while, she isn't pretty anymore. If she stays behind, every visit produces a child, and she has to bear them alone, raise them alone. It's hell, do you understand that?"

With her unique upbringing, Victoria understood more than he could possibly know, but this was hardly the time to explain that to him. "I understand what you want of me." She kept her voice even. "So why does the rest matter? I knew you didn't want a wife. You've made that very clear."

Harshly, he said, "It matters because you're a lady, dammit! I may well be a bastard, but not enough of one to give you any false promises, Victoria. I want you. I'm half out of my mind with wanting you, but I can't offer you a future."

In the back of her mind, something stirred, and

she realized then, with a surge of hope, that it was possible Falcon cared more than he knew. Morgan had taught her to pay attention to what a man said and did, to read character in behavior as well as words, and Falcon's past behavior with her was in contrast to his words now.

He had acted entirely too possessively and jealously to have felt only desire for her, and too tenderly on occasion. And then there had been his vow to "brand" her as his—again, hardly the words of a man bent on casual seduction. And the very fact that he seemed so conscious that she was a woman a man should marry rather than just bed was a telling one.

And if she was wrong? There was always that possibility, and it was a strong one. No matter how he felt about her now, Falcon could well decide his wanderer's life suited him far more than anything she could offer.

With a leaden feeling in her heart, Victoria couldn't convince even herself that there was a future for them.

"Victoria? Did you hear me?"

"I heard you." She took a deep breath and lifted her chin, realizing that it made no difference. Whatever she was, whatever he thought her, she was a woman. "And I understand."

"Do you?" His voice was restless now. "I wonder."

"I'm not an idiot, Falcon. I told you. I knew from the first what you wanted of me."

"Then I'm surprised you've been willing to go out with me."

"No, you aren't." She half-laughed, rueful. "You made certain I would."

He laughed a little as well. "Yes, I was that much of a bastard, wasn't I? You—you weren't quite what I bargained for, sweet. But that doesn't change anything."

"I didn't expect it to." Her voice was soft, calm. "I don't expect marriage, or even a future of any kind. But—lady or not—I won't pretend you don't make me feel things I've never felt before." Hesitantly, she reached up to touch his lean cheek, her fingers unsteady. And she had a sensation of burning all her bridges behind her; there was no going back, no retrieving the words.

Falcon was very still, his head bent toward her, his fingers moving gently on her shoulders. She had thrown him off-balance yet again, and he didn't know how to react. "And what about later?" His voice was husky, but the words were measured. "What will you say when your groom asks why you gave yourself to a man who hadn't married you?"

She thought of Morgan, and her voice was steady. "I'll say it was because I wanted to."

After a moment, Falcon bent his head, kissing her so deeply that she was shaking when it ended. But when he lifted his head again, his voice was rough. "Why doesn't that make it easier?" he murmured, wondering why the thought of her facing a husband on some distant day made his chest ache and his temples pound with emotion he couldn't identify.

She looked up at him helplessly. "You've told me what you want of me, and I've told you I want it too. What else can I say, Falcon? I don't really know how . . . that is, should we go to my hotel? Or yours? Or is there someplace—"

He stopped her by touching her lips gently with his fingers. "Don't." The single word was a raw sound. He was silent for a moment, and then pulled her against him, just holding her, stroking her back with hands that were a little unsteady. He felt wounded inside, torn and uncertain for one of the few times in his life. He was fascinated by her, bewildered by her. "Not what I bargained for at all," he murmured.

Victoria felt like crying, even though some part of her knew it wasn't a rejection. Unsteadily, she said, "Is this what being a lady means, Falcon? Marriage or—or nothing?"

"I don't know. I just don't know, sweet. Why don't we give ourselves a little time to think about it?"

She wanted to tell him that she loved him, but the words remained trapped, unsaid. He wouldn't want to hear them, she knew, and she was very afraid that any further complication would send him away from her instantly. And she also knew, instinctively, that there were no words to help them now. Either they would become lovers or they would not. And if they did, she thought it would result from an interlude of heated passion rather than calm decision, with no time for questions. And perhaps it was better that way, because talking would never make it seem right—even though it *was*.

Her arms slipped around his waist and she pressed herself closer to him, her face hidden in the warmth of his throat. *I love you!* He smelled of tobacco and horses and a clean wind, like the wild

Southwest she loved. He had the strength of a frontier carved from wilderness, the certainty of himself gained by half a lifetime of wandering.

And her own certainty of love was a bedrock thing—as if it had always been in her to love this man, and that love had awaited only a meeting to show itself. She needed no marriage vows, no approval from others, no golden ring. None of that mattered. Seeing no future for them, she was willing to take what she could get. She needed only him.

"I want you," she whispered against his throat, and felt him swallow, felt the tremor her words inspired.

"You aren't making this easier," he said huskily.

She lifted her head, looking up at his shadowed face. "I don't know how to do that," she said simply.

"Don't say you want me." There was a thread of humor in his deep, voice.

"But I do."

He groaned softly, but stepped back, firmly taking her hand and placing it in the crook of his arm. "I'm taking you back to your hotel."

"And then?"

"Leaving you there. Dammit."

"Falcon—"

"Oh, I'll be back, sweet." He sighed roughly. "Tomorrow, God help me."

Victoria walked at his side, outwardly demure as they joined the people moving along New York's sidewalks. Her thoughts were hardly demure, however.

She was wondering how to go about seducing a man.

New Mexico

Read tightened his horse's girth, ignoring the sounds of retching a few feet away. To Gus, he said, "It won't be easy. The bastard died too goddamned quickly."

"There's still the woman," Gus observed.

Read shook his head. "What could she know? She was a kid, and half-wild with terror; you heard him rambling about the state she was in during the trip."

"She could have noticed something."

"No." Read knew his voice had hardened, and he felt as well as saw Gus prudently abandon the idea. "We'll search every mission in Texas if we have to. We've got time before the ship sails. We'll find it."

Gus nodded. "What about Sonny?" he asked, gesturing toward the harsh sounds issuing from behind a boulder.

Sonny staggered from behind the boulder just then, his face pasty-white. "Jesus, Read," he mumbled, wiping his mouth with the back of a shaking hand. "I ain't never seen that done to a man. There ain't enough left of 'im to bury!"

Read sent him an indifferent look. "Let the buzzards have him."

"They'll be comin' after us now," Sonny whined. "Those men of Fontaine's. They'll come after us, an'—"

"They won't come after us. We'll be out of the country soon, and they won't even find him for

days, if at all. But, just in case they do, you're going
to ride a few miles east and settle down to wait,
Sonny. Gus and I will ride west a few miles before
we circle and go on into Texas. If no one tries to
follow us within two weeks, you ride on to El Paso.
We'll meet you there. That'll give us time to get to
the ship."

"But the gold!"

"You'll get your share," Read told him flatly.
"But if I find you anywhere but here or in El Paso,
I'll kill you."

After a moment, Sonny went over to his horse,
muttering. He rummaged in his saddlebags for his
spare shirt, tossing aside a crumpled piece of stiff
paper without looking at it. Pulling out a shirt that
wasn't much cleaner than the one he had on, he
changed and then stuffed the stained shirt back
into the saddlebag.

"You think he'll do it?" Gus murmured to Read.

"Think I give a damn? He didn't hear much of
what Morgan said, so he doesn't know what we're
looking for. He's half-crazy by now, and worthless
to us."

Gus swung up on his horse without another
word, and the three riders moved on, riding out of
the ravine where a broken body lay concealed
among blood-spattered rocks. A crumpled piece of
paper was stirred by the breeze, rattling dryly
across the rocks until it was caught in a crevice.
The wind tugged at it a bit longer, then gave up the
struggle.

New York

Whatever seductive plans Victoria might have created, they could hardly have been put into effect during the next two days, for Falcon gave her no chance. They spent hours together, shared meals and rides in carriages—open carriages. They walked in the park and talked of casual, uncomplicated things. They went to the theater on the second night.

They were never alone.

He collected her in the lobby of her hotel and left her there at evening's end, courteous but formal. He offered his arm whenever they walked together, his hand when she entered or left a carriage, but never once kissed or held her.

Victoria would have been appalled at this state of affairs if she hadn't realized that he was finding it as difficult and wearing as she was herself; it was in his vivid eyes, dark and hungry when they rested on her, and often his voice deepened and thickened before he was able to control it. Seeing that, she cloaked herself in serenity, responded to his politeness with bland acceptance, and awaited developments. Inexperienced in love and desire though she was, she was too wise about men in general to attempt to force anything from Falcon.

He couldn't hide the hunger in his eyes when he looked at her, but she was only too aware that he was fighting himself, that he was struggling to come to terms with the elusive but seemingly

undeniable part of her that was a "lady." Having all
but thrown herself at his feet without apparently
losing that stubborn quality, she knew that it was
he who would have to somehow deal with it.

But by the third afternoon, as they strolled in the
park, she was restless and uneasily aware that he
had been in the city for some time now; when
would he leave? The thought of his leaving was a
cold knot somewhere inside her, and she realized
for the first time just how badly she would hurt
when he *did* leave her.

"Falcon?"

"What is it, sweet?"

"They're holding a benefit at the hotel tonight.
Dinner, dancing. I thought, if you wanted to—"

"I'd love to," he said promptly.

She nodded. One more night, at least. One more
chance. And they'd be so close to her room. . . .
Her own thoughts had lost the power to shock her.

"Victoria?" He was frowning a little.

"Yes?"

"Remember the night we met? The men in the
bookshop?"

"Of course."

They had reached a bench, and he waited until
she sat down before sitting beside her. "I meant to
ask you something about them, but it slipped my
mind." He sent her a brooding glance. "Happens
often around you."

"What did you want to ask?"

"Could you tell if they were Southerners?"

"Why, yes, they were." She looked at him in
surprise. "How did you know?"

After a moment, he said, "I didn't. I just wondered if they spoke with accents, that's all."

"You're still looking for that man," she realized. "The one you followed to the bookshop."

He gazed at her beautiful, delicate face, and wondered if the niggling sense of unease he felt professionally would have been stronger or clearer had he not become involved with her. He felt edgy, restless, and these last platonic days had caused the feelings to grow like steam trapped beneath a tightly fitted lid; he was no longer sure what he felt when he looked at her, and thoughts of business had been fleeting, vague, and disturbing. When he did manage to think of business, he was aware that some instinct prodded him, some foreboding that was elusive.

He still felt instinctively that something had been set in motion, and that he had somehow, without understanding, been a part of it. After years of false trails and fruitless searching, he felt closer to the gold than he ever had before. But he didn't know *why*. If he had been able to concentrate on that, methodically consider everything that had happened since he had come to the city, he might have been able to figure it out—but that option was beyond him.

"Falcon?"

He stirred, and managed a faint smile. "Am I looking for him? Not actively. I was just curious."

"I'm curious."

"About what?" he asked lightly.

"You. You don't talk much about yourself."

"There isn't much to say."

Victoria refused to be put off. "No? You mentioned growing up near Apache camps; you've been a scout, a soldier, now a Ranger. You're obviously educated and—on the surface, at least—gentlemanly."

He acknowledged that wry hit with a smile of genuine amusement. "On the surface? Well, better than not at all, I suppose."

She gave him a pained look. "You aren't going to talk about yourself, are you?"

"I'm boring, sweet. Now, you, on the other hand—"

Victoria hardly wanted to talk about herself. She was becoming more and more conscious of the fact that Falcon knew nothing of her marriage, and with every hour that passed she found it increasingly impossible to broach the subject. How could she tell him? How could she explain. . . .

"You've gone away," he said softly.

She looked at him, aching. "Have you thought about it?" she asked, reckless.

Something kindled instantly in his eyes, dark and hot, and his face tightened. But he looked away from her. "I've thought of little else," he answered, a bit roughly.

"And?"

He shook his head, silent.

She glanced around at the park, where couples strolled and children played and there was no privacy to be found. No place where a woman could throw herself shamelessly at a man's feet, because she couldn't be left with *nothing*, not even a memory. . . . Then her gaze returned to his hard, handsome profile. "You'll be leaving soon, won't you?"

After a moment, he nodded. "A few days, maybe a week. I have to—get back to work."

"In Texas?"

He didn't know, but nodded anyway. And before she could speak again, he rose to his feet and helped her up. "It's getting late. I'll take you back to your hotel."

Victoria accepted his arm, walking beside him with her head downbent, her eyes seeing nothing. She hadn't needed to ask to realize that Falcon had not found an answer for them. And she wondered if she could have loved him if he had found it easy to take her and then walk away.

The man was big and wide, the eye patch he wore giving him a sinister appearance. Jesse's bloodstained purse was clutched in his hand, and his laugh was harsh.

"I've killed your brother, girl, bashed his head in and let the creek carry him away. I've killed your Pa over there, and your darkie. Now I'll kill you if you don't tell me where the gold is! Tell me, or by God, I'll cut your throat!"

Gold? She didn't understand, didn't know what he was talking about. They had no gold! Her heart hammered in terror, and when he lunged at her, she never even realized the knife was in her hand, until she saw it protruding from his chest, until his blood spilled onto her dress . . . blood . . . so much blood . . .

Victoria woke from the nightmare with a muffled cry, sitting up on her bed and staring wildly around the peaceful bedroom. Afternoon sunlight slanted through the window, and the silence of her room was broken by the dim sounds of activity in the hotel.

Just a dream.

She got up and bathed her face at the washstand, her heart still thudding unevenly. Ever since she had told Falcon about that day, she had relived it several times in nightmares: each time more vividly, with more of the long-buried memories remaining in her mind afterward. She could remember it all now, even though she wished that day had remained buried.

Morgan had ridden up then, she remembered, just as she'd fled the house in weeping terror, clutching Jesse's purse. Morgan had comforted her, then gone to look for the one-eyed man, discovering that he had apparently managed to live long enough to crawl on his horse and ride away. Morgan had buried her father and old Sam. He had even, at her hysterical insistence, taken her along the path Jesse always rode to Charleston, to the creek where that horrible man had killed him. They had found blood on a rock near the middle of the creek, and Morgan had told her gently that Jesse's poor body had probably been carried downstream.

She had been in shock, and hardly remembered much else. Except that Morgan had told her he would take care of her. She hadn't known his name, or anything about him. But she had put her hand in his and left her home, never looking back.

And she had never regretted it.

Victoria went to her window and looked down on the busy New York street below, wondering now, as she had not wondered then, what Morgan had been doing at Regret. He'd never said, and she, with those memories buried, had never asked. Even in her shock and grief, she had realized that Morgan had also been grieving during those days, during the long trip to New Mexico. He had lost a cherishcd dream when the South went down in defeat, and, looking back, Victoria realized that the only small piece of the life he had loved had lived, in the end, in her.

He had been so careful in teaching her not to eradicate the traits her upbringing had instilled in her. He had been openly proud that his wife was a Southerner, that her accent was soft and her manners delicate. The neighbors had said that he doted on her, and smiled because it was clear she adored her husband.

Her husband . . .

Victoria smiled, because it was better than weeping, and wondered silently if Morgan would understand what was happening to her now. She thought he would, but wondered if he wouldn't grieve because the traits he had nurtured in her had not been able to stand up against Falcon Delaney.

How odd it was. One man had taught her to be a lady, whatever that meant. Another man had taught her to be a woman, whatever that meant.

The ground floor of Victoria's hotel was taken up by many long halls and huge rooms; there were tall, fat columns and a great deal of brass and glass and fine furnishings, and intricately woven rugs cushioned the marble floor. The benefit was to take place in one of the ballrooms she had never seen, and when she came down early to explore, she found musicians tuning their instruments and ser-

vants rushing about with harried expressions.
There were a number of guests already, standing
and sitting in couples and small groups in the
lobby and hallways, talking and laughing.

Victoria had arranged to meet Falcon in the
small "reading room" just off one of the hallways,
and she made her way there now, aware that she
was attracting a good deal of attention. She held
her head up and kept moving, wondering uneasily
if this had been as good an idea as it had seemed a
few hours before. She wasn't at all sure now. There
had been no one to advise her; she was yielding to
instinct. Falcon saw her so clearly as a lady that she
had been determined to show him tonight just how
wicked a lady could look if she set her mind to it.

The gown was one Morgan had ordered from
Paris, but he had been unable to convince her to
wear it, despite his insistence that no other woman
would be able to carry it off as well as she. Made of
the finest silk, it glowed like a living thing, shimmering with trapped light. It was completely,
starkly black, with no hint of another color. But it
needed no other color. The three-quarter sleeves
were trimmed with black Mechlin lace, which also
edged the off-the-shoulder and extremely low-cut
neckline; black gauze and black velvet ribbons
decorated the skirt; and the bodice was embroi-
dered intricately with black thread. The full under-
skirt dropped almost straight in front, and was
gathered in back with lace-edged flounces, ending
in a short train; there was a short overskirt of sheer
gauze, hanging down in front, looped up at the
sides, and bunched out at the back.

Victoria had chosen not to wear gloves, and the

only jewelry she wore was a diamond tiara, which kept a sheer, lacy, black veil in place. The veil fell just over her eyes; above it, the tiara sparkled, and her wheat-gold hair gleamed in its intricate, swirling style. The dress alone was daring, both in color and style, to say nothing of the deep V neck and bare shoulders; the tiara and the brief, mysterious veil lent her an enigmatic, almost feline look, like a shadow drawn deliberately over something to conceal it.

A glance in the mirror had told Victoria that she looked a far cry from virginal. She looked wicked. Her tiny waist and full breasts were set off by the tight bodice that clung lovingly to the naked flesh beneath, and though the lace at the neckline provided a bit more cover than the black silk alone, her breasts were nonetheless bared almost to the nipples. And the contrast of the black gown and her fair hair and pale, golden flesh was so striking that it lent an illusion of more flesh showing than there actually was.

Victoria was very conscious of that illusion as she moved down the hall and into the deserted reading room, very aware that every step caused the front of her gown to mold itself to the length of her legs daringly, but she had already burned her bridges. She had been right in believing that talking of the situation between her and Falcon would change nothing. Nor would thinking about it. But she was achingly aware of her desire, and of his, and knew that one more interlude of passion between them would quite likely settle the matter for them.

The reading room was small, three walls lined floor to ceiling with shelves containing books, and the fourth wall holding the door, a velvet-covered settee, an overstuffed chair, and a small table between them. She stood, running a finger along the shelf of books, unseeing, feeling her entire body tauten and warm at the thought of lying in his arms. Wouldn't that be worth the pain that was sure to come afterward? And she loved him. . . .

"Well, well. It's Victoria, isn't it?"

She turned slowly, still half-trapped in dreams of Falcon, unaware that more than the veil shadowed her eyes and made them darkly secretive. "Yes." She looked at the other woman, a redhead dressed improbably in a scarlet gown even more daring than her own. "And you're Cassie."

"Waiting for someone?"

"Falcon."

"I see." A man might have thought Cassie was smiling; Victoria knew she wasn't. "Tired of playing the lady and decided to play the whore instead?"

Coolly, Victoria said, "We both seem dressed for that part."

Cassie lifted a surprised brow. "Have teeth, do you? Well, well. I supposed we could fight like cats over him, but I hardly think I need to bother. After he escorted you tamely home the other night, he came back to me. Did he tell you that?" Her voice dropped to a soft purr. "Did he tell you how he pulled up my skirts and took me against a wall?"

Still cool, Victoria said, "Couldn't you find a bed?"

A soft gurgle of laughter escaped Cassie's red lips. "Nice try, honey, but you went white when I told you that. You do have it bad, don't you? Someone should have warned you never to fall in love with a man like Falcon. He's a marvelous lover, but the woman hasn't been born who could get him to a preacher."

Through lips that felt stiff and cold, Victoria said, "That doesn't appear to trouble you."

Cassie laughed again. "Oh, I'm already married, honey. I have a doting husband who wouldn't see one of my lovers if he climbed into bed with us. What I want from Falcon, he's perfectly willing to give. And has. You see, I don't need a ring or a promise from him—and he knows it. And I don't have to wear black to prove that to him." Her eyes narrowed suddenly, and her voice dropped to a low note again. "He may well play the gentleman with you, but I'm the one he'll come back to." Then she laughed softly and left the room.

Vaguely, Victoria heard the musicians stop the screechy tuning of their instruments and start to play softly. She turned back to the books, unseeing now for a different reason. Truth? Or spite? It could be either, and quite possibly both. Falcon had told her himself that Cassie had "offered," but that he had sent her away. Had he indeed gone back to her?

"My bedmates are bought for the night. Whores. Do you understand? I pay for my pleasures, or else find them in some secluded bedroom or garden with a willing and knowledgeable woman who might *call herself a lady even if no one else does!"*

She half-closed her eyes, hurting more than she would have believed possible. She had no right to hurt, she knew that; Falcon had promised her nothing, after all. And just because he wanted her didn't mean he wouldn't continue to want other women. She looked down at her gown and laughed softly, bitterly. Even Cassie had recognized the dress for what it was: A costume, a defiant show of bravado.

"Victoria?"

As soon as she heard his deep voice, she knew that what Cassie had told her changed nothing. She still loved him. She still wanted him. And she was still willing to take whatever he offered her, even if it was only a night.

"Dear God," he murmured when she turned to face him.

She watched as he slowly closed and locked the door and leaned back against it, seeing the leap of hot desire in his eyes, seeing his gaze moving over her hungrily. And she was grateful for the veil that shadowed her own eyes. But she had to ask, had to know, because she was hurting, and she couldn't seem to breathe. "Cassie was here."

He pushed himself away from the door and crossed slowly to stand before her. His eyes were still hot, darkened, but he was frowning a little now. "Was she, sweet?"

"Do you call her that too?"

"No." His hands lifted to her bare shoulders. "What did she tell you?"

Steadily, Victoria said, "That you went back to her the other night. That you made love to her."

His hands tightened, and after a moment, he said shortly, "Well, she was half-right." He didn't bother to correct the euphemism. "That's what I intended to do."

"I see."

"No, I don't think you do." His voice was hard. "I

didn't want her, Victoria, I wanted you. But she was willing, and uncomplicated, and I thought she could help me to forget you."

Victoria swallowed hard. "And did she?"

He shook his head. "I couldn't feel anything for her, do you understand that? I wanted to. I wanted to take her like some rutting animal," he said harshly, "but I couldn't. *You* were the fire in my blood. There wasn't even a spark for her."

She gazed up at his taut face, the blazing green eyes, and knew that he was telling the truth. The cold ache inside her eased, and she could breathe again. Before she could speak, he was going on, his voice still harsh.

"Do you realize what you've done to me? I've been acting like a tamed cat, Victoria. I walk along beside you, the perfect gentleman; keeping my hands to myself when what I really want—"

"What do you want?" she whispered.

Falcon drew a deep breath with a rough sound. "You shouldn't have worn this dress," he muttered, looking down at the almost naked breasts that were rising and falling quickly. "You're a siren in this dress, not a lady." There was something in his voice, something savage and frustrated and barely under control.

"Perhaps I don't want to be a lady any longer."

Her soft voice filled his ears, his mind, dizzying him more potently than the finest Irish whiskey. He was touching only her shoulders, gazing down at the glint of green eyes through a shadowy veil, watching her lips part and her tongue touch them unconsciously so that they gleamed. He thought vaguely that this was sorcery, enchantment, because it was too astonishingly powerful to be anything else. His body responded like dry wood to a torch, blazing with heat. The muscles of his belly knotted hard, and desire was a searing knife cutting him up inside. Every harsh breath he drew hurt him, burned his chest and caught raggedly in his throat. And the full, heavy ache in his loins intensified until he knew he would burst with it, explode into a dozen jagged pieces.

He had thought he could control this, just as he had controlled his desires and impulses for his entire adult life, and the past platonic days had deceived him into certainty. But now, looking at her in the wicked black gown, he knew that he had never been less in control. From the instant his gaze had met her startled green eyes in a dusty bookshop, he had been adrift in a wild current, rudderless and at the mercy of something beyond himself.

His hands moved slowly along her shoulders and up her throat, and the silk of her golden flesh sent a hot tremor through his entire body. He framed her delicate face, staring down at her, fascinated by the shadow of her veil.

Victoria stared up at him, and her veil had altered him as well, leaving his lean face darker, curiously savage. The hard planes and angles of his face seemed more sharply defined, his eyes more deeply set and hooded, his mouth almost cruel. His bronze skin was drawn tightly over the bones beneath, as if every muscle was taut, and a fine sheen of sweat drew her finger to glide slowly along his upper lip. She could feel his breath, coming quick and hard, feel tension as her hand came to rest on his cheek, and her fingers trembled.

"You're hiding the lady," he said thickly. "Concealing her behind this bit of lace, in the shadows where she won't torment me."

Her body trembled. There was a heavy, stinging ache in the pit of her stomach, a quivering weakness, and she could feel a sudden heat between her thighs. Her breasts hurt—the nipples tightening, hardening until they poked against the thin silk and showed themselves in jutting desire.

"That lady's gone," she breathed unsteadily, nearly drowning in the sensations racing through her, the wild tangle of emotions gripping her heart and clouding her mind. Her body ached, as if she had held herself stiffly at the edge of a precipice for too long, muscles quivering with the strain of trying to save herself. "She's been packed away with her demure gloves and her—" *And her wedding ring.* Even that, even the knowledge that he thought she was free hadn't the power to alter her course now. And it didn't matter, after all, it didn't matter. . . .

"Victoria . . ." His head lowered and his mouth captured hers, fierce and hot, his tongue thrusting deeply. His arms gathered her close, crushing her against him, and her arms went up around his neck instantly. A sound she was hardly aware of escaped her; faint and hungry, dark colors swirling behind her closed eyes, she could feel her breasts swelling, aching against his hard chest. She wanted to move, press herself closer than she could ever be.

Falcon lifted his head at last, and looked at her with blazing eyes. His hands swept slowly down her back to her hips, and he groaned softly. "You're not wearing a damned thing under this dress," he said hoarsely, the flames in his eyes leaping higher with the realization.

The thin silk separating his flesh from hers provided a tingling friction, and she half-closed her eyes in pleasure. "No," she murmured. "Nothing. No chemise . . . no petticoats . . . nothing at all."

The promise of her words scorched his already inflamed senses, and he clamped his teeth together in an effort to maintain some tenuous control. "Jesus, don't do this to me," he got out in a thick, strangled voice. "Not here, not now. You're tearing me apart, sweet—" He broke off with a groan as her lower body shifted against him in an unconscious, seeking movement. He sought her lips again, blindly guiding them both the few steps to the velvet-covered settee.

Victoria was barely aware that she was half-lying against the corner of the settee while he kneeled on the pale Persian rug at her feet; she was too conscious of his fingers behind her, coping with the buttons of her gown, his mouth moving hotly over her breasts. Her fingers locked in his thick hair as he bent over her, her head fell back and she bit her lip, trying to hold back sounds struggling to escape wildly.

"I want to look at you," he muttered thickly, and his hands moved from behind her to tug the loosened neckline of her gown down to uncover her breasts. Victoria opened her eyes to watch his face, moved almost unbearably by the wonder in darkened green eyes, by his intense expression of pleasure. "So lovely. God, Victoria!"

She couldn't stop the moan from escaping when his hands surrounded her swollen breasts and his thumbs teased the jutting peaks until they were painfully tight and hard. He watched her response to his touch, intent and absorbed as pink flesh became dusky, until the distended nipples begged for a more intimate caress. And when his mouth closed over one of those hard buds, he felt as well as heard her moan again, and the soft, driven sound spurred his own hunger.

Christ, she was beautiful, perfectly beautiful. Her lovely breasts just fit his hands, he could span her tiny waist, and the gentle flare of her hips was so damned seductive. He could feel the slender shape of her leg as he slid his hand down, catching the flounced hem of her skirt and drawing it slowly upward. In some distant part of his mind he was aware of where they were, aware that privacy in this small room was a risky thing, despite the locked door. He didn't care. He had to see her, touch her, had to satisfy this terrible craving to learn all there was to know about her.

His hand touched her silky leg beneath the skirt, and he felt her tense in an instinctive response, but she made no protest at all this time. He felt the garter just above her knee, holding her stocking in place, and his hand slid between her thighs there, very gently parting her legs. Her knee touched his knotted belly as she obeyed the insistent pressure, and he caught his breath even as she did.

He concentrated on her breasts, his tongue rasping, sucking strongly while his hand remained still on her inner thigh, until he felt the tension ease, felt her legs widen for him. He could barely breathe at all now, every muscle aching, and the heat in his body a raging fire.

"Falcon, it hurts. . . ." Her voice almost wasn't there.

"I know, sweet," he murmured thickly, nuzzling his face between her flushed breasts briefly and then lifting his head, watching his hand disappear beneath the black skirt. "I'm hurting too." Her inner thigh was warm silk, and, as promised, there were no barriers to block his searching, caressing touch.

Victoria cried out softly when his fingers touched the heavy ache she had been more and more conscious of, shock rippling through her at the mind-numbing pleasure of that starkly intimate contact.

Falcon nearly lost his tenuous control then, but held on to it somehow, absorbed in learning her secrets, fascinated by her awakened face. The soft curls at the base of her belly were hidden from his eyes, but not his hand, and he explored gently until he found the slick heat at the core of her womanhood. He caught a second soft cry with his mouth, kissing her deeply while his finger stroked.

Dear God, he wanted her! But he was aware of their surroundings, and, suddenly, fiercely, he wanted nothing to mar their first joining. He wouldn't take her with her dress half-off, on an uncomfortable settee or hard floor in a tiny, locked room. He wanted to undress her slowly, lingeringly, kiss every inch of her golden body while she lay on the bed they would share. He wanted to take her hair down and run his fingers through the silky strands, make love to her, watch her sleep, kiss her awake.

Still kissing her deeply, hungrily, he eased his hand away and allowed her skirt to fall, and then pulled the neckline of her gown back up over her breasts. He rose to his feet, aching, and gently pulled her up and turned her around, fastening the bodice with an absolute concentration on the task.

"Falcon?" She was bewildered, hovering on the edge of hurt.

He turned her back to face him, framing her face in his hands as he gazed through the veil into darkened green eyes. In a voice that was low and rough and tender, he said, "I'm going to make love to you, sweet."

"Then—?"

"Not here." He kissed her gently. "We're going out there to that damned benefit. We'll have dinner and dance. And then we're going upstairs to your room, to your bed."

She wanted to laugh, cry, throw her arms around him. She didn't want to eat or dance. "Why not now?" she asked shamelessly.

His smile was crooked. "I need to calm down a little first, sweet."

"You look calm," she offered, dissatisfied.

He chuckled softly and tucked her hand in his arm, leading her to the door. He paused there, his free hand on the lock, looking down at her with a sudden glitter in his eyes. "My sweet, I'm about as calm as a tribe of Apaches on the warpath. If we went upstairs now, I'd tear your clothes off like an animal."

She caught her breath, and his rough voice gentled.

"That isn't what I want. I want to make love to you, all night. I want to be gentle, and I—" He swallowed. "Give me a little time, all right?"

"All right," she whispered. And when he unlocked the door and opened it, she walked calmly from the small room, with the secret knowledge of what was to come hidden behind her serene smile and veiled eyes.

6

Victoria had never felt so vividly alive, so vibrantly aware of everything around her. The music was delightful, the food superb, the colorful crowd fascinating. Falcon never left her side, and when the dancing began, his stony refusals to give her up to another partner sent many a shaken gentleman sliding away in the hopes of becoming invisible to those dangerous eyes.

And when they discovered Leon and Mary Hamilton in a secluded corner during one of the pauses between dances, Falcon was told roundly by the forthright lady that he was hardly being discreet.

"Do you know we heard a man warn his friend not to get near 'the lady in black' because he was apt to be murdered by her escort? You're about as subtle as a cobra, Falcon!"

Unmoved, he said, "I'm not trying to be subtle."

"Yes," Leon murmured, "we rather gathered that."

Victoria could feel herself flushing a little, and looked hastily around the huge room to avoid amused eyes. But she found another pair of eyes in

133

the crowd—eyes fixed intently on her face and holding a peculiar expression she couldn't read. "Who is that man?" she murmured curiously.

Falcon followed her gaze, and his expression hardened; it was easy to see who was staring at Victoria. He waited until those cool, gray eyes met his own, and sent a silent warning. He saw a flicker of a smile that might have been acknowledgment of the warning, and then the other man turned away.

"Falcon?" She was looking at him, puzzled.

He returned his gaze to her and forced taut muscles to relax. "You may have heard of him; he was a blockade-runner during the war. Marcus Tyrone."

"I had to—run an errand for Captain Tyrone, Tory. But the Raven *sails soon, and I have to get back."* Jesse had said that to her, just before riding away from Regret, and to his death.

Victoria turned her head to swiftly search the crowd, looking for that tall man. "Captain Tyrone," she murmured. Jesse's captain. Jesse's friend. She found that tall figure and committed him to memory.

"He made a fortune," Mary was saying. "He has half a dozen ships now, including that little one he used to run the blockade. What was it called?"

"The *Raven*," her husband supplied casually.

"That's it. Rumor has it that he has a heart of stone and the morals of a tomcat—"

Mildly, Leon said, "He probably hasn't found the right woman, that's all. And there is such a thing as a reformed rake."

"You should know," his wife said softly with a sidelong glance at her husband.

"I do know," he said promptly. "I found the right woman."

Mary grinned at Victoria. "He's so disarming."

Victoria smiled in return, hoping she didn't look as distracted as she felt. Tyrone. The last link to her childhood, because he had known Jesse. She wanted to meet him, talk to him.

"Falcon, why don't we go have a cigar and leave the ladies to rest their delicate feet?"

Looking at Leon's bland expression, the protest Falcon had been about to make died in his throat. He knew that expression. But he felt unsettled, disturbed by the way Victoria's gaze had searched the ballroom and fixed on Tyrone. She was distracted, preoccupied, and he felt a flare of primitive emotion because something had taken her attention from himself.

"Falcon?" Impatient now.

He carried Victoria's hand to his lips. "Excuse me for a few moments, sweet?"

She met his gaze, her own softening, and a smile curved her lips. For him. All for him now. "Of course."

"Well, well," Mary said as the two men moved away through the crowd. "You certainly have managed to tether that bird."

Victoria blinked and felt herself flush. "He has very nice manners," she managed a bit weakly.

Mary's eyes were bright with enjoyment. "Manners? I've known Falcon for years now, and I can tell you that, like his namesake, he's a hunter. He was hunting the other night, when you two came to our party, but he isn't hunting now." Her expression was thoughtful. "And I have a feeling he won't go hunting again."

A little shaken, Victoria said, "You must be mistaken. He told me himself that there was no place in his life for a woman."

"Did he, now? That's interesting." Mary smiled. "Take it from one who caught another hunter a few years back—pay attention to what a man *does*. He hasn't let another man near you all evening, and has hardly taken his eyes off you. And I have never, in all these years, heard Falcon use an endearment or seen him kiss a woman's hand."

Victoria fought a surge of hope, knowing it would only hurt more if she allowed it and Mary was wrong. She managed a smile. "We'll see, won't we? Will you excuse me, Mary? There's someone I need to talk to."

"Certainly." Mary chuckled. "And if that someone happens to be male, better you talk to him before Falcon comes back!"

"You're making a habit of dragging me away from Victoria, and I don't like it," Falcon told his boss impatiently.

"I never would have guessed."

"For Christ's sake, Leon!"

With a chuckle, Leon said, "All right, all right. Marry the girl before you go mad over her, will you? I need your mind intact—at least until we find that gold."

They were standing across the hall from the ballroom, where a smoking lounge was deserted except for themselves. The mocking words caught Falcon off guard, and his face closed down immediately. "Did you call me in here for a reason?"

"It wasn't to offer paternal advice," Leon murmured. "Since I'm only ten years older than you—"

"Leon."

He cleared his throat. "Right. The list will be here within a day or two."

"Didn't you say that last time?"

"This time it happens to be true. We had to change couriers. The first silly bastard managed to fall off his horse and break a leg somewhere in Virginia. Andrew's got it now."

"I'll be waiting for him, then." Falcon felt restless, unsettled. Two days, and then he'd have to go wherever the list led him. Victoria . . . After tonight, she'd be out of his mind—she'd *have* to be out of his mind. His chest ached, and he didn't know why. "I'll be waiting," he repeated.

"Good," Leon said politely.

"Anything else?"

Silently, Leon reflected that, if any of his other men were to use that tone with him, he would have put them in their place instantly. But Falcon wasn't one of his other men. Leon could remember the beginning, during the war, when he had met Falcon Delaney. Agents had been sent to specific parts of the South—Confederate states, or areas—to conduct the necessarily quiet search for leads that had continued after the war. But Texas, notoriously hostile to government interference, was a part of the Confederacy, and not entirely convinced that the war was over. Treasury decided an open investigation would be both politically and practically impossible. So, it was determined to send a lone agent into Texas.

After consideration, it was also determined that
the lone agent should become a Texas Ranger,
allowing both mobility and a certain amount of
authority. If necessary, he would remain a Ranger
for years, and accept whatever assignments were
given him as a Ranger. He also had to search for the
gold. To assume the role of Ranger, Treasury
needed a man very familiar with the Southwest
and its inherent dangers. A man who was indepen-
dent, coolly efficient, and tough enough to get the
job done. They also needed a Texan; however, no
such agent existed. So they got the next best thing.

A Delaney.

Leon, who had recommended Falcon, had not
regretted it. He had seen something in that younger
Union officer, something cool and tough and implacable. He had seen it since then, often. And he
had respected it. It would have been crazy not to.
There were some who said "those Delaney men"
were Indian-wild and snake-mean, but few in
Arizona said it out loud, and never when a Delaney
man was within hearing.

"Anything else?" Falcon asked impatiently once
more.

Leon wondered if that gently born lady in the
ballroom was strong enough to handle a Delaney
man. He hoped so. For both their sakes. "No. No,
there's nothing else."

"Mr. Tyrone?" She looked up into a hard face, in
which cool eyes regarded her at first with puzzlement and then surprise.

"Ma'am?" He inclined his head courteously. His
voice was deep and calm.

A little hesitantly, she said, "My name is Victoria Fontaine, Mr. Tyrone. I believe—I think you knew my brother?"

His brows drew together, but before he could speak, a bellman appeared at Victoria's shoulder.

"Mrs. Fontaine? There's a wire for you, ma'am. The desk clerk thought you should have it right away."

Victoria accepted the telegraph message and then glanced back at Tyrone with an apologetic smile. "I'm sorry; perhaps we could talk later? Excuse me."

He inclined his head again, and, frowning, watched her move back through the crowd to the door.

Falcon was too far away to hear what was said, but he saw Victoria accept something from a bellman, then smile at Tyrone and move away. He stood for a moment, staring across the room, bothered by the look on the other man's face. What was it? Surprise? Recognition? And why had Victoria apparently sought out the former blockade-runner?

Frowning himself, Falcon went after her. She wasn't in sight when he reached the hallway, and he looked into two rooms before finding her alone in the third, a small salon. She was holding a telegram in her hand, staring across the room at nothing, and her face was tight with worry.

"Victoria?" He forgot about Tyrone. "What is it? What's wrong?" He came into the room and crossed to stand before her. "Bad news?" She didn't seem to hear him, and he reached out to take the wire from her.

She started, then gasped. "No! Falcon—" But it was too late.

He stood staring down at the telegram, his face draining of color as though some awful wound was stealing his life's blood away. And when he looked at her, his eyes were as hard and bright as emeralds. "Mrs. Morgan Fontaine." His voice was soft, hardly more than a breath of sound, and toneless. "Your—husband—seems to be missing, Mrs. Fontaine. The ranch foreman appears to be concerned."

Victoria had never felt so cold. "It isn't what you think," she whispered. *Oh, God, why didn't I tell him!*

He laughed, the bare sound of something terrible. "Isn't it? How many other men have you bewitched with your innocent eyes and gentle ways, Victoria? How many other poor bastards have helped you betray your *husband?*" The final word was gritted out, raw and hard.

"You're wrong." She could barely speak through the tight pain in her throat. "I can explain."

He reached out suddenly and jerked the veil away, staring into her eyes. "Christ, it's still there," he muttered in disbelief. "Even knowing you're a liar, a cheat, it's still there."

"Falcon—"

"The body of a siren, the face and eyes of an angel. And the heart of a whore!"

She flinched. "Please! You have to listen!"

"To more lies? How you must have laughed,

sweet." The endearment was nothing of the kind now; it was harsh, mocking. "Just one more stupid son of a bitch crawling to you on his knees, hungering after you like a besotted boy. Do you enjoy that, Victoria, enjoy thinking of that power? Does it amuse you to twist us into knots until you've bloody well emasculated us? Gelded us, like poor mindless beasts?"

Falcon wasn't searching for the hurtful words; they broke out of him like jagged knives, tearing him even as they ripped at her. He couldn't stop them. Her face was white, masklike in its utter stillness, her eyes dark pools that were bottomless and opaque. She flinched from every word.

His gaze raked her black gown, and he laughed. "Showing your true colors tonight, weren't you, sweet? I should have realized you were too eager to be virginal, too goddamned responsive to be innocent. But you blinded me with your lying, cheating, *innocent* eyes. Damn you. Damn you to hell."

Victoria didn't understand how it was possible to hurt so much and go on living. He would never listen now, she thought dully, never understand or believe. She lifted her chin and said softly, "Goodbye, Falcon." Then she turned away with an effort that broke something inside her, and left the room.

Falcon didn't know how long he stood there, staring blindly at the spot where she had stood, the damning telegram crumpled in one hand and her veil in the other. Some terrible cry of rage and pain writhed inside him, tearing bloody wounds, and he wanted to smash something. Anything. He wasn't conscious of the music that droned on and on,

wasn't aware that an occasional guest stepped into
the room and then backed hurriedly out again. He
wasn't aware of anything but the turmoil of emotions that left him frozen in an anguish he didn't
even understand.

Not his, never his. She belonged to another man.

Lying, cheating. And still, it was in her eyes, that
innocence, that peculiarly undeniable look of a
lady. That look of gentler times, and fragile
strength, and dignity. How? *How?* Pale and still,
she had accepted his brutal verbal blows, and then
she had gently said good-bye and walked from the
room. A lady.

His lips twisting, he looked down at the telegram
and veil in his hands, then thrust them both into a
pocket. He moved stiffly from the room, his entire
body aching like something battered. He went back
to the ballroom first, searching, but no stunning
black gown, no fair beauty met his gaze.

"Falcon?" Mary was at his side.

"Have you seen Victoria?" The sound of his voice,
calm and even, sounded strange to him.

She touched his arm. "No, not since— Falcon,
what is it? What's wrong?"

"I have to find her," he murmured. He looked
blindly around for a moment. "The desk clerk. He'll
tell me which room . . ." He absently brushed off
Mary's hand and left the ballroom, heading for the
lobby.

"Mrs. Fontaine has checked out, sir."

"There hasn't been time," Falcon said.

The desk clerk looked at him a bit warily,

grateful there was a counter between himself and this man with the wild eyes. "She checked out, sir, just a few moments ago. The gentleman who was here when she arrived had arranged for a private coach to stand ready for her. She requested that most of her bags be sent on, and she ordered the coach." He didn't add that the lady had left still in her ball gown, a simple portmanteau in her hands and a black cloak thrown over her shoulders.

After a moment, Falcon turned away and left the hotel. He stood outside for a long time, gazing off into the night.

Days later, Falcon realized just how stunning had been the blow Victoria had dealt him. The realization came with a gray morning and a grating hangover, and he sat for long minutes on the side of his bed, a pounding head held in both hands. He felt sick and shaken, his thoughts moving sluggishly.

His Irish heritage and a naturally hard head, combined with a dislike of losing control of himself, made Falcon a man who could count the drunken nights of his life on the fingers of one hand; never before had he consciously and willfully drunk himself into a welcome oblivion.

Disgusted with himself, he pushed the nagging pain to the back of his consciousness, fighting to ignore it. He rose, splashed cold water on his face. The small mirror showed him a face that was stubbled with beard, the mouth a thin, hard slash, and the eyes red-rimmed and hot. Grim, Falcon went to soak out the poisons in his system with a steaming bath, then allowed himself to be shaved—

another occurrence he could count on one hand. With determination rather than hunger, he faced breakfast.

It was only then, after pushing his plate away and drinking hot, strong coffee, that Falcon squarely faced his own violent emotions.

He could still feel the jagged pain, though it had been confined to some dark corner of himself with the control built up over a lifetime of need. But the first shock of rage and bitterness had worn off now, and though he was conscious of the ache that wouldn't go away gnawing at him, he could at least think clearly again.

It was *wrong*, all wrong. The bile of his bitterness had washed over them both like acid, searing her attempts to explain, but now, in the tenuous but sane calm of passing days, he knew he should have listened to her. She had walked away from him, white and anguished, her eyes dark pools of blind agony, and he had known even then that hers was not the face of that heartless whore his cruel words had drawn for them both.

He still had the telegram, knew the name and location of Morgan Fontaine's ranch. He had to go after her, had to hear the explanation she offered. His jaw was aching, and he knew his teeth were locked tightly. She was his, she belonged to *him*. He'd take her away from her husband, kill the bastard if he had to.

Why hadn't she told him she was married? Was her marriage a troubled one, was that why she had come to New York? How could she look so innocent, so damned *untouched*? How? He would have sworn that she had never even been kissed with passion, never been held and touched as he had held and touched her.

He ran a shaking hand through his hair. The tenuous sanity was slipping, pain and bitterness and yearning tugging at him, pulling him into a black pit of anguish.

He had to go after her.

"You look the way I did after El Paso."

With a scowl, Falcon looked up to find an old friend standing by his table. The dining room was nearly deserted, and none of the few patrons paid the slightest attention to the new arrival. And though he had not seen this particular friend for months, Falcon, characteristically, made no overt gesture of greeting.

"In El Paso," he said, his voice dry and the scowl fading, "you worked your way through every girl in Miss Amy's whorehouse and drank half her whiskey. In three days. Next to you, I'm a saint. Sit down, Andrew." With a tremendous effort, he fought his way through the tangle of emotions to concentrate on business. The gold, always the damned gold.

Andrew Murphy, grinning, sat down across from Falcon. He was a man of about Falcon's age, cheerful and fun-loving; few had ever guessed that beneath his friendly eyes and ingenuous ways lay a methodical brain and a nose for devious plots—of which he had unraveled many. He was whipcord-lean and sunbrowned, and only his warm smile made his thin face handsome.

And, like Falcon, he was a government agent of many years.

"I will," Andrew said briskly, "have to speak to the boss about you. It's obvious that those Texas boys are wearing you down. You look like eight miles of bad road, lad."

"Thank you," Falcon responded in his most polite tone.

Andrew sighed in a long-suffering way, unsurprised to find his old friend as stoic and unrevealing as ever. "All right, I won't ask what's happened to ravage that noble face."

"Too kind of you."

"Right, then. We've got the list, Falcon." In keeping with policy—open conversation and casual meetings being less obvious than anything surreptitious—Andrew made no attempt to lower his voice and spared not a glance for the other early-morning patrons of the dining room.

Falcon was equally casual. "Have we? Anything interesting?"

"Damned annoying, more like. See for yourself." He passed a folded sheet of paper across to his friend. "Takes us years to track down that so-called 'power circle' out of Charleston, and when we finally get the names, most of the bastards are dead. Of the three left, two are unaccounted for, and only God knows where they are. The third is living blamelessly on his New Mexico ranch. A very successful ranch, so I'm told, and has been for fifteen years. From all we can gather, it's unlikely that he was involved, even though he was in Charleston during April of '63."

Since Falcon remained silent, his gaze turned

downward to the paper he held, Andrew went on. "The Bureau did its usual thorough job in investigating the rancher's finances, and came up with a depressingly successful picture. Seems this lad made his money in Europe somewhere, possibly by piracy on the high seas, but it's been thirty years and who knows? Anyway, before the war, he went to live out in the western territories. They speak highly of him out there, and there's never been the faintest smell of anything crooked. Everything honest and aboveboard as long as he's lived there.

"He didn't fight during the war. He'd have been in his forties then, so that makes sense. Seems to have been a Southern sympathizer, and married a Southern girl young enough to be his daughter several years ago. But there's not a trace of that gold anywhere near him. Looks like the end of the trail, Falcon."

Without looking up, Falcon asked quietly, "The descriptions of the two missing men—are they accurate?"

Andrew looked at him curiously, alerted by something in that still voice. "As accurate as possible after all these years," he confirmed.

Read Talbot. *A large man, black-haired, with thick shoulders and a black eye patch.* Gus Rawlins. *Tall, thin. Brown hair and eyes.* God knew who the third man in the bookshop had been. A henchman hired for a kidnapping?

Falcon cleared his throat of some obstruction. "There was a rumor of a falling-out among these men. Do we have anything more on that?"

"Well, we're pretty certain of it. Seems to have happened about the time you figured the gold got through the blockade. April of '63. Our New Mexico rancher there left Charleston about that time, and the others seemed to have either left as well or turned on each other, foaming at the mouth."

After a moment, Falcon looked up, and Andrew knew instantly that his deduction had been wrong. It wasn't the end of the trail; somehow, to Falcon, the names on that paper represented the beginning, the beginning of something bitter and painful.

"What?" Andrew asked quietly.

Hard, remote, green eyes dropped briefly to the paper, then lifted again. Falcon's voice, when he spoke, was level, almost toneless, hiding whatever it was he felt. "I'll need the necessary authority to go into New Mexico. Everything documented, giving me all the power possible. If this rancher is as popular as you say, it won't be easy to bring him out of there without a bloodbath. And I may have trouble anyway; his foreman sent Mrs. Fontaine a wire a few days ago, saying he was missing. I'll have to be a federal marshal. And I'll need federal warrants for Morgan Fontaine's arrest, and the arrests of these other two."

"You're that sure?" Andrew, cut from the same cloth as the man across from him, wasted no time in questions or astonished exclamations; he spoke as if the possible solution to the mystery of a million-dollar gold shipment stolen years before was only mildly interesting.

And Falcon, knowing very well that his instincts were undependable where the name of Morgan Fontaine was concerned, was nonetheless certain. He was sure, with a leaden certainty far more pain than pleasure, that a years-long trail was coming to its end.

A man with a black eye patch named Read had paid for a night's drink with a stolen, specially minted gold coin. And then he had slipped from a waterfront barroom and gone to a lonely bookshop, where two other men waited to execute a plan. The only customer in that shop had been a woman who was the wife of one of the men who had planned the theft of the gold shipment.

Falcon had gone into that shop, intent on following a tenuous lead, never knowing that he had indeed been closer to the gold than ever before. And those men had never realized that the man who had blundered in and spoiled their plot was a far more deadly danger to them than merely a witness to a botched kidnapping.

Victoria. Morgan Fontaine's wife. How had they found her? Chance? Hearing her name perhaps, and making the connection? And they had planned to kidnap her, possibly use her to force Fontaine to give up the stolen gold—twice stolen. And how many years had they searched, just as Falcon had, for a man quietly ranching in New Mexico?

The kidnapping had been aborted because he had entered the shop, but Read had gotten the address, and they had gone directly to the ranch in New Mexico. And Victoria had received a telegram later saying that her husband was missing. Had he run when they got too close? Or had they found him, taken him? Was Morgan Fontaine alive or dead?

Was Victoria wife or widow? What would she find waiting for her in New Mexico?

And where was the gold, the gold that had

shadowed so many lives for so long? Did Victoria know of it? Did she know her husband had likely acquired his wealth as a pirate before she was born, and had helped plan and execute a daring robbery during the war that had destroyed her world? Did she know her husband was a hunted man, hunted by co-conspirators he had apparently betrayed, hunted by a government agent who had so nearly seduced her?

A government agent who was, even now—

"Falcon?"

"I'm sure," he said.

II

1

New Mexico

Victoria stumbled back with a harsh sound and turned to lean against her horse, dry sobs tearing at her throat. She felt cold, icy-cold, and her mind was numb. Her shaking hands held on to the finely tooled leather of the saddle fiercely, and her stomach churned.

She should get her rifle from the scabbard and signal the others, she knew. Every man on the ranch was searching, just as she had been searching. This was the second day. She would explain to them that Buck had shied nervously at the mouth of the ravine, arousing her suspicion, so she had urged him on. And that the horse had picked his way warily, snorting, shying, until she had finally seen what he had sensed or smelled.

But she couldn't move yet.

She stared over the horse's back, vaguely baffled because the day looked no different—and it should have. The sky was still cloudless, so blue it almost hurt to look at it; the air was dry and cool, and a slight breeze stirred the dust-dry earth. It was the kind of late fall Southwest day she had always loved, yet now it would always remind her . . .

This time, the blood was only rusty spatters on the sunbaked rocks.

The icy numbness spread over her slowly until she stopped shaking. *Animals.* Bastards! They weren't human, to do that to a man. A good, kind man. Not even the Apaches tortured their victims as Morgan had been tortured.

Victoria steeled herself with all the strength she could command, and finally released the saddle and turned away from her horse. She didn't look at the remains of that poor body, but instead searched the area all around. The hoofprints of horses, she saw, shod horses. Not Indians, then, although she'd already guessed that. Three horses.

She realized she was crying.

The horses had gone west. She was west of the ranch house now. Had they kept on in that direction? If they had, their tracks could well be lost in the confusion of tracks left by the ranch hands and cattle during the normal course of ranch work and activity.

She heard rough, gasping sobs, and knew vaguely that they were coming from her. They hurt her throat.

What was that in the rocks? Hard to see—a dry rattle as the breeze tugged at it. She bent and retrieved a crumpled piece of paper, smoothing it out against her thigh. A handbill? Hard to see. She brushed a hand across her eyes, and her glove came away stained with wetness.

The Frigate Ulysses, late of the War Between the States, welcomes passengers as it departs Charleston harbor for Europe. . . .

Victoria looked at the date on the handbill, trying

to think. Weeks. Just a few weeks away. Would Morgan's killers be on that ship? There was a chance. Maybe the only chance she had. She would track them. If she didn't find them quickly enough, she could wait for them at Charleston.

She would wait for them.

She folded the handbill carefully as she walked back to her horse, slipping it into her saddlebag. She fumbled at her rifle scabbard, finally drawing the Winchester out. She pointed the barrel up and fired a single shot, and then slid the rifle back into its scabbard.

Then she sat down on a rock and waited for the ranch hands.

New York

Marcus Tyrone looked up from his desk as his office door thudded open. His rather cold, gray eyes searched the intruder's face. He studied that handsome and sunburned face, unaware that the habitual chill of his gaze was somewhat trying to the younger man standing before his desk.

"All right—what did I do wrong?"

"Did I say you had done something?" Tyrone's tone was mild, his eyes still coolly thoughtful.

Long, brown fingers raked through silvery hair, and the younger man sank down in a chair before the desk, deciding not to await an invitation. "There must," he said, "have been some reason you ordered me to report to you first thing. Marc, I'd like to get the ship unloaded and—"

Tyrone pushed away the papers lying in front of

him and spoke carefully; he was unwilling to raise hopes without first being certain that it was at least possible. "Jesse, do you remember April of '63? The gold shipment?"

Jesse Beaumont laughed rather wryly, and lifted a hand to touch the crooked scar high on his right temple. "Remember? Hell, yes, I remember! That bastard got a knife in my ribs, then brained me with a rock. I must have been carried a mile downstream before I was able to crawl out. If it hadn't been for a hard head and a little luck, I'd be dead."

Tyrone thought it had been more than luck; even now, he didn't like to remember the condition Jesse had been in when, uneasy over the boy's delayed return from delivering the gold to Morgan Fontaine, he had ridden inland from Charleston harbor to find Jesse crawling along a deserted road and bleeding his life away. He shook off the memory.

"Before that, though, on your way back from delivering the gold, you had visited your family's plantation?"

Jesse nodded, eyes abruptly bleak.

"You told me that you spent some time with Morgan Fontaine after delivering the gold to him. Did you tell him you were worried about your family? About your sister in particular? Wasn't her name Victoria?"

"Yes." After a frowning moment, Jesse nodded. "He asked about my home, I remember. And he seemed—kind. Interested. I told him all about the family and Regret, where it was, and that it would come to me even though I didn't want it. I told him I was worried about Tory."

Tyrone reflected that that would have likely been enough to rouse Morgan Fontaine to sympathy. But, would he have gone to Regret? With all his plans in splinters, the group of powerful men to which he belonged at each other's throats? Probably. He was an unusually kind and caring man, as Tyrone himself had cause to know. And the woman's name . . . Dammit, everything fit! Still, he wanted one last fact to be certain. "Jesse, what did your sister look like?"

It was a moment before Jesse answered, and then his voice was rough and a bit unsteady. "Like me. But her hair was more golden, and her eyes were lighter. She was more delicate, of course. Her features were finer. But we were only three years apart in age, and people had mistaken us for twins more than once when we were younger."

It told Tyrone all he needed to know, really; he was virtually certain. "You went back there to the plantation when we returned to Charleston—about a month later, wasn't it?" He waited for the jerky nod, then went on in a deliberately impersonal voice. "You said there were two new graves, that your father and sister had vanished."

Jesse nodded, his eyes pained, but an expression of puzzlement was beginning to draw his brows together. It wasn't like Marc, he thought, to deliberately rake up old and painful memories. Some called him a hard man, but Jesse knew from experience that there was a great deal of kindness under that tough and sometimes curt exterior.

"Yes. The house had been looted, but there were stains in several rooms. Bloodstains. None of the neighbors knew anything, but there had been

violence on more than one plantation in the area.
I've never found a trace of them, so they must have
been killed. Marc—"

Tyrone held up a hand to halt the inevitable
question, and then answered it. "Jesse, I don't know
what happened at Regret, but I'm positive your
sister is alive. I met her less than a week ago; the
resemblance is uncanny."

And while shock held Jesse silent, Tyrone explained what had happened, finishing with, "I was
about to ask her if her maiden name was Beaumont, but a telegram was delivered to her and she
excused herself. When I looked for her a few
minutes later, she was gone. I got the impression
that she believed *you* were dead, which would
explain why she hadn't tried to find you before now.
She said, 'I believe you knew my brother,' as if it
were a long time ago."

He remembered, abruptly, that Falcon Delaney
had been there at the benefit too, remembered that
he had seen Delaney while looking for Victoria, and
that his hard face, so expressionless before then,
had held shock, a grinding bitterness, and something that might have been pain.

He had felt then, Tyrone remembered, a cynical
amusement that his almost-nemesis—not punishing, but shadowing—clearly had problems of his
own. And he wondered now if those problems had
something to do with Victoria Beaumont Fontaine.
He had been with her earlier in the evening, and
had shown all the signs of a very possessive man.

And if that were indeed true, the entire situation,
Tyrone thought with a short inner laugh, was
absurd . . . and dangerous. He knew only too well

that Delaney was still after the gold; his wary attitude toward Tyrone, as well as the pointed visits and pleasant, veiled questions, were proof enough of that. And if he were unknowingly involved with the wife of the man who had planned the theft?

He put the speculation aside as Jesse's voice, shaken but delighted, finally made itself heard.

"Alive? And married to Morgan Fontaine? But how in God's name could *that* have come about?"

Tyrone shrugged. "You'll have to ask your sister or Morgan about that. I assume that to be your plan? She's not in New York; she left days ago, but her hotel gave Morgan's ranch in New Mexico as a forwarding address."

Jesse didn't have to ask if his employer would give him the necessary time to find his sister; Tyrone's attitude made his willingness obvious. And though he had never been further west than the Mississippi River, Jesse thought nothing of possible hazards. He would, he thought vaguely, simply take a train out to the Fontaine ranch.

Tyrone could have warned him, and would have, except that his mind was somewhat occupied with speculation. He was thinking of a gold shipment that still, after all these years, had the power to haunt too many people.

In checking for Victoria's whereabouts at her hotel, he had also looked quietly for Delaney—who had left New York only yesterday. Tyrone had his own sources, and he had found out that a man answering Delaney's description had indeed been seen escorting Victoria Fontaine about the city, and to at least one ball, where several others had marked his possessiveness toward her. And Tyrone couldn't help but wonder now if an almost-forgotten crime was about to be solved by the simple mischance of a wife's lighthearted visit to New York.

Tyrone would have been willing to bet that Delaney's interest in Morgan's wife was entirely personal; what if he followed her to New Mexico? What if, somehow, after all these years, that very determined man stumbled upon the principals in that long-ago plot? What if the past were to be uncovered now?

How many would be hurt?

He looked up as Jesse stood to leave, still abstracted and faintly uneasy. "Jesse, there are still people seeking that gold. A very determined man named Delaney, for one. Be careful out there."

Jesse nodded, but he was looking ahead eagerly to the meeting with his sister; the warning went virtually unnoticed.

New Mexico

It was not, Jesse discovered days later, quite as easy as he had supposed to reach the Fontaine ranch. He took the train as far as he was able, then purchased a horse, asked directions, and set out— feeling more than a little appalled.

He could, certainly, ride, but he had never in his life been forced to ride from morning until night, and he had spent little time at all in the saddle these last ten years. And he had never before cooked over an open fire, or ridden—quite literally—for days without seeing another human being.

Accustomed to temperamental seas and booming cities these last years, he found the vast and empty landscape of the West not so much interesting as unsettling. It was so damned *still*. Not a movement anywhere to hint at life. He did not like it. He longed, with still nights following still days, for the comforting, pulsating sea beneath his feet.

Everything was strange to him, from the hat he wore and the saddle on his horse to the raw scenery and slow-talking people he had met. But Jesse wanted very badly to find Victoria, and he rode on with the same determination that had made him crawl doggedly on after being left for dead.

He was actually on the ranch before he knew it, and found out only because three suspicious ranch hands hailed his fire one night and asked, with rather studied politeness, where he was bound. A cheerful and open man by nature, and thoroughly tired of his own company, Jesse told them readily, and was somewhat chagrined to be told that he was sitting on the Bar F, and that he would have ridden off it within a day or two, given his direction.

They asked, still with that studied politeness, his reasons for coming to the ranch, and he told them. His answer, he noted, seemed to surprise them. But when morning came and the sunlight showed them his features clearly, there were three identically startled blinks, and then an immediate relaxation of their obvious suspicions.

And then they were troubled.

"We've been out on the range for near a week," Tony Bannon told him, riding beside Jesse while the other two rode ahead. He was the foreman of the Bar F, he had explained. "Con, Wade, and me, we've been rounding strays." Then he fell silent for a while, frowning.

Jesse, who had missed human company recently and had rapidly gotten on a first-name basis with the hands, felt the older man's uneasiness and wondered at it. "I met Morgan Fontaine years ago," he said. "Before he married my sister. Just a brief meeting, during the war."

Tony glanced at him, then said softly, "He's dead, Jesse. We buried him a week ago."

Jesse remembered the man who had spoken kindly to him years before, the man who had apparently sheltered and cared for his sister, and he was saddened that he would have no opportunity to meet that man again.

His own voice soft, he said, "I'm sorry, truly sorry." And then, more softly still, "She's alone again."

For an essentially expressionless man, Bannon could look fierce, and did. "No. She's got all of us— every man jack of us on the ranch, including Morgan's man, his servant, I guess he is—he'll look after her too. The Bar F is her home, and she's happy here. I watched her grow from a girl, and I know she's happy livin' on the ranch."

Jesse realized that the older man feared he would take his sister back east, and he quickly disclaimed that notion. "Of course she belongs here, if that's what she wants. And since she's been here so long—" It was an opening, an invitation to talk about just how long Victoria had lived with Morgan, how it had all come about. But they topped a rise just then, and the ranch house lay before them.

In the excitement of being so near his sister after so long, Jesse promptly forgot his questions. Eagerly, he spurred his horse into a gallop and headed for the sprawling ranch house.

He was, had he only known, just a few days behind Falcon Delaney.

Jesse had time only to realize that the Bar F was a wealthy ranch, evident from the beautiful house that was made of adobe and Spanish tiles, and stood gracefully near the bank of a stream in the shade of tall cottonwoods.

A man stepped outside as they drew up their horses, a man who was tall and stooped, with graying hair and hooded eyes and an earring in his left ear. A man Jesse dimly remembered; he was Morgan's servant, and had been present the day Jesse had delivered the gold. And when he spoke, Jesse stopped looking at the house.

"Miss Victoria is gone."

"Gone?" Jesse felt a crawling chill. "Gone where?" he demanded.

The hooded eyes looked at him and blinked once, the only sign of emotion. "She has, I believe, gone after her husband's killers, sir."

Tony Bannon emerged from his frozen stillness to grab for his horse. "Goddammit, Galen, you—"

"No." The man named Galen spoke quietly, but with a curiously firm inflection. "She left orders. You and the men are to care for the ranch in her absence. Winter is here; it will take every man to work."

Bannon hesitated, his jaw working, eyes anxious and undecided. "How long, Galen?"

"Days. It is unlikely that you could find her before she finds—them."

"Why in hell did you let her go?"

Galen looked at the foreman, expressionless; it would have been impossible for anyone who didn't know to guess that he had been fiercely devoted to Morgan and his young wife. "She did not ask my permission, Mr. Bannon." He was, invariably, formal to the ranch hands.

"Killers." It was Jesse's voice. "Murdered? My sister's husband was murdered?"

Galen looked at him, clearly unsurprised by the information Jesse had supplied; whether he remembered him or not, he did, it was obvious, know who Jesse was. "Savagely murdered, sir." There was no inflection in his voice at all.

Jesse's jaw firmed. He forgot his weariness, forgot his earlier, wistful thoughts of a bath and a decent bed to sleep in. "Which way did she go?" he demanded.

"When she left, she headed west," Galen replied.

"Jesse!" Bannon knew he was too late, even as he called, even as he made a fruitless grab for Jesse's reins.

"Let him go." Galen stood, watching emotionlessly, as Jesse's horse disappeared far away over the rise.

Bannon turned on him, furious. "He's a babe out here! No more fit to take care of himself than—"

"Than his sister?" Galen shook his head briefly.

"You know better. And neither of them would thank you for interfering in their affairs."

Tony Bannon stared at him for a long, hard moment. "Sometimes," he said in an even tone, "I wonder what rock Morgan found you under." Then he took up his horse's reins and stalked toward the bunkhouse.

No one saw Galen's twisted smile, or heard the thoughts he was so adept at keeping to himself. He turned and went quietly back into the silent house, there to await Victoria's return. He had no doubt that she would return, for he had watched his master teach her, carefully, how to survive.

He wondered briefly if Jesse would ride west steadily, or if he would somehow discover that it was not his sister's ultimate direction. Galen could have told him that there was a place, many days east of the ranch, where Victoria would likely end up. A place in Texas.

He could have made it easier for Jesse.

That he had not done so was due simply to his loyalty to Morgan Fontaine, and the promises he had made that man. When Victoria returned, he would tell her the story only if she asked him, obeying the instructions Morgan had issued long ago. He would discharge his final duty to his master, regretting only that he was himself too old and stiff now to avenge his death.

Galen wondered if Morgan had realized that Victoria would do that, if he had realized that his young wife would set out on a grim trail alone, where she was likely to learn things about her husband she had not known while he was alive. Somehow, Galen doubted it. The single thing Morgan had kept from Victoria during the years they had been together, the one secret of their marriage, was the knowledge that his own actions had destroyed what was left of her family.

Morgan Fontaine would have taken that knowledge with him to the grave—had he died naturally. But he had not died naturally. Only Galen knew the whole story, and he had promised not to reveal it to anyone. Unless . . .

"They might catch up to me, old friend, if I live long enough. Some of them had to have survived. They don't know where to begin looking for me, but I've noticed fate has a way of tying up loose ends in life. They may well find me some day. But I won't tell them where the gold is. If something should happen . . . you tell Victoria the truth if she asks. I'm—not strong enough to tell her. But if I'm killed, she'll need to know. She'll need to protect herself from them."

And Galen had meant to tell her, but Victoria had simply and quietly left the ranch, to avoid any protest. She had gone the day after Morgan's funeral, leaving only a short letter of instruction for him and the ranch hands.

So he would have to tell her when she returned. When she found Morgan's killers.

Texas

The trail led eastward.

Not a breath of wind stirred where she sat, immobile as a statue, on her horse. The big, rawboned buckskin blended with the arid landscape until he would have been invisible from a distance; his stillness guaranteed it. The poncho she wore covered her effectively, and hid her as well as her horse's natural color hid him. Her flat-brimmed hat was pulled low over her eyes, shading them, and those green eyes scanned the horizon keenly. She heard the packhorse shift restlessly, and soothed him with her voice without turning. When he became still again, she continued to study her surroundings.

Her head turned only a bit, and slowly. She had already studied her back trail with cautious eyes, and had found no sign that she was being followed. No sign, in fact, of any living thing for miles. Now she was looking out over land still to be traveled, and uneasiness was growing in her. There was so little time left, and if Morgan's killers escaped to Europe, she might never find them. But there was something else as well, something bothering her. She searched her mind for reasons and found, besides her awareness of time passing, only a niggling agitation.

She felt vaguely worried, abstracted, as though she had seen or heard something that had not been fully noticed at the time, but was now perturbing.

And she was also uneasy because instincts and senses honed to animal sharpness warned her that a storm was coming. A day, she thought, maybe two. The air had grown steadily colder these last days, and winter was surely coming to shake an icy fist over an already barren land. Her horses had grown winter coats quickly, and that alone told her that there would likely be bad weather—and soon.

There was so little time. She would have to cut short her search soon and head toward Charleston, especially if the weather worsened; she couldn't afford to be snowbound somewhere along the route, at least not for long.

She put aside that worry, knowing that there was little choice for her.

Perfectly still, blending easily with the calm around her, she considered the situation. She carried food for herself and grain for the horses, enough to last a couple of weeks, if need be. And if shelter could be found. She pulled memories from her mind and examined them one by one, recalling the talk of ranch hands and her own knowledge, culled from Morgan's teachings, recalling trails and water holes and the rare empty shelter to be found. There was little enough of the latter in this rough Texas land; with range wars to the north, desert and Indians to the west, and Mexican bandits to the south, there was, in fact, little of anything that could be called safe.

Especially for a woman.

She thought little of that. The fact that she was a woman had not influenced her to this point; she would not allow it to influence her now. Instead, she concentrated on the immediate problem. Shelter. She sifted through information gathered by many people over the years and shared in saloons and around campfires here and there, her mind gradually narrowing that information to pinpoint this area.

And after a while, she remembered hearing a drifter from Tombstone mention the existence of an old homestead near here. She considered the information, examining it for potential problems. Then, with a sigh that misted before her eyes, she lifted the reins, and the buckskin moved ahead with his mile-eating walk.

She found it two hours later, just as a weak sun was at the halfway point of its daily journey. Only a charitable soul would have called it a homestead, and only an optimistic soul would have named it shelter.

Winding the packhorse's lead around her saddle horn, she dismounted and dropped the reins to groundtie her horse. The horse stood between her and the two ramshackle structures, and she remained there for a few moments, studying her surroundings. After a while, she relaxed just a bit, but her green eyes were wary and both hands remained beneath the concealing poncho while she stepped out and headed first for the building that must have been built as a barn.

It was large, as such buildings sometimes were, its back to the north and a tumbledown corral beside it. A shed stuck out bravely from the side to shelter a small corner of the corral, one of its support posts leaning precariously and gray sky showing through the roof. The barn proper was, unusually enough, completely enclosed, but one of the doors hung askew by the last threads of a leather hinge.

She bent and picked up a rock, tossing it inside the barn with enough force to strike the back wall sharply. Listening intently, she heard no sound, no rustle of animal inhabitants. After a long moment, she walked inside the building and gazed thoughtfully around.

There were three open stalls along one wall, all with mangers. On the opposite wall hung various pieces of rusty equipment and bits of rotted leather. In the loft above, she could see plenty of loose hay, which lifted her spirits; the horses would have shelter and her supply of grain would last longer. The roof seemed solid enough, but she made a mental note to check the hay carefully for mold.

She smiled a little to herself, satisfied, before turning to retrace her steps to the door. The buckskin and sorrel packhorse stood as she'd left them—Buck's head up as he watched her, and the packhorse standing wearily on three legs while he rested the fourth. She headed for the house, still moving cautiously and alert for any suspicious sound. The animals would be sheltered; now she had to make certain of shelter for herself.

It was little more than a sod shanty with a dirt floor, but there was a rock fireplace, a roughhewn table and bench, and a cot with mostly rotting leather straps beneath the stained and musty straw-filled mattress. The door had long since parted company with its leather hinges, and now lay in the dirt outside, but the roof had only a few holes, and the walls seemed sturdy.

An hour later, she had picketed both horses nearby to get what grass they could, and carried her gear into the house. Using rusty nails found in an old can and strips of leather she carried in her pack, she repaired the door and fixed a latchstring, then set about making the place reasonably weathertight.

It was hard work, and make-do, since scant materials for repairs could be found. There had once been glass in the single window near the door; she used a section of canvas from her pack to close out most of the drafts. She made a rough broom with straw from the barn and a long stick, then swept out the filth accumulated by animal inhabitants over a long period of time. Along with the dirt, she swept out any crockery that couldn't be burned or cleaned. She rolled up the filthy mattress and set it near the fireplace; it was dry, so it would burn. Clean straw from the barn piled on the repaired cot made a fresh mattress; over this she placed a huge pelt that had once belonged to a bad-tempered grizzly, and over that her bedroll. It would be a comfortable bed.

Within another hour, a fire burned in the hearth and coffee was making. The house would never be spotless, but it was neat and reasonably clean, and warming rapidly.

She made several trips outside, to check on the horses and fetch water from the nearby spring and wood from the pile behind the house. On this last she cast a thoughtful, measuring eye, then raided the barn for what pieces of wood could be used for the fire. By the time she was finished, she had a sizable woodpile, and a comfortable certainty that she could weather a storm of up to a couple of weeks without ever leaving this place.

But no more than that. Any longer than a couple of weeks, and she would miss the ship leaving Charleston. Any longer than a couple of weeks, and Morgan's killers might escape her forever.

But *they* were still out here, she was sure of it. The trail she had followed was no more than a few days old, and those men would have to seek shelter, just as she had. But she'd have to move on during the first break in the weather, move on and close the distance between herself and them.

She had to find them.

She took the horses to the spring for water, and then to the barn, tossing them hay and finding some corn in an old crib. With the corn and her own supply of grain, she decided, the horses would make out very well.

The last thing she did before darkness fell was to make a complete circle a hundred yards out from the buildings, on foot and cautious. She studied the layout of the place with wary eyes, coming finally to the conclusion that the homesteader who'd built here had chosen well. The place was in more of a hollow than a valley, but it was not a small hollow. Hills reared up all around, far enough away to provide a certain amount of protection from the elements, and from hostile guns. There was no cover near the buildings sufficient for anyone caring to creep up on the house unseen, and the trail leading here was disused to the point of being nearly gone.

Satisfied, she returned to the cabin. She closed the door and pulled the latch inside, then removed her poncho at last and hung it on a peg by the door.

If there had been a mirror in the cabin, and if she had cared to look at her reflection, she would have seen a sight that was becoming something of a legend the length of her back trail. Her boots were old and worn, boy's boots on small feet, and no spurs jingled to advertise her movements. In a plain holster on her right hip was a Peacemaker Colt, a gun that any man would have realized had been used and cared for, and it was tied down in the manner of gunfighters.

She unfastened the thong and the belt, then hung it over the tarnished bedstand. Faded jeans clung to slender legs and hips, worn jeans, with the shiny seat of someone long in the saddle. A heavy coat joined the rest on the wall, and its absence took away twenty or so pounds from her appearance, revealing her as a fairly tall woman, and slender. Her blond hair was worn in a single, long, thick plait down her back, tied at the end with a rawhide thong; she had chosen the style for the sake of convenience, but an impartial observer would have noted that the plain, severe style emphasized her delicate bone structure.

A man would have instantly noticed that her leather vest and faded blue shirt did nothing to hide a body that God had been generous with, but she noticed only that a button was missing. She untied her bandanna and cast it onto the table with a sigh, then hung her hat by the door and went wearily to pour herself a cup of coffee.

Stretched out on the cot, the only light provided by the crackling fire, she sipped her coffee and allowed her tired body to relax. Somewhat. There was a part of her that never slept now, a part born in grim, grieving necessity and kept alive out of need; that part of her was alert with the senses of a hunting or hunted animal.

Her only meal that day had been a jackrabbit roasted in her morning campfire, but she wasn't hungry. She was too tired to be hungry. After a while, listening to the building wind outside the cabin, she slept.

* * *

Her unease grew as the storm outside intensified. Time . . . she needed time! It did no good to reassure herself that the men she hunted had likely taken shelter and were as immobile as she was herself. Time was her enemy.

She went out at least twice during the following day, but there was nothing to be seen or heard in the blowing snow. She knew her restlessness was rooted in some definite cause apart from passing time, but she also knew that her mind, in an effort to avoid thinking of recent events, could well be unreliable in the recognition of possible dangers.

She was tired.

There was so much she could not bear to remember! The time in New York with Falcon, colored only faintly by her own guilt. The shock of the telegram; Falcon's bitterly accusing eyes, and her own pain; her swift, anxiety-ridden trip back to the ranch. And, finally, what had awaited her at home and now pursued her as demons in her dreams: the horrifying sight of Morgan when she had found him.

It was, she tried to tell herself, hardly surprising that uneasiness plagued her. It would have been a miracle if she had *not* felt tired and sick and shaken, if she had *not* felt the itch between her shoulder blades that grew stronger with every passing day. A miracle.

She was tired, her emotions numbed by everything that had happened since she had begun that joyful, unconcerned trip to New York. Her mind, for the most part, remained blank, because there was too much that hurt unbearably to think about.

She didn't want to think, because the pain would come, the pain of Falcon and Morgan. The pain of loss that had left her so hollow and alone that she couldn't bear to think about it. Not now. Not yet. She wanted to hold on to the blessed numbness as long as possible, because there was something she had to do, and pain would distract her from that.

Perhaps it was wrong, and Morgan would certainly have disapproved, but she felt a terrible sense of guilt about his death. She had been away enjoying herself—with another man—in New York, while enemies had torn her husband apart. Morgan hadn't believed in revenge, but he had believed in justice. So did she. Lawful justice. But the law had failed to provide that for her, so she was going after it herself. She was tracking the men who had killed Morgan.

And she intended to find them, even if the trail led into hell itself.

It went against her very nature to deliberately set out on a hunt for men she intended to see punished. Nothing in her life had prepared her for something like this. So, of course she was uneasy and restless.

Of course.

But when the trouble came, Victoria realized that the root of her anxiety had indeed been a sight unnoticed at the time. Because when the door burst open, she caught a glimpse of a pinto outside the door—a horse she had glimpsed once while riding from the ranch, and a second time in a town she had passed through. And all her instincts had been trying to tell her that, signs or no, someone had followed her from the ranch.

She was one step too many from her gun when

the door slammed against the wall, and she froze without having to be told; he held a gun that was pointed levelly between her breasts, and she couldn't doubt he would use it.

He was—or should have been—an ordinary-looking man; the gun made of him something deadly. He was of medium height and lean, his shaggy hair, filthy clothes, and beard-stubbled face telling of days in the saddle. And his close-set eyes were hot and hard, with a gleam as wild as unreason. He stepped into the room, kicking the door shut and staring at her.

And she remembered him. This man had struck Falcon down in a dusty bookshop in New York a lifetime ago, had later whined that he wanted to go into the cellar and crawl between her legs. What was he doing here? What—

"The gold!" His voice rasped. "Tell me where to find the gold!"

Victoria had no need to feign bewilderment. "Gold? What gold? Who are you?"

He didn't seem to hear her. His eyes darted around the cabin, as if he would find what he sought. "You know where it is. You were with him. All the way, you were with him. You must have seen him hide it!"

For the second time in moments, the door slammed open. Victoria dived for her gun instantly, grasping it and falling to the floor, rolling to make a lesser target of herself. From the corner of her eye, she saw the stranger whirl with a hoarse cry, and two sharp reports echoed within the space of a heartbeat. The stranger cried out again and fell heavily, his gun clattering against the stone hearth as it dropped.

Victoria, on her stomach, raised her gun toward the door—and froze.

Falcon leaned against the jamb, the hand holding his pistol slowly dropping to his side. Their eyes locked—his bitter, and hers astonished, bewildered. In that still instant, she saw the other side of the city gentleman, a man dressed roughly in jeans and a heavy coat. A man with the weariness, dirt, and stubble of days of riding covering him.

Then she saw the blood reddening the shirt beneath his coat, and her own gun clattered as she thrust it aside and scrambled to her feet. She tried, desperately, but failed to reach him before he fell.

2

New Mexico/Arizona

It occurred to Jesse only when the Fontaine ranch lay far behind him that he had no idea at all of how to find his sister. He realized vaguely that he was heading toward Arizona, about which he knew absolutely nothing, and wondered for the first time if there was danger about. He was carrying a rifle on his saddle, but wore no handgun; the provisions in his saddlebags were running low; and though he could navigate by the stars as adeptly as any ship's captain, tracking a horse and rider across barren terrain was somewhat beyond him.

It had been eight years since he had seen Victoria, eight years since he had accepted her apparent death, and the knowledge that she was alive—and bent on finding her husband's killers—drove him on, despite his lack of familiarity with this bare, arid landscape. He had come of age in a brutal war, and had spent the years since primarily at sea, working his way up rapidly to become one of Marcus Tyrone's few trusted captains. He could find her. Like Victoria, he possessed a stoic strength integral to what he was, and a dogged determination that took little notice of hazards.

So Jesse merely buttoned his coat against the chilly winds and rode on toward the western horizon. He ran out of provisions on the second day and could find very little food; though he was a good shot, game was increasingly scarce. Winter was blowing into the Southwest early and in an unusually severe mood, and both animals and humans had read the signs and taken shelter.

All except for a lone, tired man on a weary horse. If it hadn't been for his sturdy and trail-wise chestnut, Jesse would have died quickly; but he had sense enough to give the horse his head, as long as they moved in a generally western direction, and the gelding found water where Jesse would have found nothing. With water at least, they could press on steadily.

It was on the fourth day, and somewhere in east Arizona, when Jesse topped a rise and looked down on an Indian encampment. He was saddlesore, bone-weary, hungry, and inclined to be furious at his own lack of experience. He felt like the rawest tenderfoot, and didn't relish the feeling.

The chestnut nickered loudly when he sensed others of his kind, and began to pick his way down toward the encampment. Jesse gave him his head.

The Indians had been tamed, hadn't they? He remembered reading it somewhere. Not that it really mattered to Jesse. He needed food and help, and wasn't too proud to ask for it. He needed help in order to find his sister quickly, and it would have taken more than a numerous band of Apaches to turn his steps from the first sight of other humans in days.

Beginning to feel more cheerful, Jesse rode on.
Into Geronimo's camp.

Texas

The wind was wailing, snow blowing angrily—a
noisy storm that allowed no other sound to penetrate inside the dimly lighted room. From a seemingly great distance, as if he were at the bottom of a
deep well, he heard a voice. It was a familiar voice,
but it was saying words that surprised him somehow. He had said such words, he recalled idly, a few
times in his life. When things had been desperate,
when he had known gnawing anxiety and gut-level
fear. He had sworn then, as she was swearing now,
and in the same unsteady, toneless kind of voice.
  She?
  Her voice changed, becoming soft and crooning,
and even though he didn't hear the words, he
responded to that voice. He managed to get his feet
under him, leaning on a slender, fragile strength to
replace his own. He was dimly aware of moving,
slowly and haltingly, aware that the voice urged,
and that he couldn't deny her anything, no matter
how much it hurt.
  And then he sensed he was lying flat on something soft and yielding, and wondered idly what it
was.
  Very quickly, though, he forgot sound, forgot
puzzlement. His body was wracked by pain, fiery
waves of it. When he opened his eyes, the pain
seemed to shimmer like heat waves before him. He
felt something touch him, causing an agony that

lanced through him, and a groan locked behind his teeth. The pain was unendurable, and he had no strength to push away the touch that brought agony. Someone was stabbing him, over and over again, using a razor-sharp hot knife that seared as it sliced raw flesh. He could not even breathe; all his remaining energy was taken up with merely outliving the torment.

Then the agony faded to mere pain, a dull ache that pulsed throughout his body, and he felt the relief of respite after torture. His eyes opened and sight was hazy; he blinked, blinked again. He saw a face hanging over him, familiar, but strange in its deadly pallor. It was a lovely face, with wet, green eyes and bitten lips.

And of course she was stabbing him; he could hardly blame her for that. After what he had said to her in New York, the only wonder was that she apparently hadn't killed him. But she probably meant to let him die slowly, the way an Apache would . . . and he couldn't blame her for that either.

She had cut off one of his arms, because he couldn't feel it anymore, but the other was there, and he lifted it with all his remaining strength so that he could touch her pale, wet cheek. "How beautiful you are," he said clearly, wanting to tell her so much more, but unable to find the breath to push words out.

"Goddamn you, live," she whispered.

Falcon heard a thick laugh and knew it was his own. Of course she wanted him to live; a quick death would cheat her. He wanted to say something, comment on her unladylike swearing, or ask why she was crying. She shouldn't be crying over him, that wasn't right. No woman had ever cried over him. And he wanted to say . . . something else. Something terribly important. But her face swam before his eyes hazily, and he felt unable to say anything at all. He was hurting again; the arm she had cut off hurt dreadfully now, and his chest too, and he was hot and very tired and he just wanted to sleep.

His eyes opened occasionally, fevered and un-seeing, and muscles in his arms and legs jerked at her every touch as she carefully bound his wound. When she finished, she covered him, then brought a cup of the tea she had brewed and managed to get some down him, even though her hand trembled.

Lifting the lamp, she carried it back to the table and placed it there. She stood there for long moments, staring at the cot holding Falcon, then went to build up the fire. He'd need the fire, need warmth. His fever was increasing, and there was no one but herself to deal with that. She had never been forced into a situation like this, had never felt the awareness that only her own skills could mean the difference between life and death.

She had never felt so frightened, so alone. He could die here; the wound a handgun made in human flesh at close range was a terrible thing, and the risk of infection so great.

She put that out of her mind. He would live, he *would*. She built up the fire, checked on Falcon again, and put on her coat.

After that, she stoically dealt with the dead stranger.

The rest of the day passed almost in silence, except for the steadily building roar outside. She gave Falcon hot tea several times, checking his forehead lightly with the back of her hand on each occasion.

By nightfall he was burning up, and his eyes no longer saw her at all.

She was no doctor, but she knew more than the average woman about wounds and fevers. She also knew medicines and healing herbs, that knowledge culled from a wide range of people and situations she'd encountered, including Morgan's teachings. But her expertise was—in the end, she knew—useless after a point. His wound was clean and she rebandaged it once during the day; it looked healthy enough. It was the shock and fever that were dangerous.

She kept him warm, wrapping the ends of the grizzly pelt around him, as well as her extra blanket. He remained still and quiet, not rambling even in his delirium; there was, she thought, something shut-in and remote about him. He gave nothing away.

She sat near the cot, watching him, trying to fight off the pain that his arrival here had resurrected. Why was he here? Following her? Or following the man he had killed in this room? She couldn't think about that man, that stranger who had been in the bookshop in New York; her mind was totally occupied with thoughts of Falcon, and there was room for nothing else.

The bitterness in his eyes just before he fell haunted her, hurt her terribly. And yet, when he had been wracked with pain, his strength all but stripped away from him by the loss of blood and shock of his injury, he had touched her cheek and called her beautiful.

During the night, she slept little. She unrolled his own bedroll and placed it on the floor near the fire, getting up several times to check on him. His pulse was fast, his breathing raspy, and his fever increased. By dawn, she was fearfully aware that even his own strength might not save him. He had been tired even before the injury, his face thinner than she remembered, his eyes rimmed with weariness. Too tired to fight off the shock of a terrible wound.

She sat on the edge of the cot, bathing his face, praying silently for the Power greater than herself to give him the strength he needed. He had only one fairly lucid interlude that day, and it was while she bathed his face and looked down at him in helpless anguish.

"Don't cry," he murmured, cloudy green eyes gazing up at her as a puzzled frown drew his brows together. "You shouldn't cry over me."

Victoria hadn't even been aware of the tears. Swallowing, she said unsteadily, "You have to get better. There's no one but me, and I've done all I can. Please fight to get better."

"I have to get better." His voice was idle, conversational, and his clouded eyes moved over her face intently. "You look so tired. You should rest."

"I will." She brushed a lock of raven hair off his forehead, aching inside because she thought that never again would she see him like this, gentle and vulnerable.

The opacity of his eyes increased until they were

unseeing again, and his hand suddenly found her wrist and held it hard. "*I didn't mean it!*" His voice was low and harsh, raw.

"I know," she soothed, with no certainty of what he was talking about. "I know you didn't. It's all right."

His hand tightened. "No, it isn't all right . . . it was never all right. My cursed tongue . . . I say things I don't mean . . . I hurt her. I hurt her, and she went away."

"It's all right," she whispered.

"Tell her." His hold loosened and his eyes began to close. "Tell her . . . I didn't mean it."

Victoria hadn't been able to cry when she had fled New York with Falcon's harsh words ringing in her ears. But she cried now. She cried for both of them, for mistakes and deceits and guilts, for love and anguish, for words that should have been said.

She buried her face in the soft grizzly pelt covering Falcon's chest and cried for all of it.

She went out to feed and care for the horses, noting that his wore a brand. A shamrock. It awoke vague memory in her, and she remembered why after a while. Shamrock Ranch. The Delaney family. So he was one of *those* Delaneys, those tough, hot-tempered, hardheaded men. The Bar F was in western New Mexico, and the Delaney homestead in southeastern Arizona, so they were neighbors of a kind. And she had heard much of the Delaneys, news of large and powerful families being the sort that traveled.

Realizing who he was gave her a flicker of hope. The Delaneys were known for many traits, not all of them good ones, but they were certainly known for their hell-bent strength. The voyage to America hadn't killed them, the journey across a rugged new frontier hadn't killed them, and, word had it, the Apaches had given up trying to kill them long ago. Not all had survived the years, of course, but the Delaneys beat the odds, it was said.

And Victoria, remembering that, couldn't believe that Falcon Delaney would die now because of a weaselly madman with a lucky shot. She refused to believe that.

By the following night, she was exhausted and drawn herself, and Falcon was deeply unconscious. She did what she could for him. She fought to break his fever, using every scrap of knowledge she could remember. She kept tea and stew hot. She didn't pace, because it wasn't in her to move needlessly, but she watched him through the hours.

From time to time, she dug the handbill from her saddlebags and sat looking at it, smoothing the paper. Just a chance, of course, that one of Morgan's killers had left this behind. Just a chance she could find them in Charleston, if not before. But it was a chance she believed in strongly, and she was, on some cold level of herself, conscious of the time ticking away.

Once the storm passed, only one thing would keep her here. Only one thing could. Falcon. In truth, he was the only man on earth who could have interrupted her determined search.

When she rose to check him near dawn, his stillness and silence made her heart leap in agonized fear, but when she touched his forehead, relief swept over her so suddenly that she nearly fell. His skin was damp and cool, and he was breathing normally.

He would live.

Looking down at him, she didn't think, somehow, that he would make any more unguarded comments. He wouldn't, she thought, say again that she was beautiful. He probably wouldn't laugh. He wouldn't say that he hadn't meant it, hadn't meant to hurt her.

She wondered again—why was he here?

When she went out to feed the horses, she saw that the storm had passed. Snow lay everywhere, blanketing the harsh landscape in a sparkling whiteness. She gazed around for a moment, feeling an abrupt surge of loneliness. Then she shook off the unusual emotion and went into the barn.

When she returned to the cabin, she stood for a few moments at the window, a corner of the canvas lifted so that she could see out. She moved away finally and retrieved the handbill from her saddlebags. Smoothing it out against her thighs, she stared down at it for a long time. If she began moving again within a week, there was still time. Time to find those men before they headed for Charleston.

But a wounded man recovered slowly. Even a hell-bent Delaney man. How long? Two weeks? Three weeks before he was well again? How long before he was strong enough to care for himself, to ride if he had to?

Victoria sat at the table and lifted her gaze to the man lying so still on the cot. After a long time, she looked back at the handbill. She folded it up carefully, and returned it to her saddlebags.

Sometimes, she realized, there was no choice to make.

When Falcon came to his senses, he realized immediately where he was and what had happened. But she . . . After what had happened in New York, he wasn't sure of anything where she was concerned. He felt a savage bitterness that he now owed her his life, and the power of his own emotions kept him silent during those first hours of convalescence.

Still, he couldn't help watching her. And thinking. She fascinated him. She was miles from anywhere and alone. She dressed like a man, and wore a gun tied down in the manner of gunfighters. And she had been tracking two men on horseback with the skill of an Apache.

But her hands were gentle in their touch, and there was nothing hard on her face, nothing cold or brittle in her manner. When she moved, it was with the clean, economical grace and coordination of muscles under unthinking control. She was alert to her surroundings, each sound obviously noted, without being at all nervous.

Her face was calm, tranquil; her eyes gazed levelly with a thoughtful air of intelligent perception. There was a curve of humor in her lips, and a hint of vulnerability. Fine breeding was apparent in her delicate features, and strength in the proud tilt of her head. Her lovely face was almost imperceptibly thinner than he remembered, and there was, in her eyes, a hint of strain and the shuttered look of control.

She was the woman he had met in New York—and yet she was not that woman. She was quite different now. He could see the strength in her, the strength that had been concealed beneath the silks and gloves and hats of New York. And it wasn't that fragile strength of a young girl that he had glimpsed more than once; this was something bedrock inside her, something that had always been there but never needed.

Until now.

What fascinated him the most was that, for all her masculine attire, it was obvious that this woman knew she *was* a woman. It was in the straight, proud way she held herself, in the slight sway of her hips when she moved, and, most of all, in her eyes. She knew she was a woman, an attractive woman, and she was comfortable with that knowledge without being overly conscious of it. This was no woman hankering to be a man; she was female from her long, braided, blond hair to her small, booted feet.

But she was here. Alone. Wearing a gun while she tracked someone. Her husband's killers? Falcon had heard of Morgan Fontaine's death before he could reach the Bar F, and he had seen Victoria as she had ridden a day or two out from the ranch. It hadn't taken him long to realize that she was tracking two men—white men, because the horses were shod—and he was certain that the men she sought were Read Talbot and Gus Rawlins.

A third man, Falcon had quickly realized, was also tracking someone. Victoria. And Falcon had tracked him, edging closer cautiously until the storm caught them all and the other man had hurried on recklessly. He hadn't been given much time to study the man he had shot here in this shanty, but he had heard enough before he had burst in, and knew that the third man of the New York trio was now dead. He had also heard Victoria's bewilderment when gold was mentioned, and he was almost positive that had been genuine. She knew nothing of the gold.

But what kind of woman was she, in truth? So much a lady in New York that her deception had shaken him badly, yet here she was, clearly skilled in survival in an extremely hostile land. Alone. What kind of woman would discard her dresses to ride like a man and wear a gun?

She asked him not a single question, and a glance told him that she had not disturbed his saddlebags; there was still mud encrusted on the buckles. Quiet, she seemed not to want conversation; seemed, even, to avoid it, and busied herself inside the cabin with cleaning her gear and, later, his own saddle and bridle.

A fairly silent man himself, he discovered that the silence of the little cabin began to grate on him. There was, he knew, too much between himself and this woman. Too much left unsaid, unexplained. Too many feelings that had exploded between them with too little time to explore, to understand. Too many puzzles. Too many questions.

Too much pain.

"You're alone now." It was a statement, but a question as well. And a harsh one. He could still feel the shock of learning she had a husband, the betrayal of lies. The sickening knowledge that she belonged to another man.

She was sitting at the table, repairing his shirt with neat stitches, while he lay on the cot and watched her. He was still weakened by the wound, dependent on her and painfully conscious of that fact.

She folded the washed and mended shirt and laid it to one side. Those unreadable green eyes appraised him. "I'm alone," she confirmed quietly. "But I can take care of myself." Her voice was matter-of-fact and without arrogance.

He wanted to say it more clearly, wanted to tell her that he knew her husband was dead. He remembered wet, green eyes and bitten lips, and wondered where that woman had gone. She had put a wall between them—or maybe he had, in New York. And in the riot of his emotions, he didn't know how to break through it, or even if he should.

She rose and went to the fire to stir the bubbling contents of the cooking pot. She had gone out just after dawn, returning sometime later with a jackrabbit, already skinned and cleaned. He had heard no shot, and assumed she'd set snares.

An unusual woman. God, what an understatement!

He felt awkward, uncertain, almost baffled by her and by himself. Had he apologized to her for what he'd said in New York? He thought he remembered doing so. She had saved his life when she should have let him die, had watched over him, bathed him, fed him, seen to his needs. She had said not one word about what had happened—and

almost happened—between them, and her unreadable eyes made no accusations, no reproaches.

But Falcon felt what was unsaid. And he was torn
by his own knowledge of what she apparently had
no awareness of. The gold. As much as he had
wanted to destroy her husband upon finding out
that she was married, he was reluctant now to
tarnish a man unable to defend himself. And, even
more than that, he was strongly reluctant to be the
one who told Victoria the truth about Morgan
Fontaine.

She had haunted his days and nights since that
first meeting in the city. She had driven him nearly
mad with wanting her, drawn tenderness from
some place inside him he hadn't even known
existed—and she had lied to him by omission. And
he wanted to punish her savagely for doing that to
him, for cutting him up inside. He wanted to tear
down the wall between them and get his hands on
her, he wanted to hold her. Kiss her. Touch her.

He wanted to know, no matter how much it hurt
him, how she had really felt about her husband. He
had to know. He had to know that because it was
tearing him apart not to know.

His strength was growing steadily, thanks to her
deft care and good cooking, and he'd been on his
feet several times as the days passed—unsteady
feet, to be sure, but both were working.

He should have been thinking only of the gold.
He had to have his answers. All his answers. Had to
understand the enigma that had haunted him since
New York. The instincts he had depended on for

most of his adult life were in turmoil, leaving him unsettled and uncertain.

What was he feeling?

Grimly, he waited for his strength to return. And it came quickly, because he willed it to come. On the fourth day after the fever had broken, he prowled around the interior of the cabin, fully dressed but for his boots. She had placed his guns near him as soon as he'd regained his wits; they were cleaned and loaded, and she made no comment. Her own gun was always within reach, worn in its holster whenever she went outside, and never more than a step away inside the cabin.

He asked, finally, a question that had troubled him. "The man. The one I shot. Did you—?"

She glanced up. "I buried him."

The ground was still frozen. Falcon thought about that, but made no comment. He stood by the window, a corner of the canvas pulled back slightly, looking out at the snow and absently fingering the dark growth of beard on his jaw. He didn't know how to talk to her, how to begin to ask the questions he needed to have answered. And he knew that his hold on his emotions was precarious, to say the least.

"Would you like to shave?"

He turned to look at her where she sat by the fire, mending a broken strap on her pack harness. She was watching him, one brow lifted slightly.

Falcon fingered his jaw again and nodded. "Lost my knife," he confessed, hearing the rusty, unused sound of his voice. Had the silence gone on that long? It had.

She rose and put water on to boil, and while her

back was to him, he saw a slight movement he couldn't interpret. When she turned back, a knife lay in her hand. The haft was about four inches long, the blade six inches, and it looked razor-sharp and deadly. He hadn't seen a scabbard, but realized instantly that she carried the knife somewhere on her person—always. She laid the knife on the table.

"There's soap in the washbasin," she said, nodding toward the battered tin basin placed on a small, sturdy table beside the water barrel. "I'm going to ride out for an hour or two and see if anyone's passed this way."

He watched her buckle on her gunbelt, then reach for her coat and hat. He wanted to tell her to be careful, but he somehow knew that she was always careful. Always cautious. Always guarded. And where had she learned that? When the door closed behind her, he started to clean up.

It was just under two hours later that she returned, and Falcon had found time to trim his hair, as well as shave and wash up. He'd told himself it was a simple matter of feeling better when he was clean and neat, but an inner voice jeered at him.

Her eyes rested on his face, somewhat surprised, while she discarded coat and hat. "You look better."

He felt his ears warming, and swore silently. For Christ's sake, what had happened to him? Where was his rage, his bitterness? "I feel better."

She went to pour herself a cup of coffee, still wearing her gun. She seemed a bit distant, pre-occupied. He watched her.

"Another storm coming." There was restlessness in her voice.

"When?" He had a feeling she'd know.

"Tonight." She was frowning just a bit, gazing at the cup in her hand, a grim set to her delicate lips. "Worse than the last, I'd guess."

Falcon wondered if she was implying it was time for him to leave, and the thought made his stomach muscles tighten in a sudden spasm of pain. Then she was going on. He relaxed.

"We've enough food for a week or so, even if the snares catch nothing," she said slowly. "Enough feed for the horses. If the storm lasts more than a week, we may have to start taking the barn apart, to burn the wood."

He blinked, then caught the faint gleam of humor in her fine eyes as she glanced at him. After a moment, he asked, "Any sign of company?"

Victoria leaned a hip against the table and gazed at him. Her face was as serene as ever, but the green eyes were abruptly shuttered. "No."

He went to pour a cup of coffee for himself, gesturing silently at her knife, lying on the table near her. "Thanks for the loan."

"You're welcome."

She didn't reach for the knife, which both disappointed him and caused his respect for her to reluctantly edge up yet another notch. Somewhere along the way, he realized, in her traumatic girlhood or since, this woman had learned that a hidden weapon is effective only as long as the hiding place is secret; she wouldn't show him where she carried it.

He didn't want to think about that, didn't want to

wonder where she had learned that. He looked at
her and felt his stomach muscles tighten again,
knot, felt heat spread through him. She was so
beautiful, even in her man's clothes, and his body
ached with wanting her for so long. He hadn't
forgotten that, not even weakened by shock and
pain, and not now, when he was healing physically
and so aware of her.

Wet, green eyes and bitten lips.

She was so calm now, so emotionless. He wanted,
suddenly, to destroy that calm. To force her to feel
the savage emotions he felt himself. But the words
that emerged from his mouth were not those he
would have chosen if he had given himself a
moment to reflect—even though they did force a
response from her.

"I heard your husband was killed."

Her body went stiff. "While I was in New York."

"The telegram." He didn't want to remember
that night, what he had said to her, didn't want to
remind them both of what had happened to them.
But they were acting like strangers, and he couldn't
bear that.

"Yes. He'd just been found missing then." Her
eyes were unreadable again, but there was a white
look of strain around her lips as she stared at him.
"I didn't find out the rest until I reached the ranch."

Falcon knew what the rest was, but he made it a
question. "He was murdered? And you're after his
killers?"

"Yes." Her eyes darkened, something like horror
stirring in their depths. "Oh, yes, they murdered
him. And I'm after them."

"Why not let the law—"

Her laugh—soft, flat, empty—interrupted him. "The law? Our local sheriff made a show of looking for Morgan's killers. Gathered a posse. Followed tracks for a day or two. Then he came to me just before the funeral, hat in hand, his eyes full of pity, and told me the trail had vanished. He told me Morgan had probably been killed by drifters, by outlaws already long gone. He told me he'd send out handbills, except that there weren't any witnesses, and, so, no descriptions. He told me to be brave. He told me to go on with my life. I was young, he said. And lovely, in case he hadn't mentioned it. And I'd need a man around the place." She laughed again. "You're a bright man, Falcon; I'm sure you can follow the direction of his very unselfish thoughts."

Falcon could. "You could have contacted a federal marshal," he told her.

"And be told the same thing again? No witnesses, no descriptions, no trail, no killers. And no need to waste a marshal's time."

"How can you hope to find them?" Falcon asked reasonably. "If you don't have any more to go on than that?" He was wondering about the gold, wondering, still, if she could possibly know about that.

"But I *do* have more. I followed a few trails myself. And I came up with a terrified eight-year-old boy . . . who saw everything. The son of one of our ranch hands. The *law* wouldn't believe him. I do. I know him. And I know he gave me a better description than most men could have given, even though he didn't see the men clearly. I know what their horses look like, and that's enough."

She felt a sudden chill. A pinto. The boy had seen

a pinto, just like the one now in the barn. The man from New York—one of Morgan's killers? It didn't make sense; none of it made sense to her! What was it all *about?*

"On the word of a child, you're hunting men? What will you do when you find them, Victoria?" He wasn't conscious of using her name for the first time since seeing her again. "You have no evidence—"

"I will have," she said, her voice remote. She pushed the speculation to the back of her mind in order to deal with Falcon now. "I'll have evidence. His killer may still be wearing the ring he took from Morgan's finger."

"And if there's no ring? No evidence? Will you use that gun to get your justice?"

Victoria looked at him for a long, steady moment. "Falcon, the men who killed Morgan will pay for what they did. But I'll shoot no man down in cold blood. I'll face them and I'll be sure—very, very sure. If I can, I'll take them in alive. If not, they'll go in dead." She frowned a bit, adding almost to herself, "I have to know *why*. An Apache couldn't have approached Morgan without his knowing; these men disarmed him because he let them get close enough."

"Men make mistakes," Falcon noted, watching her.

She shook her head. "Not Morgan. Not that kind of mistake." Her voice was utterly certain. "I think he knew them, that he let them get that close for some reason. But *why* did they kill him like that? And the boy said he heard them mention gold." Gold again, always gold. What did it *mean?*

Falcon stiffened, but kept his face expressionless. "Gold? The man who followed you here—didn't he ask about gold?"

"Yes. Gold. I think, no, I'm sure that he was one of the men who killed Morgan. But he was one of the men in the bookshop in New York, the one who struck you down. Why would he have come out here and killed Morgan?" She was obviously bewildered. "And why would they have thought he knew where gold was? Why would they think that? Morgan was a wealthy man; he didn't want or need gold. He didn't care about it."

"Are you sure your husband knew nothing about it?" Falcon was treading warily now, every sense alert, trying to ignore the pain of naming another man her husband.

"Of course I'm sure."

"And you know nothing about it?"

She stared at him, her green eyes suddenly wary. "I know nothing."

"But you connect the gold with your husband's death?" Falcon asked softly. "Why?"

Her reaction to that startled him. Green eyes darkened, horror stirring in them again, and her face drained of color. Huskily, she said, "Because Morgan wasn't just murdered. He was tortured to death." She drew a deep breath. "Obviously, they wanted to find out something from him."

Falcon agreed with her silently. "You think it was the gold?"

"I don't know what else it could be. But I don't believe he knew anything about it, and I don't understand why they believed he *did* know." She sighed, a weary sound. "I think Morgan died because of some horrible mistake. He was a good man; he didn't deserve to die that way. No one deserves to die that way."

"You saw—"

"Of course I saw!" Her breath caught on a sob, but almost instantly, she was calm again. "I'm the one who found him. There wasn't much left."

"I'm sorry."

She looked at him, but said nothing.

"I heard that Fontaine was quite a bit older than you." He was driven; he *had* to understand.

"Almost thirty years."

Falcon watched as she moved over and sat down on the cot, leaning back against the wall. He sank down on the bench at the table, gazing at her. An older, indulgent husband? There was no trace in her of the spoiled, petted wife, and yet— He didn't understand, and he had to. That innocence in her eyes, the surprise at his passionate caresses. But it couldn't be. She was too beautiful and vital a woman to share a man's home without also sharing his bed.

Unerringly, she picked up his train of thought. "Some of the townspeople were certain I'd gone to the city in search of a younger man; they made their beliefs painfully obvious, even before I left for New York."

"Had you gone looking for a younger man?" he asked bluntly, half-dreading the answer.

"No."

Just that, just the simple denial. Falcon felt a painful kick in his stomach, reflecting that she must have loved her husband very much, that a man thirty years her senior could have commanded such loyalty from a young and vital woman . . . at least until she had been thrown into a cellar with a stranger.

Falcon tried not to think about that, tried not to remember. He was having trouble keeping his voice steady, and cleared his throat harshly. "So. On the word of a young and frightened child, you're hunting men. What about this?" He kept his gaze fixed on her face.

Victoria looked at the handbill he had pulled from his shirt pocket. Her eyes flicked to her saddlebags, then returned to him. She was somehow unsurprised that he had taken advantage of her absence to look through the saddlebags. "I found that near Morgan's body."

"You believe one of his killers left it there?"

"It's a possibility." She drew a deep breath. "That handbill hadn't been left out there in the rocks any longer than—than Morgan had."

Falcon opened the handbill and looked at the date of departure, then refolded the paper and laid it aside on the table. One thought, one realization, filled his mind. "You should have left days ago," he said softly.

"I have time." She kept her voice even. "A few days, at least. I can swing south to avoid the bad weather, and—"

"Why didn't you leave, Victoria? The storm ended three or four days ago. By staying, you've gotten caught by a second storm. Why did you stay?"

Victoria remained silent. There was no answer

she could give him. What could she say? That she had stayed because she loved him still, despite everything? No, she couldn't say that. He'd never believe that.

Roughly, he said, "You stayed because of me, didn't you? You dug a bullet out of me instead of taking that knife and gelding me, and then you stayed here to take care of me instead of leaving to catch the ship. Why, Victoria?"

"It doesn't matter." She shook her head. "I would have done as much for any man."

"Would you?"

Desperately, she ignored the question. "I still have time. They must have taken shelter too. I'll find them."

He looked down at the untasted coffee in his cup. He heard his voice speak harshly. "You found me in New York." He had to hear her admit that he mattered to her, *had* to.

"No," she said very quietly, holding on to her composure with all her will. "I found a man I was drawn to, in spite of myself. And you found a lady you were drawn to. Two different people, in another time."

"You're saying we're no longer drawn to each other?" He looked up at her, his eyes glittering.

Victoria looked down at her coffee. "I'm saying we can't go back to being those people, existing in that time." Her voice was low. "I lied to you by omission, even though I never meant to do that. I let you believe I was free. In a way, I was free, but I don't expect you to understand that."

"Victoria . . ." He hesitated, then finished

roughly. "I still want you." Immediately, he wondered if she'd suspect him of being interested in her dead husband's wealth. It only then occurred to him to wonder if she'd suspected he was after her own obvious wealth in New York. But when she spoke, he realized she was thinking along other lines.

"You wanted that lady, that other person. I'm not her anymore."

"As you said," he muttered, "we can't go back."

"No, we can't." She sounded tired. "We know too much about each other—and too little. Too much has happened. And Morgan is dead."

Falcon felt his jaw aching, and knew his teeth were gritted tightly. Every time she spoke the name of her dead husband, it was like a knife stabbing him. He couldn't think clearly of anything but that. Years of work, of painstaking search, filtered through his mind, yet he couldn't grasp a single thought. He just sat looking at her, absently setting aside his cup, standing up and taking a step toward her. His jaw hurt, and there was an ache near his heart, and he badly needed something—anything— to wipe out the betrayal of New York.

"You felt something," he said, "when you dug a bullet out of me. You felt something then."

Wet, green eyes and bitten lips.

Victoria kept her eyes lowered, afraid to meet his. Afraid he would see too much truth. She could feel his gaze, feel awareness of him in every nerve of her body. The room was suddenly too hot, too close, and she couldn't breathe. Grimly, she fought for control, knowing that if she gave in to desire, she would only be confirming this man's low opinion of her.

She lifted her head at last, staring at him proudly even as her knees weakened at the very male expression in his eyes. "Whatever I feel or do not feel is my own concern, Falcon. I will find the men who killed my husband . . . and nothing else matters."

3

❦⟡❦

"**I** don't believe that." His voice was taut. "I don't believe nothing else matters to you."

"I can't help what you believe."

He took another step toward her. Brutally, he said, "You wanted me in New York, Victoria. We were going to spend the night together in your room, remember?"

She half-closed her eyes, struggling to hang on to some semblance of control, of pride. He had already told her what he thought of her, and nothing could take back those words. "I made a mistake," she said steadily. "It was foolish of me." *End it, just end it now!* "I betrayed my husband!"

"You betrayed *me!*" He was there, suddenly, yanking her up and sending her coffee cup flying, hauling her against him with punishing force. And his kiss was punishing, cruel and bitter. He kissed her with an angry force that sought to wipe away another man's memory, holding her head firmly so that she couldn't escape him.

She struggled at first, wildly, matching her strength against his in an unequal contest. He was larger, stronger, furiously angry, not even his healing wound holding him back. She couldn't escape him, but wrenched her mouth free, and the protest screaming inside her emerged only in an anguished whisper. "No, not like this, not in anger!"

"Any way," he uttered thickly against her throat, his hands dropping to her hips to pull her lower body tightly against the swelling fullness of his arousal. "Any way I can get you. And you want me, Victoria, as much as I want you."

He was right and she knew it, knew her body was responding wildly to his, weakening, yielding. The overpowering desire he had instantly ignited in New York was a raging fire she couldn't damp, couldn't put out. But he was angry, and she couldn't bear that, couldn't bear that he would take her in his fury. And it was that she protested, not his desire *or* her own. "You promised once that you'd never hurt me," she whispered, trying to reach him, trying to drain the black rage from him.

"You hurt me." He lifted his head, eyes blazing. "You stuck a knife in my gut!"

She shook her head a little, confused, unwilling to believe what she heard. "You wanted my body, Falcon, not my heart! You had no right to be hurt, no right at all. Angry, yes. I knew you'd be angry, but—"

"*I loved you!*" The words burst out of him, raw and violent, shocking them both.

Victoria was utterly still, gazing up at him. "You . . . you never said . . ."

"I didn't know." His face was white, his eyes burning like live coals, and a muscle jerked in his hard-held jaw. "It never happened to me before, and I— Goddammit, Victoria, I nearly *died* when I read that telegram!" His voice was rough, unsteady. "I was half-crazy, ready to kill him, ready to lock you away somewhere until I could make you love me."

"I do." Her voice almost wasn't there. The hands that had pushed against his chest slid upward, around his neck, and her body yielded to his even more now. "I thought you knew. I was willing to break all the rules, forget everything I'd ever been taught." For the first time since New York, her eyes were alive again, glowing with feeling. "I loved you so much that nothing else mattered."

He caught his breath, unable to tear his gaze from her softened, tender face. He wanted to question her words, doubt them, deny them, because she had been married. He wanted to ask how she could love him and yet be so determined to find the men who had killed her husband—an action that had to be motivated by extremely powerful emotions. But he loved her, and he wanted to believe that she loved him.

"Victoria . . ."

Huskily, she said, "I know I killed it, what you felt for me. I know you don't love me now."

He made a rough sound and kissed her. "Killed it?" His voice was shaken. "You didn't kill it, and I couldn't, no matter how I tried." There was no anger in him now, only an aching need that had been a part of him so long it was a familiar thing. And there was too much to think about, too much still unanswered; he wanted to just feel.

Victoria was in the same state, her mind numbed by it all but her body achingly alive and aware. She had fought not to love him, not to give in to his desire and her own, and had been defeated in New York. In this small, dark room, she had fought to save his life, even though she had believed he hated her, and she had triumphed. Now she was conscious of nothing but the overwhelming need to belong to him.

He was still holding her hips, pressing her body against his, and his face was taut, his eyes dark. "I don't think I can wait this time," he said thickly. "I've wanted you so long, sweet, so desperately."

"Your wound," she managed, breathless as his hands slid over the tight jeans to shape her buttocks.

"What wound?" he murmured, just before his lips covered hers.

Victoria forgot it as well, mindless in the stark need of his kiss. Her breasts ached against his hard chest, and her lower body throbbed even as his did. The shocking intimacy of his subtle movements against her sent her senses into a dizzying spin, until she was aware of nothing but him, his body against her, his mouth claiming hers with the driven impatience of something held in check for too long.

She could barely breathe when he lifted his head at last, and stared up at him dazedly. He pushed her gently back onto the fur-covered cot and then knelt before her, pulling her boots off and setting them aside, removing the thick socks. Victoria wouldn't have believed that such a matter-of-fact action could have been erotic, but it was, and when his thumb brushed her sensitive instep, she caught her breath.

His eyes gleamed beneath the hooded lids as he

rose and pulled her back up. His fingers trailed down her thigh and unfastened the leather thong tying her gun down; then he unbuckled the heavy belt, and dropped her gun near the discarded boots. "I've wanted to do this," he murmured, his hands lifting to her hair, "since the first moment I saw you." He freed her braid from the thong and ran his fingers through her hair, spreading it in a pale curtain over her shoulders, and watching as the firelight glimmered off the pale strands. "Beautiful . . . I knew it would be." Her leather vest was slipped off, and fell unheeded to the floor. He unbuttoned the tight cuffs of her shirt, and chuckled softly when his fingers found the scabbard strapped to her forearm.

"So this is where you hid the knife. I wondered. Who taught you to wear a knife?"

"My brother, during the war," she murmured, hardly aware of the question.

Falcon unbuckled the scabbard and tossed it aside. Her shirt was tugged free of the waistband of her jeans, and he began slowly unbuttoning it from the top.

Victoria was caught, trapped in the darkness of his eyes, and it was a familiar feeling. Her heart was pounding heavily, her breath coming fast between parted lips, and the hollowness deep inside her was filled only with an aching heat. She listened to his deep, rough voice and gazed into his compelling eyes, and she couldn't have turned away from him then even if it had been the price of her life.

The shirt was pushed off her shoulders and dropped, and Falcon caught his breath as he stared at her. He had seen her before, in a darkened carriage and garden, in a book-lined room. But not like this. Those shadowy glimpses paled beside this. Naked to the waist, the firelight flickering over her golden flesh, she was more beautiful than any person or thing he had ever seen. "God, Victoria . . ." His hands surrounded her full breasts, and he watched intently as his stroking thumbs brought the sensitive tips hard and erect. He heard her gasp, felt her sway toward him, and the feverish need to see her totally naked blazed through him.

Victoria twined her finges in his thick hair, feeling his mouth move slowly downward between her breasts, barely conscious that he had dropped to one knee. Then she felt his fingers unfastening her jeans, and knew a moment of instinctive panic, aware that she was vulnerable as never before. But the panic faded as he smoothed the coarse material down over her hips, faded because he was moving his lips over her quivering belly, and the sensation drove everything else from her mind.

Then she was lying on the cot, with no memory of being placed there, watching him swiftly discard his own clothing. His eyes were sweeping her body, hot and glittering, and she had never felt so much a woman as she did in that moment. Vaguely, she thought that she should have been shy or embarrassed, because she had never lain naked while a man looked at her, but it was a fleeting thought and untroubling. Her body burned, and she looked at his in wonder as the clothing fell away, fascinated by his power, by hard planes and angles and muscles that rippled with every movement.

Black hair covered his chest, arrowed down his hard, flat stomach to the thicket over his loins, and she caught her breath in surprise. Beautiful—he was beautiful with the strength and pride of a wild stallion. She'd never known a man could look like that, never realized such beauty existed. His desire was obvious in the jutting fullness of his manhood, and she let her gaze move slowly back up to meet his darkened eyes.

So this was desire, this terrible hunger for something she couldn't even put a name to. He was so beautiful, and she wanted him so desperately.

But his wound. The bandage was starkly white against his bronze flesh, wrapping his upper chest and one shoulder, and the thought that he might tear the wound open and start bleeding again was a worry she couldn't ignore.

"Falcon, you haven't healed yet—"

"You'll heal me," he said thickly, joining her on the narrow bed.

"But you might start to bleed!"

"I won't," he promised recklessly, and kissed her before she could protest again. Her flesh was silk beneath his touch as his hand stroked lightly beneath her breasts, her response instant and total, and he ignored the dull ache of his healing wound. Other aches were more insistent, driving him. His heart was thundering, his breath a rasp, and the fullness of his loins a fire that was burning him alive.

Victoria bit her lip to hold back a wild cry when his mouth trailed down her throat and between her breasts, a restless heat filling her until she wanted to move, wanted to plead with him to hurry, to stop torturing her like this. But the ache grew stronger, maddening, until her entire body was taut and she couldn't breathe, couldn't hear for the pounding of her own heart against her ribs. She gripped his shoulders without even feeling the bandage under one hand, all her burning senses concentrated beneath his lips as they moved over her breasts.

She lost what was left of her breath when he finally stopped tormenting her and captured a throbbing nipple in his mouth, but that was another kind of torture, and she moaned with the sweet agony of it. Her body shifted restlessly, burning, and she moaned again when his hand slipped down over her flat belly.

She could feel his touch there like a hot brand, moving lower, until she arched against him with a broken cry when his fingers moved through the pale curls at the base of her belly and slipped between her thighs. It was too much, it was . . . Her thighs were taut, trying to force his hand away from the exquisite sensitivity he was so close to because it was too much. And then it wasn't enough, and her legs parted for him, and the pleasure jolted through her like madness.

"Falcon . . . make it stop . . . it's getting worse, make it stop," she pleaded huskily.

"I will, sweet," he murmured against her breast, flicking the distended nipple with his tongue and then drawing it into his mouth hungrily. She was so sweet, so soft and warm, she was driving him out of his mind. His palm covered the satiny curls of her womanhood, his fingers probing, and he could feel the slick heat of her response to him.

Victoria was on fire, her flesh burning her, and

the erotic touch of his fingers only fed the blaze instead of diminishing it. She knew she was dying, knew it because her heart had gone wild and she couldn't breathe and the flames were consuming her. Her stomach muscles knotted painfully and her head lashed, and he was killing her instead of making it better. "Falcon . . ."

"Shhh. I know, sweet," he murmured thickly. He took one of her hands, carrying it to his lips briefly and then to his body. "I'm hurting too."

Her fingers closed around him, and her feverish eyes widened in surprise. So warm and hard, alive in her hand, and he responded to her touch just as she had to his, a groan escaping his lips and his stomach knotting in a hard spasm.

"Oh, God! Don't—" He gently moved her hand away, his breath rasping as he fought to get the words out. "I can't take it. Not now. I wanted to go slowly, but—"

Victoria felt her legs gently widened, felt him there, and she caught at his shoulders. A blunt pressure, hot and hard, and she could feel her body stretching, feel the tension that was a building ache.

"Relax, sweet," he murmured, a tinge of surprise in his rough, deep voice. He was braced above her, kissing her deeply again and again, and she couldn't find the breath to tell him her body's resistance wasn't a conscious thing. And she was too involved in the sensations even to be able to form the words that would have warned him.

It felt so strange. But hard and hot, and what her body craved in its terrible hunger. The pressure increased, and a flash of pain tore a gasp from her

lips, but there was a deeper, burning ache, a need
he was so close to satisfying. She could feel his
surprise, feel his big body shudder, and see a
dawning, baffled realization in his eyes, even as his
face tautened in stark pleasure.

"God, you're so small," he whispered. "So . . .
tight. Victoria? Relax, sweet, you—" He didn't
believe what his body was telling him, couldn't
believe. He pushed harder, deeper.

The pain was worse now, stealing her breath, but
need was stronger, and instinctively she met his
sudden thrust, arching upward. She cried out even
as he went still, and she was conscious only of the
throbbing fullness of him deep inside her. There
was no pain now, just the hot satisfaction of
merging, joining, and the tension of hovering,
waiting for . . . something.

"Victoria?" His elbows braced on either side of
her, he touched her face with one shaking hand,
and she could see the shock on his face, the glitter
of something wild in his eyes, hear it raw in his
voice.

She didn't want to talk. There was more, she
knew that, knew the pleasure had only begun. The
heaviness of his body was wonderful, the pulsing of
him within her spurring the tension higher and
higher, and she moved impatiently beneath him.
"Falcon, please."

He groaned, and his lips covered hers. His tongue
dived deeply, filling her mouth in a stark caress,
and he began to move in a hot, smooth rhythm that
stole her breath all over again. The burning ache
inside her was magnificent now, maddening, and
she half-sobbed as she held him with all her

strength. His powerful rhythm filled her mind, her swirling senses, her shaken world, until there was nothing but that, nothing but this pulsing, jagged pleasure surging within her.

Falcon tried to be gentle, but her response shattered his control. His body was wild for hers and his mind was chaotic, his emotions reeling with the knowledge that there had been no other man in her bed, not husband or lover.

She was *his*, all his, and he hadn't known until then just how much it meant to him.

There was no time for thought, no time for astonishment and wonder. Her body sheathed his with a molten tightness that was almost agony, a sweet agony that drove him to thrust harder, deeper into her welcoming heat. And then he heard her broken cry, felt her body convulse around him in an ecstatic rhythm, and a guttural groan tore its way from deep in his chest as he buried himself in her, shuddering . . . dying.

They both became aware of their surroundings again in the same moment, and Falcon lifted his head to look down at her as the wail of the wind reached his ears. The fire in the hearth had died down and the shanty was chilly, the storm outside building loudly in the fury she had predicted.

He touched the flushed curve of her cheek, and a pang of tenderness such as he had never known went through him. So much to talk about, to understand. Her eyes were fixed on his face, wide and wondering and glowing, and a tiny smile curved her lips. He didn't want to leave her, never

wanted to leave her, but the fire had to be built up
before they froze.

He bent his head and kissed her gently. "We'll
freeze," he murmured.

"Will we?" Her voice was dreamy, soft.

Falcon chuckled and moved carefully until he
was off the bed and on his feet, very conscious then
of the chill in the room. "I'll build up the fire. Get
under the covers, sweet."

She didn't want to move, but with the warmth of
his body gone, she realized it was necessary. She
wiggled beneath the heavy grizzly fur and lay on
her side, watching him as he built up the fire. She'd
never known a man could look like that. He was so
beautiful . . . so— "Falcon? Your wound?"

He returned to the bed, sliding in beside her and
drawing her close. "Fine."

"Let me see." She wouldn't be denied, and
carefully examined the bandages to make certain
he hadn't reopened his wound. He had, but just a
little. "I should rebandage it."

"It's fine, sweet." He raised up on his elbow to
look down at her, reaching to trace the curve of her
bottom lip with one finger. And it was time, now,
for questions. "He wasn't your lover."

She heard the wonder, the bewilderment in his
voice, and knew that he had to understand her
relationship with Morgan, knew it was important.
"No. Husband in name, but never more. It was just
for appearances, because there was no other woman in the house and I wasn't kin to him. But he
promised to set me free when I met someone else.
That's what I meant when I told you that I *was* free

in New York. I was. Morgan would have understood."

He shook his head a little. "How did you meet? How did it come about?"

She took a deep breath and told him steadily about that day years before, about her brother Jesse's visit, and about the man who had come later, the man with the bloodstained purse, the man she had killed. And about Morgan's arrival, and his gentle invitation. "I don't remember much about the trip to New Mexico," she finished softly. "And perhaps it was wrong of me to go with Morgan when I didn't even know his name, but I've never regretted it."

Falcon was gazing down at her with an odd expression in his eyes, something a bit distant and preoccupied. "The man who attacked you that day, did he say anything about gold?" he asked slowly.

Victoria was startled. "Why, yes. He had Jesse's purse; I suppose he meant that gold, that he knew somehow Jesse had left some of it with me."

"Jesse left some gold with you? Was that usual?"

The question surprised her. "Well, he always tried to send some of his pay home to us. But that day, he said he'd been paid for an errand. He left a bag of gold with me, and took some with him in his purse. Odd, I'd forgotten all about that. I hid it in the house and never thought about it again, not even when I left with Morgan."

He was still tracing her lip slowly, watching his finger now, frowning slightly. "The man who attacked you. What did he look like, sweet?"

She shivered. "He was frightening. Tall, with

wide, thick shoulders. Black hair. And an eye patch."

"When you fought him, did you cut his cheek?" Falcon's voice was slow and still.

Victoria half-closed her eyes. "The blood . . . I cut his face, and then . . . I stabbed him in the chest and he fell."

Falcon leaned down to kiss her gently, then raised his head, murmuring, "It's all right, sweet. It was a long time ago. And Fontaine took you away that day?"

She was disturbed by his still face and soft voice, bothered by something she sensed in him, something almost detached. "Yes. I was running from the house when he saw me, caught me. And he was very kind. He calmed me down, asked me what had happened. He seemed—well, almost as upset as I was when I told him about the man and Jesse. He went with me to look for Jesse's body, but we never found it; the stream had carried it away. He—he buried Papa and old Sam."

"But not the other man?"

Victoria blinked and felt uneasy suddenly. "No. He said the man must have made it to his horse and rode away. But there was so much blood—"

"It's all right, sweet. Don't think about it anymore." Falcon kissed her again, gently, and then eased down and pulled her into the circle of his arms so that her head rested on his shoulder. He changed the subject abruptly, but in the same quiet voice. "Tell me about him. About Fontaine. About your life together."

"Falcon—"

"I need to know, sweet. I need to understand."

She realized that. And, quietly, she told him. She told him about the shock of a new life in a place vastly different from her childhood home. About Morgan's teachings, his insistence that she learn to survive no matter where she was, and yet never forget the gentle upbringing of her childhood. She told him about learning to hunt and track and find or build shelter. She drew a loving image of a man who was intelligent and kind and strong, and it helped ease her grief to talk about him to someone who had never known him.

"You love him," Falcon said finally when her voice trailed away.

She lifted her head to look at him gravely. "I love him. I always will. I would have died without him—or something worse. He gave my life back to me. Can you understand that?"

Falcon's eyes were dark, somber. "Yes, sweet. I can understand that."

Victoria was uneasy nonetheless, listening to the storm building outside and wondering why she felt it inside as well, inside Falcon, as if pressure were growing where it couldn't be seen, but only felt. "Falcon? I love you." Her voice was unconsciously imploring, afraid.

He looked at her with those somber eyes, and the smile that curved his lips was tender and loving and almost sad. "I love you, sweet. More than you'll ever know." He swallowed hard. "Don't forget that."

It should have reassured her, but frightened her instead, because the look in his eyes was achingly familiar. Morgan had looked like that, she remembered, when he had talked about what the South was like in her childhood. When he had talked about something that was lovely and gentle—and forever out of his reach.

What had Falcon suddenly lost to bring that terrible look of pain and grief to his eyes?

"Falcon."

He drew her head down and kissed her, at first gently, and then with growing desire. "Slow this time," he said thickly, drawing her closer. "Slow and sweet."

But it wasn't slow and sweet, their lovemaking. It was wild, driven, hungry. Desperate. It was a violent storm, capturing them both, tossing them furiously on surging waves until they were left at last, drained, on a peaceful shore.

"Victoria?"

"Hmmm?" She was almost asleep, her head pillowed comfortably on his chest.

"You said your brother had to hurry back to his ship that day. What was the ship called?"

She snuggled closer. "The *Raven*," she answered drowsily. "Captain Tyrone's ship. I wanted to talk to him in New York, about Jesse, but I never got the chance."

A rough sigh lifted his chest, but his voice remained soft.

"What was the date, sweet? Do you remember?"

She started to say no, but then she did remember. "It was—April 14. April 14, 1863." She felt as well as heard another sigh from him, and was dimly troubled, because he was holding her as if he expected someone to tear her away from him. . . .

* * *

The storm raged for two days, battering the little house with sharp winds and snow. Outside was a frozen wasteland; inside, a warm, quiet haven.

Victoria knew there was something wrong. He was too quiet, too contained. He made love to her with hunger and told her often that he loved her, but she was aware that he hardly slept at all, aware that he watched her with brooding eyes when he thought she didn't see. He was restless, on edge. He went out to take care of the horses several times a day, taking over those tasks from her. He ate what she prepared automatically.

Several times she saw him go to his saddlebags and stare down at them, only to turn away with an abrupt motion. He asked quiet questions of her childhood and her life with Morgan, and grew more and more silent as she answered honestly.

Victoria knew something was wrong, and she was cold with fear. Even though he held and kissed her, even though she believed that he loved her, he had put a distance between them, as if he were guarding himself. She could only believe that he was ready to move on again, to wander as he had told her it was his nature to—and he didn't want her with him. She was afraid, and afraid to ask, reminding herself again and again that he had made no promises, after all, had even warned her in New York that he couldn't offer her a future.

And what had changed since then? Nothing, except that he had admitted to love. Nothing . . . except that she didn't know if she could go on without him now.

* * *

"Storm's breaking." He hung up his coat and hat, moving to stare broodingly down at the fire.

Time. Victoria managed to keep her voice calm. "Those men will most likely have taken shelter during the storm. I may have to circle for a few miles, but I'll pick up their trail easily enough. I can still find them before they make it to Charleston, I think." He would tell her now, tell her he wouldn't be going with her.

Falcon sent her a look she couldn't read, then returned his gaze to the fire. "I want to tell you a story," he said abruptly.

She braced herself inwardly, going over to the cot and sitting down. "All right."

"During the war, there was a group of men in Charleston. A group of powerful men." His voice was level, toneless. "They could see the war was going in favor of the North, and they were determined to save the South. They needed money, a lot of it. So they planned and executed the theft of a gold shipment in the North. A million dollars in gold."

Victoria was frowning, puzzled. This wasn't what she had expected. "I don't—"

"Hear me out." He drew a deep breath, and then went on in the same toneless voice, staring into the fire. "In that shipment, by mistake, was a chest of specially minted three-dollar gold pieces; they had been ordered melted down, so none were in circulation. Somehow, that one chest wasn't melted down; it wound up with the rest of the shipment, and was stolen. The shipment was transported to the coast, and then onto a blockade-runner, which made it into Charleston. And then something happened.

There was a falling-out, a betrayal. One of the group took the gold and vanished—I don't know why. I was a major in the Union army then, but I was also a Treasury agent—and I still am.

"I've been on the trail of that gold for eight years. Becoming a Ranger was a part of that. We followed leads, but there was nothing to show for the work except a handful of those special coins that had found their way into circulation. I was in New York, waiting for another agent to contact me; we had finally gotten a list of names, the names of those men who'd planned the theft. And one night, while I was at the waterfront, a coin was given to me in change. A three-dollar gold piece. The barkeep pointed out the man who had given the coin to him, and, because it seemed a good lead, I followed him from the bar."

"To the bookshop?" She felt a prickle of foreboding, an instinctive realization that she wouldn't like what he had to tell her.

"To the bookshop. You know what happened when I arrived. The man and his partners were gone, and I couldn't find a trace of them. But I was bothered by what you'd overheard. It seemed I had stumbled into something, ruined their plans, but I had no idea what those plans had been. I never connected any of it with you, because it seemed absurd."

"With me? But I was just looking for a book."

"At the waterfront. The last place in the city for a woman alone, especially a lady. Who told you to look there, and when?" He kept his gaze on the fire.

"The desk clerk at my hotel. I'd spoken to him earlier that day about the book, and he said he might know of a place. There was a message from him later."

"Written?"

"Yes, a bellman brought it to my room."

After a moment, Falcon said quietly, "I saw that desk clerk several times. Middle-aged, fatherly. Do you really think he would have sent you to a waterfront address alone? With no warning of what you might encounter?"

Victoria hesitated. "I never thought about it."

"Was there anyone in the lobby when you talked to the desk clerk earlier?"

"A few men, I think. I didn't really notice."

Falcon nodded slowly, but still didn't look at her. "One of them was always around, I'd guess, since they'd somehow spotted you. I don't know *how* they spotted you. Maybe they just chanced to hear your name. And Talbot would have remembered you. It would have been enough. It was probably one of the other two watching you at the hotel; you would have recognized Talbot, I think, even after all these years."

"Talbot? Falcon, what are you talking about?"

"You were lured to the bookshop, Victoria. They meant to grab you there, kidnap you. But I blundered in and spoiled it for them. They didn't want a witness, and didn't dare take the chance of killing me."

"Why would they want me?" she whispered.

Falcon's shoulders tensed, and his face hardened, went remote. "They could have used you to force your husband to talk. To tell them where he'd hidden the gold years before. It was just an idea, something they decided to try. They'd gotten the address of Fontaine's ranch, though, probably from your hotel, so when I spoiled their plan, they headed for New Mexico. He'd done a good job of covering his tracks, you see, and they'd had no more luck in finding him and the gold than I'd had. Even though they had known him then, he apparently told them nothing of his background. Anyway, it seems they hadn't known much about him when he joined their group, since he wasn't from the South, and when he disappeared, along with the gold, they didn't even know where to start looking for him. Then they somehow found you in New York. And they knew where he was then. They knew where he was, and they went after him."

"No." Her voice was strained, disbelieving.

Falcon flinched. "I didn't know any of it until I met my contact, after you'd left the city. Then the pieces began falling into place. There were only three men on the list still alive. One of them was the man I followed to the bookshop, the one you never saw in New York—Read Talbot. The second was the man who posed as the shopkeeper when you came in—the tall, thin man. Gus Rawlins."

Victoria felt cold. "And the third name?"

Harshly now, Falcon said, "If you'll look in my saddlebags, you'll find a federal warrant for Morgan Fontaine's arrest."

"You're wrong." Her voice was quick, anguished. "You have to be wrong. He wasn't that kind of man, he wouldn't do something like that!"

Falcon was white, his face strained, and he looked as if every breath he drew hurt. His voice was still harsh, even though it was quiet. "There's more."

"I don't want to hear it!" she said, a little wildly.

"You have to." He closed his eyes briefly. "It's the truth, and you have to hear it."

"No—"

"The shipment was brought into Charleston on the *Raven*, Victoria. On April 14, 1863. Your brother did something for Tyrone, ran an errand for him, and he was paid for it. I think he delivered the gold to Fontaine that morning, and he was on his way back to Charleston when he stopped at Regret. Remember the coins he gave you? They were odd coins, like none you'd ever seen before, weren't they? Three-dollar gold pieces. Fontaine must have paid him. And Talbot must have seen or suspected that Jesse had delivered the gold. He attacked Jesse on his way back to Charleston and killed him. Then he backtracked and found his way to Regret. He was after gold, you said, and he had your brother's purse."

Victoria's mind was whirling. "But you said Talbot was the man in New York."

"He was." Falcon turned his head, looking at her finally with hot eyes. "You didn't kill him. He carries the scar you gave him, but you didn't kill him."

She met his eyes, her own bewildered, hurting suddenly. "But that means Morgan caused it. Papa and Jesse died because . . . because of what he did."

Roughly, Falcon said, "I'm sure he knew that; you said once that he was upset that day. Jesse must have mentioned you, and Fontaine rode to Regret to check on you. When you told him what had happened, and described Talbot, he knew. He knew it was his fault. So he took you away from there and gave you a new home, to replace the one his own actions had destroyed."

"His fault." Her voice was soft and anguished. "He lied to me all these years."

"Maybe he wanted to protect you." Falcon was looking back at the fire again, his face strained. "He was all you had and you loved him."

"Papa . . . Jesse . . ."

"He paid for it, Victoria. He paid for it all. Talbot finally caught up with him."

She felt as if she'd been battered, beaten. She was cold, hurting. Morgan. Had he done it out of guilt, raised her, taught her, cared for her? No, not entirely. Even now, confused and hurt, she couldn't believe that. At first, perhaps. But he had loved her, she knew that. Whatever his original motives, he had loved her.

And Falcon?

She looked at him, stiff and silent by the fire, not looking at her. *He didn't want to tell me.* He had listened to her talk of Morgan, and he hadn't wanted to be the one to destroy her image of that man. Without thought, she went to him, sliding her arms around his waist. "I love you," she murmured.

His arms closed about her, hard, and he made a rough sound. "I didn't want to hurt you, sweet," he said unsteadily. "He was so important to you, and I didn't want to take that away."

Victoria drew back far enough to look up at him. "You ·didn't," she said gravely.

"I thought you'd hate me." He framed her face in his big hands. "I was so afraid you'd hate me."

The coldness was seeping away, and she smiled slowly. "Never. I love you. I'll always love you."

"Always," he murmured, looking into her soft eyes as if he found his ·soul there. "That might be long enough."

4

Time. The storm had delayed them, and they could only hope it had also delayed Morgan Fontaine's killers. They had perhaps three days before they would have to abandon the trail and head quickly for Charleston, and a ship departing for Europe. If Morgan's killers had managed to learn from him where the gold was hidden—and Falcon thought it likely—then they were most probably engaged in a feverish search of their own.

Both Falcon and Victoria knew that if the men found that gold, and managed to reach the ship and set sail, it was doubtful they could ever be found again.

They found the tracks a day out from their abandoned haven. The storm had passed and the temperature was rising steadily, though it remained cold at night. But by the second day, they had advanced much farther south in following the trail, and they saw snow only in melting patches. They made camp that night in the lee of a hillside, picketing their four horses—they had kept the pinto as a second packhorse—to graze.

Victoria woke first, and lay looking up at the clear, blue sky, feeling loved and secure in his sleeping embrace. She had been struggling to remember that long-ago trip west, trying to think of where the gold could be hidden, but had been unsuccessful.

Her mind had refused to allow those memories to surface. But it came to her now, in the silence of morning, the memory she had not recalled for eight years. The memory of the trip west, and one stop that had lasted longer than the others.

"Falcon?"

He was instantly awake, and she knew it, but only one eye opened to peer at her and then he shut it again, drawing her closer. "It's barely dawn," he murmured.

She pushed herself up onto an elbow and gazed down at him. "You have to wake up, love, I've thought of something."

A smile curved his lips. "Must be the drawl."

"What must be?"

"The feeling I get every time you say 'love.' Like a shot of raw brandy."

She leaned down and kissed him, but drew away quickly when it became obvious he was waking up with a vengeance. "Falcon! I think I know where the gold is."

He opened his eyes reluctantly. It was a chapter in their lives that had to be finished, but he'd been wishing that gold in hell for weeks now. "Near?"

"A day's ride, if we start now. I don't think the other two know where it is, not exactly. I don't think Morgan would have told them. And they aren't heading in the right direction." She sat up and pushed the heavy grizzly pelt away. She had gotten so accustomed to waking up naked at his side, that she became aware of it this morning only because a sudden, chill wind struck her bare flesh. Before she could move to find her clothes, Falcon growled and pulled her back down.

"Falcon—"

His mouth was at her breast, nuzzling a nipple that the cold wind had tightened into a hard bud. "You don't expect me to ignore this, do you, sweet?" he asked hoarsely.

Victoria caught her breath, and her hands lifted to tangle in his thick hair. "No. Oh, no," she murmured. "I wouldn't expect you to ignore that at all."

And they were only an hour late in getting started.

"This is more familiar territory to you, isn't it?" she asked as they mounted the horses.

"Familiar enough, after years."

Victoria pointed in the direction the tracks led, slightly northeast. "Is there a mission that way?"

Falcon frowned a little. "Two of them, within a few days' ride."

"We passed by an old, abandoned mission yesterday, remember? The tracks were all around it."

He nodded slowly. "So that's what you thought of—a mission? Did Fontaine stop at one on the way to New Mexico?"

"Yes. I'm pretty certain it's southeast of here, between San Antonio and the Mexican border. I remember it was the only place we stopped other than a town or out in the middle of nowhere. We spent the night, and I didn't see much of Morgan. And—" She drew a deep breath. "—we left a wagon behind there."

Falcon looked at her gravely, and then glanced at the trail leading off. "These tracks are a few days old, at least. If they went on to both the missions, they could just be turning south now, assuming they even know of the other mission. That would put us in the right place a couple of days ahead of Talbot and Rawlins. *If* they really don't know where they're going. But they could be ahead of us."

"I know," she said in a steady voice.

"You don't have to do this, sweet. We can ride to San Antonio, and I'll have a cavalry regiment greet those bastards at the mission."

She looked at him as he sat easily on his big horse, a handsome, tough man with gentle eyes, and she knew he would do that for her. He'd ride away from the end of a years-long search, leaving the gold for someone else to uncover in triumph, to spare her the pain of certainty and the danger of facing the men who had killed Morgan.

Softly, she said, "We both have to finish this, love."

Their horses were standing side by side, and he didn't have to lean far to kiss her. "Then we'll finish it," he said in a quiet voice.

Their horses moved out in perfect step, the packhorses trailing behind them as they headed southeast.

* * *

Victoria was looking at the abandoned mission as they topped a rise, but Falcon glanced back over his shoulder with a frown. It was almost sunset, and impossible to see much behind them in the glare, and he swore softly.

"What is it?" she asked, looking at him.

After a moment, he said, "I think we're being trailed."

She was startled. "Talbot and Rawlins?"

"I'd say not. The direction's wrong. They couldn't have gotten south of us so quickly. Maybe bandits; they could have come up out of Mexico. Indians, even. The packhorses could have convinced them we're carrying something valuable." He studied the mission as they approached it, and shook his head a little unconsciously. "This is not a good place to stand off bandits or Indians," he muttered.

Victoria could see what he meant. Like many of the missions in Texas, this one had been built around a hundred and fifty years before, but it had been abandoned. That the mission was even recognizable was surprising; the roof had fallen in, and only two walls were left standing. An old well was little more than a hole in the ground and a tumble of stones, and a battered stagecoach rotted, cock-eyed, on two broken wheels. There was a graveyard off to the east in the wispy shade of a lightning-blasted cottonwood, what had once been a picket fence around it now no more than a few ragged stakes in the ground.

But when Falcon glanced at her questioningly, she nodded. This was the place. "It was occupied then, and pretty much in good repair," she told him. "I remember that cottonwood, and the way lightning had split it."

"Do you have any idea—?"

"The gold?" She sighed as they drew up near a standing wall. "I was exhausted when we got here. It was late at night, and the padre took me away to sleep in a little room. I didn't even see Morgan until late the next morning. It could be anywhere."

He nodded. "We'll start looking in the morning." Handing her the packhorses' lead ropes, he added restlessly, "I'm going to ride out and take a look around. I don't like the idea of having uninvited company during the night."

"Be careful."

He smiled and leaned over to kiss her. "I will. And *you* be careful too, sweet."

Victoria was grateful that he didn't try to wrap her in cotton wool; clearly, he respected her ability to take care of herself, even to the point of making no objection over her intentions to confront Morgan's killers. That warmed her, made her feel more confident. It would take a strong woman to walk or ride beside Falcon. She watched him ride off, and then sighed and dismounted, ground tying her horse and leading the packhorses over to what had once been a hitching post. Warily, she moved around, her hand always near her gun, until she was satisfied that the place was indeed deserted, of animal as well as human life.

Inside what had been the mission was surprisingly free of rubble near the standing walls, and she decided on that spot to build their campfire. She

felt a little edgy, and on each trip out to unload the
packhorses she glanced around carefully, but saw
and heard nothing alarming. The horses were led a
little distance from the building, and picketed to
graze on sparse grass.

She was still edgy. Falcon hadn't been gone long
enough for her to begin worrying, so that wasn't it.
*The last time you felt like this you nearly got shot—
and instead, Falcon did!* She walked outside the
mission, staring around, bothered. The faint wind
changed direction just then, and she saw the
packhorses start, saw her buckskin move nervously
to the end of his tether. In the same moment, she
caught the foul odor coming from the old well.

"Oh, God," she murmured. Just some poor animal, it had to be that. Just some—

"I've been waiting for you."

She was half-prepared for the voice, but not the
memories. In a flashing instant she was fifteen
again, terrified, fighting for her survival. Holding
on to control, she turned slowly to face him, hoping
her fear didn't show.

He was a big man, with bulky shoulders and
graying black hair, one eye covered by a black
patch, and the opposite cheek scarred terribly. He
was standing only a few feet away from her,
smiling a twisted smile, and the hand holding a
gun pointed at her stomach bore a ring she recognized. Morgan's ring. Victoria didn't dare move,
didn't dare reach for her gun.

She swallowed hard. "You couldn't have followed me. Your tracks were heading north, and you
were days ahead of me." Did he know about
Falcon? She didn't think so.

Read Talbot seemed pleased. "I thought that'd throw you off, Mrs. Fontaine. You see, we heard, back before those two damned storms, that you were trailing us. A woman who puts on britches and wears a gun gets herself talked about, and we heard about you back at Fort Davis. We also talked to one of those Spanish priests, who mentioned an old mission with a split cottonwood at the edge of a graveyard. Morgan . . . mentioned . . . a tree like that. He died before he could tell me exactly where he'd hidden the gold, but when I knew you were following, I figured you could help. Now, Morgan didn't seem to think you knew where he'd hidden the gold, but I had an idea you might."

"You tortured him." She spoke from between stiff lips.

Talbot chuckled obscenely. "He talked a lot about you, Victoria. In between screams. Of course, I already knew the most important thing about you." His free hand lifted to touch the scarred cheek. "That you're a rebel, just like me. That's why he married you. Because you were a rebel."

"The war made rebels. I'm a Southerner." She lifted her chin as she said, and realized it was true.

Tilting his head to one side, Talbot studied her curiously, and a glint of admiration showed in his single, cold eye. "So you are. And a damned fine lady. I knew that in New York. That's why I wouldn't let Sonny have you in the cellar. Where is Sonny, by the way?"

"Dead."

"Morgan must have taught you well. Sonny was a fool, but a good shot, and not above turning his gun on a lady."

She ignored that. Time, she needed time, time to distract him. "There was another man."

Talbot's gaze flickered toward the well. "There was," he agreed blandly.

Victoria felt sick. Not just some poor animal, then. . . . "You wanted all the gold."

"It's mine," Talbot told her in a sharpened tone. "The assassination was *my* idea."

"Assassination?"

"Lincoln. If we could have gotten him during the war, everything would have been different. But that bastard Tyrone got suspicious of the shipment, and when he met me at the harbor, he'd left the gold on the *Raven*." Talbot's voice was rising now, tautening. "The son of a bitch didn't take sides in the war, but he couldn't stomach assassination plots, he said. He knocked me cold and left. He went straight to Fontaine, and agreed to deliver the gold to him. And when I came to, the gold was being taken out of the city. Some kid drove the wagon."

"Jesse." Her voice was toneless. "My brother."

"Yeah, I remember." Talbot was indifferent. "It took me a while to find a horse—there weren't many left in the city. By the time I started to follow the boy, he'd already delivered the gold, and I didn't know where."

"You killed him."

"He had some of the gold in his purse," Talbot said reasonably. "And I found more at the plantation when I came back later. After I'd healed from what you'd done to me."

Victoria felt an anger such as she had never

known burning through her like a fire. "You killed my father." Her voice shook with rage. "My brother. You would have killed me. You tortured Morgan to death, killed your own partner. How many times will you kill for that gold?"

"It's a million dollars," he said, as if that explained everything. "We'll need it for the ranch, Victoria."

Even through her fury, her skin crawled at his implication. "We?"

"Of course." He smiled at her. "We'll go to Europe first, like I planned. And then we'll come back to the ranch, and everyone'll think you met a fine gent over there. I told Morgan what I meant to do. And he heard me, even through his screams. I told him I'd take the gold, his ranch, his woman. He destroyed my life; it's only fair that I take his."

Her heart ached at the thought of Morgan dying in agony with that horrible promise ringing in his ears. All she could do for him was to make certain Talbot's triumph never came to pass. Her rage turned cold, and her mind worked quickly. She kept her face serene; he seemed to admire and respect her, thinking her ladylike even in her man's clothes, and she needed every edge she could get. "I see. And have you found the gold?"

He chuckled. "You'll tell me where it is."

She feigned surprise, glancing toward the well. "I assumed you'd found it."

Talbot's eyes narrowed, and he glanced at the well also. "What are you talking about?" he asked sharply, his cold eye shifting from her to the well.

Coolly, she said, "You should have checked the well before you threw your partner into it."

"What?" He was only a few feet from the well, and immediately moved toward it, greed twisting his features. In that moment, he forgot revenge, forgot her. "It's in there? It's in there with Gus?"

He might have caught the flicker of motion from the corner of his eye as Victoria's hand dropped to the gun on her hip. He might have realized in some part of his mind that her behavior was wrong, all wrong, that the fifteen-year-old girl who had nearly killed him would not have become a woman who wouldn't finish the job. Or it might have been sheer animal instincts shrieking a silent warning, as he stood at the edge of a crumbling well with his back to a woman whose husband he had horribly killed. He pivoted wildly, his gun hand coming up in a jerky reflex as he came around to face her.

She shot him.

"Victoria!"

She rose from the newly kindled fire inside the mission, relieved to hear Falcon's voice. "In here," she called. She was vaguely aware that there was too much noise for just his horse, but didn't think much about it as he strode quickly through the skewed doorway and into the flickering firelight. It was nearly dark now, but she saw his strained face ease the moment he caught sight of her.

"We heard a shot," he said, coming to her quickly and hugging her tightly. Then he drew back and gazed down at her face. "What happened, sweet?"

"This time, I killed him." Her voice was quiet and calm, and there was no horror in her eyes, just the sure knowledge of something done that was right.

Falcon framed her face in his hands, and after a moment, he smiled a little and nodded. "Tell me how it happened."

She told him, beginning with her realization of what was in the well, and finishing with what was there now. "He couldn't turn fast enough or get his gun pointed at me in time. The shot carried him backward into the well." She drew a deep breath. "So it's over. And . . . I think I know where the gold really is. I'll take you out there in the morning."

Falcon held her for a moment, then smiled down at her. "I have a surprise for you."

"What?" She looked toward the doorway as Falcon stepped back and half-turned, her eyes narrowing and then widening, as a tall figure carrying a rifle came into the light.

"Tory?"

Victoria caught her breath, "Jesse? *Jesse!*" The clock turned back as she threw herself, laughing, into his arms, half-crying in happiness, exclaiming.

And it took a while to get the stories sorted out, beginning with the fact that he hadn't been killed by Talbot, but only wounded, and ending with Marcus Tyrone's recognition of her in New York, and Jesse's trip west to find her.

She was about to ask how on earth he'd managed to track her from New Mexico, when she caught sight of another man, and was startled to recognize an Apache. "Jesse, who—"

"Oh, that's Sam," Jesse told her cheerfully. "The chief was kind enough to lend him to me as a guide. And I don't mind telling you, he came in handy. I might have ended up in California without him."

Falcon, who had made no effort to intrude on the reunion, sank down rather abruptly on a fallen beam by the fire and began laughing softly. Victoria went to sit beside him, while Jesse eyed him a bit balefully.

"That's the second time you've gone off," he said. "What the hell were you and Sam jabbering about all the way back here?"

Falcon cleared his throat and sent a look brimful of laughter to Victoria. "His name's Running Wolf, Jesse."

"Oh." Jesse looked with interest on his guide as the young Apache obeyed Falcon's gesture and joined them at the fire, sinking down cross-legged. "Well, how was I supposed to know?" Jesse demanded, taking a seat on another beam. "Nobody spoke English, and I didn't spend more than a day in their camp."

The Apache spoke suddenly and at length to Falcon, his impassive face lighting up in a grin, and Falcon laughed again.

"What is it, Falcon?" Victoria asked in puzzlement.

"I thought the Delaneys were lucky, sweet, but your family must have it in buckets. Told you had headed west after leaving the ranch, your brother rode off alone after you. A few days later, lost, weary, and out of provisions, he came on an Apache camp—and rode blithely in."

"Whose camp?" she asked with foreboding.

"Geronimo's," Falcon murmured.

"*What?*" She turned her head to stare at her brother. The fact that he was still alive was nothing short of a miracle. "Oh, Jesse!"

A bit testily, Jesse said, "So? I don't know who the chief was, but he was nice enough. A little nervous, maybe."

Victoria looked wonderingly back at Falcon. "How on earth did he manage to get out alive—much less with a guide?"

"According to Running Wolf," Falcon supplied gravely, "it seems that Geronimo was convinced the smiling white man was possessed of evil spirits. Obviously, no sane man would ride into his camp completely alone in broad daylight. He didn't want the spirits to depart Jesse and possess the camp, so he wasn't about to kill him. Which is why Running Wolf volunteered to guide him—as far away as possible."

Victoria started laughing.

"Look, it got me here, didn't it?" Jesse demanded. "And Sam—I mean, Running Wolf—taught me a lot about tracking." He eyed Falcon again suspiciously. "What I'd like to know, is how he knew *you* were about. We crossed a lot of tracks, days back, before we headed south to avoid the storm. At least, I think that's what he was trying to do. Anyway, he got very excited, and every time we made camp, he'd draw a shamrock in the dirt and try to explain something to me. It didn't make sense, until he hailed you like a brother, and I saw the shamrock brand on your horse."

Falcon smiled a little. "What he was trying to tell you was that one of his relations was also tracking your sister. How did you manage to explain who you were looking for?"

"A lot of sign language and drawing in the dirt," Jesse said with some feeling. Then he blinked. "You're related to him?"

"A cousin by marriage. His cousin, Rising Star, married one of my brothers years ago."

"Oh." Jesse frowned. "That doesn't explain how he knew it was you just by looking at the ground days ago."

Blandly, Falcon said, "The Apaches know the mark of every Delaney hoof in the Southwest—and my horse has a distinctive narrow fore. Running Wolf recognized it."

Jesse looked at the faintly smiling Apache with increased respect. "Did he, now? I was barely sure we were following a *horse*."

Victoria laughed again, and Jesse looked at her with a smile. His eyes were grave, though. "Falcon told me part of the story on the way here," he said abruptly. "And I heard what you told him a little while ago. I'm sorry, Tory. If I hadn't delivered that gold to Morgan Fontaine—"

She shook her head. "You couldn't have known we'd all be tangled in it. You weren't much more than a boy yourself then, and just did what your captain asked you to do."

Jesse looked at Falcon then, and his eyes hardened. "This is just between us, you know. I won't testify against Marc, which means I won't incriminate myself."

Falcon nodded. "I know," he said quietly. "Recovering the gold is the important thing. For the rest . . . I've been eight years on the trail. I want to know what happened—for myself. As far as I'm concerned, everyone involved in the theft is dead."

Jesse studied him intently for a moment, then nodded. "I can't tell you much. I know Marc wasn't told what he was transporting, because he was mad as hell when a chest broke open at sea and we found out it was Union gold. When we ran the blockade and made Charleston, he went ashore. Came back to the ship a few hours later and asked me if I'd be willing to drive a wagon out of the city. I was, and did. Delivered the gold to Morgan Fontaine. You know the rest."

"I don't know why Fontaine apparently turned on the group and took the gold." Falcon sent Victoria an apologetic glance, but she was smiling with understanding.

Jesse shook his head. "I don't know either. Marc might, but I can't see him volunteering the information."

"The hell of it is," Falcon said wryly the next morning, as they stood just outside the mission, "I can't see Tyrone offering an explanation either." They were watching Jesse and Running Wolf ride off toward San Antonio, where they would deliver a message from Falcon to the army, which was to provide armed escort for the transport of the gold to Washington.

"Could you force him to?" she asked reluctantly.

"With no evidence? And besides that, I believe Jesse was right. I don't think Tyrone knew what he was carrying until too late."

She nodded, then watched as he stepped aside to pick up a shovel leaning against one of the walls.

"Ready?" he asked quietly.

Victoria nodded and took his hand, and they walked together past the well that he, Jesse, and Running Wolf had filled in with stones earlier, past the rotting stagecoach, and up the little hill to the graveyard.

"He was out here that morning," she said softly as they stood looking at the few crooked head-stones. "Out here all alone, just staring at one of the headstones. He saw me coming toward him, and went to meet me. I never knew what he was looking at."

Falcon remained silently by the cottonwood tree while she moved slowly among the graves. This was something she had to do, and he knew it. He watched without moving, still even when she stopped and gazed down at one of the headstones.

"Falcon?"

He went to her then, slipping an arm around her as he joined her and looked down at the grave. It clearly hadn't been disturbed in years; the head-stone was roughly and shallowly carved, the words almost invisible after only eight years. But they could both read what was written there.

Morgan Fontaine
April 14, 1863
buried with Regret

"The day his dream died." Victoria sighed softly. "I think a part of him *is* buried here. He was never a rebel, you know. He didn't care about secession. He just didn't want the South to die."

Quietly, Falcon said, "Then maybe it was that assassination idea of Talbot's that tipped the balance. Maybe Tyrone wasn't the only one who couldn't stomach that."

"Maybe."

He turned her toward him and bent to kiss her. "I love you, sweet," he murmured.

She smiled up at him. "I love you too."

He touched her cheek lightly, and said in a very calm voice, "When we get this damned gold to Washington, you and I are going to have a serious talk about our future."

Secure in his love, she said innocently, "I thought we already had that talk. It seems to me you told me very bluntly that you couldn't offer me a future."

Falcon gave her a look, and began taking off his coat in preparation to begin digging. "Don't throw my own words back at me, sweet. A man never likes to be told what a total ass he made of himself."

"I'll keep that in mind," she murmured.

Falcon gave her another look, but grinned when she laughed, and began digging. Some time later, his shovel struck the first chest, and within minutes a dozen of them had been uncovered.

Falcon bent to lift the first out, and his eyes rose swiftly to meet hers as he straightened to place it on the side of the pit he had dug. Victoria, alerted by that look, came closer and watched as he lifted the chests out, one by one. Then he used the shovel to smash the locks and opened the chests, one by one. And they looked at each other, baffled.

The chests were empty.

Don't miss the enthralling sequel to this book, *Velvet Lightning*, also by Kay Hooper and part of the concluding trinity of THE DELANEYS, THE UNTAMED YEARS.

THE DELANEY DYNASTY

Three of Bantam's bestselling romance authors, Kay Hooper, Iris Johansen and Fayrene Preston, have established a unique event in romance publishing—the creation of the Delaney Dynasty—a family filled with fascinating male and female characters whose love stories are deeply sensual and unforgettable. Each author's work stands alone, but read with the other books is part of a panoramic picture of a colorful, exciting, and heartwarming family.

The stories of the members of the Delaney Dynasty began with the publication of THE SHAMROCK TRINITY, the first trio of contemporary love stories of the Delaney brothers—*Rafe, The Maverick* by Kay Hooper; *York, The Renegade* by Iris Johansen; and *Burke, The Kingpin* by Fayrene Preston. These three romances received such wide acclaim and generated such a clamor for more stories of the Delaneys that our authors soon gave us the next three contemporaries—THE DELANEYS OF KILLAROO: *Adelaide, The Enchantress* by Kay Hooper; *Matilda, The Adventuress* by Iris Johansen; and *Sydney, The Temptress* by Fayrene Preston.

The authors' fascination with the Delaneys grew and, particularly, they were captivated by the daring and romantic ancestors who started it all. Thus, the Delaney historicals were created, one of which you have just read.

Setting the stage for the trilogy THE DELANEYS, THE UNTAMED YEARS, though, was THIS FIERCE SPLENDOR by Iris Johansen. In the pages that follow we are giving you excerpts of THE DELANEYS OF KILLAROO, THIS FIERCE SPLENDOR, and two of the other books of the trilogy THE DELANEYS, THE UNTAMED YEARS. We hope these excerpts will tempt you to get any of the books you may have missed . . . as well as to look forward to the second and last set of historical novels that will follow up THE UNTAMED YEARS and be published in the late fall of 1988.

ASK FOR THE BOOKS OF THE DELANEY DYNASTY SERIES AT YOUR LOCAL BOOKSTORE OR GET THEM THROUGH THE MAIL BY USING THE COUPON AT THE BACK OF THIS BOOK.

The Delaneys of Killaroo:

Adelaide, The Enchantress

by Kay Hooper

He probably wouldn't have noticed them except for the
koala. It wasn't, after all, unusual to see a horse at a
racetrack, or even a girl walking beside a horse. And it
wasn't that unusual to see a koala in Australia.

But he'd never seen one with four leather gloves
covering its paws and riding a horse.

He didn't know much about koalas, but this one
seemed a fair example of the species. It looked absurdly
cuddly, with tufts of ears and a round little body, button
eyes, and a large black nose.

Shane Marston turned his astonished eyes from the
koala to the horse that walked quietly, obediently, beside
the girl holding his lead rope. He wore no blanket or leg
bandages, and seemed not to mind the koala clinging to
his back.

The girl stopped just inside the wide barn hall and
dropped the lead rope, and while the horse stood calmly
she held out her arm toward the koala, calling, "Sebastian."

The little creature reached a gloved paw toward her,
not completely releasing the horse's mane until he could
grasp her arm. Then he left the horse in a smooth
transfer to the girl's back, his limbs firmly around her
neck.

Shane stood very still, gazing at the girl and feeling
the shock of her voice still echoing in his mind. It was the
sweetest, most gentle voice he had ever heard, and it
touched something inside him, something that had
never been touched before. His throat felt tight and his
heart pounded, and he was bewildered because suddenly
he couldn't breathe very well.

She was not thin, but she was small and looked
amazingly fragile. Her skin was very fair, almost translucent. The only color she could boast of was the vibrant
red of her short hair; and though that hair was a badge of

passion and temper, in her face was reflected only gentleness and calm.

She was not, he realized on some uncaring level of himself, a beautiful young woman. Her mouth was too wide for beauty, her eyes too large. Yet that tender mouth would always draw the gaze of a man, and those dark eyes would haunt his dreams.

"You want to meet her?"

Shane started at the sound of Tate Justin's voice. Tate didn't wait for an answer, but started walking forward.

Shane fell into step beside him, eager to meet the girl with the soft, gentle voice and the fiery hair.

"Addie." Tate smiled rather sardonically. "A guest of ours wants to meet you; he's an American horse breeder. Adelaide Delaney, Shane Marston."

Shane, peculiarly sensitive to undercurrents, saw something flash between them, something genuinely humorous on Tate's part and somewhat pained on hers.

She turned to Shane, looking up at him. "Mr. Marston."

Shane held the small hand, instinctively gentle, his fingers tingling again while a faint shock registered at the back of his mind. Her name . . . Was it possible? No . . . half a world away . . . "A pleasure, Miss Delaney," he said, releasing her hand when it occurred to him that he had held it too long.

"I'll leave you two to get acquainted," Tate said, and then walked away.

She gazed after him for a moment, then gave Shane an easy, friendly half smile. "You're interested in Australian horses, Mr. Marston?"

"Shane. And yes, I am."

"Breeding stock, or racers?"

"Primarily breeding stock." Shane reached out to pass a hand down Resolute's sloping shoulders. "He's a fine animal."

"Yes, he is." Her voice gentled even more with the words.

Shane chuckled suddenly and gestured to the koala asleep with his chin on her shoulder. "And unusual, since he allows the koala to ride him."

"Sebastian's the unusual one." She reached up to trail a finger along the koala's foreleg, and a tufted ear twitched sleepily. "He was orphaned young, and instead of climbing trees he took to people and horses. Some people, mind you, and some horses. He's a bit temperamental—but then, so is Resolute." She smiled. "I believe American racehorses sometimes choose odd stable companions?"

"They certainly do," Shane said, remembering the moth-eaten cockatoo at his stable.

Shane looked down at her lustrous coppery curls and felt his heart turn over. He was conscious of an abrupt sense of urgency, a fiery prodding along his nerve endings.

Addie frowned a little and touched his arm in a seemingly instinctive gesture. "Are you all right?"

He looked down at her, feeling her touch clear through to his bones. "Yes. I suppose I haven't recovered from jet lag yet, that's all."

The dark eyes searched his briefly, but she nodded and dropped her hand. "It was nice meeting you—" she began.

Shane smiled broadly. "Oh, I'll be around for a while," he said. "In Australia—and on the tracks. You're riding this afternoon?"

Addie nodded. "Yes, and tomorrow." She didn't seem surprised that he knew she rode. "Then up to Sydney with Resolute for the weekend races."

Shane bit back what he wanted to say. "I see. Well, I believe I'll watch you ride today." He grinned. "Should I bet on you?"

Seriously, she said, "I intend to win."

"Then I'll bet my kingdom."

She laughed a little, the sound once again running through Shane like a haunting song, then waved casually and walked away. He stood stock still for several minutes, gazing after her. Suddenly aware of the increasing noise that heralded the beginning of the afternoon races, he headed toward the track.

Addie had just won the last race on a horse improbably named Catch Me If You Can. She went through the routine of unsaddling, weighing out, and speaking to a delighted owner and a somewhat stunned trainer. Then, tiredly, she headed back for the changing room. She showered and changed into jeans and a light blouse.

Shane was outside, waiting for her.

"I won some money," he said, smiling at her. "And I was hoping you'd go out with me somewhere to celebrate."

"I'd like that." Addie was a little surprised by her instant acceptance, and frowned briefly. "Let me check on Resolute first, all right?"

"Where would you like to have dinner?"

Addie started a little. "Oh, wherever you like. Somewhere casual, please; I travel light on the circuit, so I never pack dressy things."

"Fine. We can go in my rental car, and pick up your Jeep later."

"All right then, and thanks."

"My pleasure." He watched her lock up the Jeep and pocket her keys, then took her arm courteously as they headed toward the parking area near the stables.

Shane didn't try to fool himself into believing that manners had compelled him to take her arm; he was, in fact, very well mannered. That had little to do with it, however. He had taken her arm because he knew he'd go out of his mind if he couldn't touch her even in a polite and casual way. And though it might have seemed just that outwardly, he was very conscious that there was nothing casual in his reaction to the touch.

He felt a sizzling jolt when he touched her, his breath catching oddly and his head becoming curiously light. The strength of his own feelings distrubed him, not in the least because she seemed almost too frail to withstand the powerful force of such vital desire. And it did no good at all to remind himself that she was quite obviously a strong woman; her soft voice, her shimmering halo of silky red hair, small size, and magical gift with animals made her appear ethereal, and all his male instincts urged him to believe in frailty rather than strength.

Shane had always taken his attraction to women lightly in the past; he enjoyed their company, whether casual or intimate. He had a great many female friends, and the lovers in his past tended to remain firm friends after the affairs had ended. Though in a position of comfortable wealth and gifted with blond hair and green eyes that caused the American tabloids to persist in referring to him as "the sleekest, sexiest Thoroughbred in racing circles," Shane had never cared much for casual sex.

Not since his experimental teens had he taken a woman to bed without first having genuinely liked her—and if those invited declined, they never lost Shane as a friend.

What he had seen and heard of Addie, he certainly liked. He liked the frank gaze of her dark eyes, her quick smile and fluid grace. Her voice held a strange power to move him; and her gift with animals and—apparently—people fascinated him.

Yet, for all that, he knew almost nothing about her. Nothing to explain why his very bones seemed to dissolve when she looked at him or spoke to him. Nothing to explain the rabid fear he only just had managed to control while watching her race. Nothing to explain this urgent, driving need to touch her.

Shane knew what desire felt like, and he had even known the feeling to occur spontaneously when first meeting a woman—but that was like comparing the rumble of thunder to the violence of a hurricane.

You'll frighten her to death, he told himself fiercely. If he let go. If he gave in to desires urging him to tumble them both into the nearest bed and violently explore these feelings he had never felt before . . .

She was too gentle and frail, he told himself, to respond to that kind of savagery. Too magically ethereal to want anything but tenderness and gentleness. She was sheer enchantment.

Shane knew dimly that he was already placing her on a pedestal, already setting her like some Greek goddess on an Olympus where an earthy hand could never mark her.

And he hardly heard the inner voice reminding him that the ancient gods and goddesses, for all their divinity, had been remarkably human at heart and quite definitely earthy in their passions.

Beneath the magic.

The Delaneys ouf Killaroo:

Matilda, The Adventuress

by Iris Johansen

"What the hell! There's a woman standing in the middle of the road!" Roman's foot stomped on the brakes of the Jeep. The vehicle swerved and then skidded to the side of the road. He could hear the screech of brakes from the long column of trucks and trailers he was leading. The sound was immediately followed by the blistering curses of the drivers.

"Well, there goes tomorrow's shooting." Brent gingerly touched the bruise he'd just acquired on his forehead from banging his head on the dashboard of the Jeep. "Unless you'd care to write in a barroom brawl. I'm going to have a devil of a bruise on my matchless profile."

"Are you all right?"

The breathless question came from the woman who had run up to the Jeep as soon as it had come to a halt. Her tousled cinnamon-colored hair, sparkling as though touched by a golden hand, shimmered in the headlights; Roman was fascinated for a fleeting instant by that brilliant halo of color. He shifted his gaze to her face. "What the hell did you think you were doing? I almost ran over you."

"Lord, I'm sorry. I didn't realize you were going so fast. I just wanted to . . ." Her eyes widened in amazement. "You're Roman Gallagher. How wonderful. I've always wanted to meet you."

"Yes." Hell, not another would-be starlet, he thought. He'd had his fill of actresses throwing themselves into his path in the hopes of getting a part in one of his films. As his gaze touched her he was startled to feel a swift and incredible desire for her. It didn't make a damn bit of sense to him. She wasn't even sexy. Yet his reaction had been undeniable. A tingle of annoyance went through him.

She smiled, and he inhaled sharply. Warmth. Lord, her

smile illuminated her thin face like the Southern Cross illuminated the night sky.

"I love your films," she said. "I thought *Fulfillment* was terrific, and I've seen all your documentaries. My favorite was the one you did on the Barrier Reef."

He tried to mask his surprise. She had clearly done her homework. He hadn't made a documentary in seven years, and at that time his audience had been extremely small. "Thank you. I enjoyed filming it, even though the subject of the reefs had been done a hundred or so times before."

"But not like you did it. The underwater scenes were . . ." She took an eager step closer, her brown eyes shining in the reflected beam of the headlights. She met his gaze and suddenly her eyes widened in curious surprise, and she forgot what she wanted to say. Then she shook her head as if to clear it and laughed uncertainly. "There aren't any words to describe that film. I wanted to hop on the next boat to the reef."

"I'm surprised you didn't."

She whirled to her left, and faced the man who had just stepped down from the truck directly behind the Jeep. She squinted into the shadows as she tried to match a face with the familiar voice. "Dennis?" Then, as the man came into the perimeter of the headlights, his gray-flecked sandy brown hair and rough-hewn features became clearer. She flew across the road and into his arms, and gave him an enthusiastic hug. "Dennis Billet, what on earth are you doing here?"

"I could ask you the same thing." His hazel eyes were twinkling down at her. "Except I've given up being surprised at the places you turn up. Nowadays I just accept the fact that if there's excitement or trouble or danger around, sooner or later you'll be there."

"I hate to interrupt this reunion, but I have a location to set up." Roman's tone was caustic. For some irrational reason he was displeased at the sight of the golden-haired woman in Billet's arms. "You know this woman, Dennis?"

Dennis nodded. "We go back a long way." He placed his arm companionably around her waist as he turned to face Roman. "Manda Delaney, this is my boss, Roman Gallagher."

Manda was frowning. "Location? You're going to set up a movie location here? But you can't do that!"

"I have a drawerful of permits back in Sydney that says the opposite." Roman's lips tightened. "I'd damn well better be able to do it. Are you saying you have a prior claim?"

"No, not exactly." She ran her fingers through her shining hair. "I tried to get one, but the authorities said the entire area had already been leased. I thought it was a mistake. No one comes to Deadman's Ridge anymore. There haven't been any opals found in this field for over twenty-five years."

"Which is why I had no trouble obtaining a three-month lease on the ridge."

"You're going to be here for three months?" The dismay on her face was unmistakable. "Look, can't you go somewhere else? I know I don't have a legal permit, but I was here first, and my business is very important."

He was staring at her in disbelief. "Do you realize how much money I'd lose per day looking for another location?"

She made a face. "No chance?"

"No chance." His eyes narrowed. "May I assume you're not an actress then?"

"Me?" She was astonished. "Why would you think I was an actress?"

He stiffened. "What's your business here? Are you a newspaper reporter?"

"What is this? Twenty questions?"

His lips twisted. "I know you people consider questions the prerogative of the press, but you should have thought of that before you decided to trespass on my land. Lord, I thought I'd gotten away from vultures like you."

"I'm *not* a reporter."

"Then just what is your business here, Miss Delaney?"

"Manda." She smiled and again he felt warmth radiate through him. "I'm afraid my business is of a private nature. However, I assure you it's most urgent. I promise I won't get in your way if you let me stay." Her voice dropped to wheedling softness. "I know you'll understand."

Dennis Billet suddenly burst into laughter. "Manda,

you never change. Be careful, Roman, she'll be talking you out of your mobile home in another minute."

She had come very close to getting what she wanted from him. Roman felt a flare of anger when he realized that if he hadn't been jarred by Dennis's obvious amusement, he would probably have let her stay. "I can't help you. I've made it a rule to close my set to outsiders." Roman got back into the Jeep and started the ignition. He noticed Dennis's arm still held the woman in a casual embrace, and he found his pilot's familiarity with Manda Delaney oddly annoying. The woman was obviously an accomplished charmer and accustomed to getting her own way with men. Well, she would find he distinctly disliked being used by anyone, women in particular. "I'll give you one day to pack up and get off the property."

"But you don't understand. I can't—" The rest of her sentence was lost as he revved the engine of the Jeep. "I *have* to stay here. There are reasons. . . ."

The Jeep jumped forward as he pressed the accelerator. A few seconds later he'd driven several yards down the road.

"You weren't very polite," Brent drawled. "You didn't introduce me, and I got the distinct impression that something about the lady annoyed the hell out of you. Pity. She could have been very entertaining to have around. You could have thought about *my* convenience, Roman. You drag me out here in the wilds with an all-male cast, forbid me to seduce any of the women on your production crew, and then send packing the only alluring woman who crosses our path. How inconsiderate can you be?"

"I'm sure you'll survive. Besides, she wasn't all that pretty."

"You don't think so? Personally, I prefer the unconventional type."

"Too thin."

"But she really fills out a T-shirt."

"I didn't notice," Roman said.

Brent glanced sidewise at him, and then smiled. "Oh, yes, you noticed all right. Is it okay if I go after her and offer her my sympathy, my gorgeous body, and anything else she'll accept?"

"Why should I care? She's nothing to me." Roman's hands tightened unconsciously on the steering wheel. "Though I don't think it's worth your while. She'll be gone tomorrow."

"Long enough. Haven't you heard I'm irresistible? All my press clippings say so." The amusement was abruptly gone from Brent's expression. "If you want her yourself, I'll back away, Roman. My role in your film means too much to me to jeopardize our professional relationship over a woman."

For the briefest instant Roman was tempted to tell him to back off, to keep away from her. The instinct was brutally primitive. Lord, what had gotten into him tonight? There was no way he was going to involve himself with Manda Delaney. Her appearance in his life had been entirely too coincidental, and her reluctance to tell him the purpose of her business in the opal field was distinctly suspicious. She could be anything from a con artist on the make, to one of the paparazzi out to get an exclusive interview. This was sheer madness. He forced himself to relax and the moment of insanity passed. He shrugged. "Do what you like. She doesn't appeal to me."

Manda laughed softly as she stood in the middle of the road watching the receding taillights of the vehicles of the caravan. The desert was no longer tranquil, and the entire situation was fraught with complications. Yet she was still feeling a familiar shiver of excitement. Change. Things were changing, events were going to occur, people would act and react. How she loved adventure and change and this time the potential was more exciting than ever before.

Because a difficult, sensual man named Roman Gallagher was leading that caravan and she had suddenly realized he just might be the greatest adventure of all.

The Delaneys of Killaroo:

Sydney, The Temptress

by Fayrene Preston

One floor above the casino, from behind the one-way glass, Nicholas Charron watched her, as he had every night for the past three nights.

Her name was Sydney Delaney. He had gotten this information from the registration card she had filled out when she had arrived on the island three days ago. Alone.

With each night that passed his curiosity about her grew. She seemed intensely interested in the games, but she had yet to place a bet. And he had seen several men approach her, but with scarcely a look she had sent them on their way.

From his remote observation post he had a complete view of the entire casino. Men and women dressed in their evening finery milled below him in a rhythm of bright color and swirling motion, uncaring that just beyond the casino's wide expanse of windowed walls lay the wonder and the glory of the Great Barrier Reef. Their disregard of the natural beauty of the reef and the star-brilliant night above it amused him. While most casinos were windowless, his was not. He deliberately had had the windows included in the design as his own private joke—just as he had giant seawater aquariums set in the long wall that ran across the back of the casino. Although the aquariums featured the vividly patterned fish that swam in the waters of the reef, he knew that to the majority of the people in the casino, the fish provided little more than an exotic backdrop for the real reason they had come to the island—the gaming.

He understood people, their vices, their greed. Soon, Nicholas promised himself, he would understand Sydney Delaney.

He turned away from the window and walked to the long row of monitors that provided coverage of the entire casino. With a quick flick of a series of switches, four screens glowed simultaneously with her image.

Sydney Delaney was clearly beautiful, but there were many women in his casino tonight who were as beautiful, if not more so. Yet there was something about her that had drawn his attention to her and had kept it there. Unprecedented for him.

Once, a long time ago, he had seen a figurine of a young girl in a Chicago store window, so fine and delicate, she appeared translucent, so fragile and expensive, a glass dome had protected her. He had wanted the figurine. The woman below reminded him of that figurine.

He looked closer, trying to decipher, to take apart, and thus explain, the pull she was exerting on him. Her hair seemed a dark burgundy and hung in a lustrous mass to below her shoulders. He frowned, for the color seemed to contain a depth that the screen of the monitor couldn't satisfactorily register.

In the monitor that caught her profile he saw a straight nose and a clean sweep of jaw. Another monitor showed him finely shaped brows arched over wide, light-colored eyes of an undiscernable shade and a disconcerting mouth, full and perfectly formed to fit under a man's lips.

A third monitor revealed a full-length picture of her. The long dress she wore was of cream-colored slipper satin. The neckline was high, but the back dipped to the waist, exposing skin that, on the monitor at least, appeared flawless. In involuntary anticipation of the time when he would touch that flawless skin, his fingers curled one by one, into his palm.

Experience told him that most of the gowns on the women in the casino revealed more and cost more than the one she wore, but it didn't matter. Any clothing would look marvelous on her, he concluded.

There was an elegance about her and a grace, even as she remained still, and motion and noise swirled around her—like the sea that surrounded the island . . . his island, the Isle of Charron.

Did she have that much command over her emotions and nerves? he wondered. The question intrigued him.

His mind returned briefly to the glass dome that had surrounded the fragile figurine years before. Glass could be broken.

If a panther could live on a tropical island, his name would surely be Nicholas Charron, Sydney decided. She had never seen him, but she could *feel* him—like a violent disturbance in the atmosphere.

Strangely, she never questioned why she felt he was there above her, watching. She just did. She knew that he paced in his control room above the casino, and she sensed his eyes on her, like a warm breath across her skin.

The fact that he was observing her from behind a one-way mirror made her feel exposed, unprotected, and it was a feeling she hated above all else. But she dealt with the vulnerability he was opening up in her as she always did—with absolute control over her body and her mind.

As was her way, she never went into any situation blind if she could help it. Before she had come to the Isle of Charron, she had researched the island, the casino, and the man who owned both. She had learned a great deal, but not all.

Nicholas Charron was a mysterious man. It was known that he was an American expatriate, but exactly what he had done from the time he left America to the time he bought the Isle of Charron was shrouded in mystery. However, over the last five years he had developed an island resort and casino like nothing Australia had seen before, especially on the Great Barrier Reef. They called his casino and hotel complex Charron's Glass Palace—like everything else on the island, his name was attached, whether he intended it to be or not. As a result, the Isle of Charron had gained an international reputation among jet setters and high rollers. They came to spend money, to have a good time, and if possible to see Nicholas Charron.

Speculation ran high, and extraordinary things were whispered about him. He had an aura that was as dark as the night, and to the thrill-seeking gamblers, his mystique was as big a draw as his casino.

But he never came down onto the casino floor, and only rarely did he invite anyone to his apartment at the top of the resort complex. Unless . . .

People talked and word spread. She hadn't been on the island more than a day, when an excited lady she had encountered on the beach had told her that sometimes Nicholas Charron would stand in his control room above the casino floor and scan the action below him to choose a woman for the night.

Sydney had watched women do things she knew were calculated to attract the attention of the dark man everyone talked about but very few ever saw. Somehow she had known the women wouldn't be successful. Somehow she had known it was *she* he watched.

She was being pursued by someone who couldn't be seen, only felt, but Sydney refused to give in to the agitation that ran through her veins with a singing excitement. She had to keep her mind on her purpose for being in the casino. Since she had been on the island, she had carefully studied the action of each of the games, and tonight she had chosen craps to observe. It was a fast-paced game, and the chances of winning large amounts of money seemed good. Wondering about the odds, she opened her purse and pulled out a small calculator.

Within the space of a few seconds two men stood on either side of her.

And watching from the control room, Nicholas Charron reached for the phone.

One man was big and muscular and had a face so grooved and pitted, it looked as if it had been pulled straight off the side of Ayers Rock. The other man, an Oriental, was short and wiry with flat black eyes that stared at her without expression.

It was the larger of the two men who spoke. "I'm sorry, miss, you'll have to come with us."

"Where exactly is it that you're taking me?" she asked as they halted before a set of black stainless steel doors.

"To Mr. Charron's apartment."

The doors swished open, and they stepped into a lift. The doors closed, sealing her and the strange men by her side off from the comfort and familiarity of the crowd in the casino.

Three floors above ground level, the lift glided to a stop, the doors opened, and Sydney was facing the silent sanctuary of the owner of the Isle of Charron. Slowly she began to walk forward.

She was truly lovely, Nicholas thought, watching her.

Exquisite. Instinct had told him that she wasn't like the women he usually summoned to him, and he had been proved right. When she had first looked up and seen his men on either side of her, his theory had been confirmed. Her expression had changed from composure to fear. For an instant she had looked so defenseless, that something like pain had twisted inside of him. To his mind, it hadn't seemed right that the first strong emotion he saw on her face should be fear. On a beautifully carved table a crystal swan swam on a mirror lake.

"Good evening."

She started at the deep voice. She hadn't even seen him, yet there he was! He was standing on a level above her, in front of a window, and for a moment she couldn't separate him from the night. They seemed as one.

As she had trained herself to do, she waited a beat before answering him. "Good evening."

Three long strides brought him down to her. "Thank you for coming."

"Did I have any choice?"

His mouth curved with humor. "Not really, but I won't apologize. I never apologize."

THIS FIERCE SPLENDOR

by Iris Johansen

It is 1870 and the Scottish beauty and scholar Elspeth MacGregor has traveled to Hell's Bluff in the Arizona Territory to hire Dominic Delaney to lead her to the magical lost city of Kantalan. Elspeth assumes her business with Dominic will be simple—but learns quickly that nothing is simple about this magnetic man-on-the-run who is the only person who knows the location of the fabulous city of dark mysteries and magnificent treasures. He refuses to guide her. He refuses even to speak with her again. But his nephew Patrick, a mischievous young man, is Elspeth's ally and has hatched a plan to create a confrontation between her and his uncle.

"Firecrackers?" Elspeth eyed with alarm the stack of slender sticks linked with long fuses. She had been curious about the large blanket-wrapped bundle since Patrick had picked it up from Sam Li's shack, but she had never imagined it contained anything as exotic as firecrackers. "What are we going to do with firecrackers?" she asked again.

Patrick was busy tying the fuses together. "You said you wanted to get Dom's attention and make a statement of your determination." He looked up and grinned at her. "This will make a very resounding statement, I guarantee."

"I'm sure it will," she said faintly. She glanced at the large whitewashed house across the street. "But I had a more sedate statement in mind."

"You want Dom jerked from his lair and forced to confront you in the fastest possible way." His nimble fingers moved to the second string of firecrackers. "This is the only way I could think for you to do it."

"The only way or the most interesting way?" she asked dryly. "I think you're planning on enjoying this."

"Sure, I always did like a good show."

Elspeth wished she could think of something else. She had an idea Patrick's plan had elements more explosive than the firecrackers. "Your uncle is going to be very angry."

"Yep."

"But he'd probably be angry at my coming here anyway."

"Uh-huh."

"And it's really his own fault for being so narrow-minded and uncooperative. This is a very important undertaking; it can add greatly to our fund of knowl—"

She was interrupted by his low chuckle. "I think you're trying to talk yourself into something."

She grinned back at him. "I think I've done it." She knelt beside him. "Let me help you."

"Very well. You take these two packets and run them from the front door down the steps and into the street. I'll take the rest inside and string them along the hall on the second floor and down the stairs to the front door."

"No."

He lifted his head. "What?"

"I said no. This is my responsibility. I'll be the one to set the firecrackers inside the house and light them. You're clearly trying to spare me the risk of being discovered."

"What I'm trying to do is spare you a sight that might shock the bejiggers out of you. I think you'd better wait outside until I call you."

"No." She took the larger stack of firecrackers from him. "Do I light each one as I put it in place?"

He sighed with resignation. "All you have to do is to light the long fuse on the first packet. Place that one at the end of the corridor on the second floor. The fuse will allow you enough time to trail the firecrackers down the stairs to the front hall."

His enthusiasm was contagious. A tiny flare of excitement began to smolder beneath Elspeth's apprehension. "Is the front door left unlocked?"

Patrick nodded. "Rina wouldn't think of discouraging business, be it day or night."

"Then I guess I won't have any problem." She hesitated, then squared her shoulders and started across the street.

"You might have one problem," Patrick called out.

Elspeth stopped and turned to face him with swift alarm. "What?"

"Matches." He took a box from his pocket and grinned. "Catch." He tossed the box across the few feet separating them. "It's hard to light a fuse without them."

Ten minutes later she was standing in the foyer laying the last of the strings of firecrackers on the bottom step. The house was still in half darkness.

She wished there was more light. She would have liked to have seen if the furnishings of a bordello were as exotic as she had imagined. Perhaps when the firecrackers went off she would be able to see more.

The front door opened quietly to reveal Patrick's thick hair outlined against a pearl-gray wedge of sky. "All set?"

"Yes," she whispered. "I lit the first fuse just as you told me. Shouldn't it have gone off by now?"

"Any second." He closed the door behind him.

"What do we do now?"

"We get out of the line of fire." He drew her to the corner of the foyer farthest from the staircase. "And then we wait."

They didn't have to wait long. Patrick had scarcely gotten the words out when there was an explosion!

"Here we go," Patrick murmured over the barrage of explosions. "How's this for a statement, Elspeth?"

The first explosion jerked Dominic from sleep. Gunfire. In the hall outside. He moved with the sure instinct that had guided him for the last ten years. By the time of the second explosion, he was on his feet reaching for his gunbelt. When the third explosion rocked the hall, he was at the door.

"Dominic," Rina said sleepily. She sat up and brushed a shining brown lock of hair from her cheek. "What the hell—" She broke off as another explosion jarred her fully awake. "No, Dom, don't go out there." She jumped out of bed, reaching hurriedly for her lacy peignoir.

Dominic wasn't listening. All his senses were strained toward the danger in the hall. God, he was tired of this. Tired of never going to sleep without worrying if he'd face gunfire when he woke. He yanked open the door, stepping quickly to the side to avoid a possible spate of gunshots. The explosions continued, but there were no bullets sailing through the air, impacting floors and woodwork. He cautiously looked around the doorframe. The hall was filled with smoke and the explosions weren't coming from a gun. He stared blankly at the string of explosives on the floor going off one after the other. "Firecrackers!"

"What?" Rina was beside him. "Who would do a thing like this?"

He didn't have to consider the possibilities for more than a minute. He had been in the Nugget when Patrick and his friends had ridden through the doors on horseback throwing firecrackers right and left. "For Patrick, every day is a day for celebration," he said dryly. "I imagine this was his way of bidding us a fond good-bye until next week. But, if I know my nephew, he wouldn't be able to resist staying and watching the fun." He was striding down the hall following the exploding string of firecrackers. "And when I catch up with him, I'm going to tie a string of firecrackers to *his* tail." The explosions had reached the head of the stairs and so had he. He called down into the dimness at the foot of the stairwell. "Patrick, I'm about to lift your scalp."

He thought he heard a shout of laughter amid the explosions sparking down the stairs. It didn't improve his temper. He started down but was forced to move slowly to keep behind the exploding firecrackers. "Did you consider the possibility you might have set the house on fire? Or that someone could have started shooting before they realized it was a tom-fool trick?"

"It wasn't Patrick's fault, Mr. Delaney." Elspeth moved out of the shadowed hallway to the foot of the stairs. She stood very straight, her eyes fixed on him as if mesmerized. "This was entirely my idea."

She could barely get the words past her dry throat. She had never seen a real live man naked, and Dominic Delaney was boldly and unashamedly naked. "I've come to ask you to reconsider."

The expression of stunned surprise on his face was superceded by a fierce look. "The hell you have." He started down the steps toward her, each word punctuated by the explosion of the firecrackers. "I don't like women who use their sex as a shield to invade a man's privacy and put him at a disadvantage. I don't like it one bit."

"You said you wouldn't see me. I had to do something to change the state of things."

In case you didn't hear me the first time, the answer is *no*." His blue-gray eyes glinted fiercely through the smoke. "But you knew it would be no, didn't you, Miss Elspeth MacGregor?"

"Yes, but it appeared to be the only way to get you to take my offer seriously."

"Dom, what's going on?" asked a lovely brown-haired woman clad in a blue lace peignoir from the top of the steps. Her gaze fell on Elspeth's prim, black-gowned figure at the bottom of the stairs. "Jesus, what's happened?"

"Nothing to concern you, Rina. Go on back to bed." Dominic Delaney's gaze never wavered from Elspeth. "I'll take care of this."

There were other faces peering over the banisters now, but Elspeth was scarcely aware of them. All her attention was focused on the naked man coming down the stairs toward her. She was exquisitely conscious of everything about him. The sleek ripple of the muscles of his thighs, the way his chest moved in and out with each breath. His strange eyes gazing at her with insolence and anger and something else.

The Delaneys, The Untamed Years:
WILD SILVER

by Iris Johansen

Mikhail, Nicholas's servant and friend, threw open the door to the cabin and strode into the stateroom. Nicholas rose easily to his feet, his gaze on the bundle over the giant's shoulder. "Good Lord, Mikhail, did you have to use two blankets? She must be smothering."

"I should have used ten," Mikhail muttered as he strode across the room and dropped his burden on the bed. "And I should have let you come with me. I should have let an army come with me." He unwrapped the blankets with two quick jerks and Silver tumbled free, rolling over to the opposite side of the bed. Her wrists were tied behind her back and a handkerchief gagged her mouth, but her eyes blazed up at them as she continued to struggle to free herself. Mikhail tossed the blankets on the floor and reached over to pull the gag from Silver's mouth, quickly jerking his hand away as her strong, white teeth snapped at him. "She is a wild animal." There was a curious note of pride in his voice as he gazed down at Silver's face. "If I had not taken her by surprise, I do not think I would have been able to overpower her. She is a fine, strong warrior." He carefully brushed a strand of hair from Silver's eyes, his expression gentle. "It is all right now. No one is going to hurt you."

"But *I* will hurt you." Silver glared up at him fiercely, still struggling desperately against her bonds. "You can't do this!"

"It appears that he can, because he has." Nicholas strode forward to stand over her. Her long hair was lying in wild, silken disarray against the peach-colored velvet of the spread, and he felt a sudden thrust of desire tighten his groin. He had been sitting there, imagining how she would look lying on his bed, and the reality was even more erotic than his vision. "Though not without some effort."

"You!" Her light eyes glittered with rage as she began to curse him with venom and amazing proficiency.

He lifted a brow. "My, my, she's quite talented, isn't she, Mikhail? The last time I heard a vocabulary so explicit was from my groom at the estate on Crystal Island. Should we release her, do you think?"

"Only if you wish to relieve yourself of a few fistfuls of excess hair," Mikhail said dryly, gingerly touching his own tousled red mop. "Before I got her hands tied I was sure she would strip me bald. Best wait until you have talked reason to her."

"Reason?" Silver struggled into a sitting position. "There is no reason connected with this outrage. It's madness, as I'll soon show you."

"I'm sure you'll try." Nicholas smiled. "And it will be fascinating to watch your attempts. I may even be sorry to see you depart after you tell me where your uncle has disappeared to."

"You'll be sorrier to see me stay," Silver hissed.

A flicker of anger crossed Nicholas's handsome face. "I believe you're beginning to annoy me. So far you've cursed me, threatened me, and insulted me."

"Let me loose and I'll do more than that to you. I'll stick my knife in you, as I did your friend."

Nicholas stiffened. "Knife?" His gaze flew to Mikhail. "She *stabbed* you?" His attention had been so absorbed with the girl he had scarcely glanced at Mikhail. Now he saw that the Cossack's tunic was torn, and a rivulet of blood stained the whiteness of the left sleeve.

"A pinprick." Mikhail bent down, pulled a small dagger out of his boot, and tossed it to Nicholas. "Yet it might be wise to remember she is not without fangs."

"Like all vipers." Nicholas looked down at the dagger, his beautifully molded features hard as the marble of a tombstone. "She could have killed you. I should have gone myself, my friend."

A touch of anxiety clouded Mikhail's features. "A pinprick," he repeated. "She was only defending herself. The wound will be gone by tomorrow."

Bewilderment pierced Silver's seething fury. It was clear the big Russian was defending her from Nicholas Savron's anger. Why would he help the prince abduct her and then rush to her defense?

"Do you need a doctor?" Nicholas asked gently. "I'll have Robert dock again and send someone for help."

"The woman—"

"The woman is not worth one drop of your blood." Nicholas gave Silver a glance as cold as winter sleet. "I will deal with her later."

Mikhail shook his head. "I have no need for a doctor. She did not hurt me."

"Only because you—" Silver broke off as Mikhail shook his head warningly at her. "I *will* speak. Do you think I'm afraid of either of you?"

"You obviously have no need to fear Mikhail. It seems he's been foolish enough to take a liking to you," Nicholas said softly. "But you'd do well to be afraid of me. I value Mikhail, and I don't think I've ever been quite so angry with anyone in my entire life."

"Liking? He *abducted* me."

"On my orders. And he insisted on going alone, because he felt it would be safer for you."

"Or because you were too cowardly to go with him," Silver said contemptuously.

Mikhail inhaled sharply and took an impulsive step forward, as if to place himself between Silver and Nicholas. "Nicholas, she is only a woman. She did not—"

"Only a woman," Silver repeated indignantly. "A woman can do anything a man can do! She can do more! Why do—"

"*Shut up!*" Nicholas shouted, enunciating with great precision.

"I should not have taken the gag off her." Mikhail sighed morosely. "I should have known her tongue would be as sharp as her dagger."

"Go take care of your wound." Nicholas's gaze was narrowed on Silver's face. "I have a fancy to prove myself to the lady."

Mikhail gazed at him helplessly. Nicholas was dangerously infuriated, and it was evident that Silver Delaney was not about to try to placate him. "You gave your word."

Nicholas glanced at him incredulously. "Good Lord—she stabbed you and you're still defending her?"

Mikhail's jaw squared stubbornly. "You promised me."

Nicholas muttered something fierce and obscene beneath his breath. "And I'll keep my word, dammit."

Mikhail turned toward the door, and then glanced over his shoulder at Silver, a gentle smile lighting his craggy features. "I will be back soon. Do not be afraid."

Silver gazed at him. "I'm not afraid and I need no protection."

Mikhail slowly shook his head and shut the door quietly behind him.

Silver immediately turned to Nicholas and opened her mouth to speak.

Nicholas raised his hand. "Not one word, or I'll put the gag back on you."

She hesitated, and then pressed her lips together.

"Very wise. I'm holding on to my temper by a very precarious thread, Silver."

He sat down on the bed beside her, not touching her, but close enough so that she could feel the heat emanating from his body. The faint scent of musk, brandy, and tobacco drifted to her nostrils.

"I'm about to give you the rules that will govern your stay while you're on the *Rose*. Are you listening?"

She gazed up at him mutinously.

"I see you are." He smiled faintly. "First, let's discuss why you're here."

"You want Dominic."

"Exactly. I suppose I should give you the option of telling me where he is."

"Would you let me go if I did?"

"I'm afraid I'd be forced to do so. Do you wish to oblige?"

Silver drew a deep breath. Lord, she hated lies. Still, if it would give Dominic a little more time . . . "He and Elspeth went back to Killara, in the Arizona Territory."

Nicholas's expression hardened. "I see you're as prone to falsehood as the rest of your sex. Randall's investigators ascertained that your uncle was most definitely not at Killara. It's obvious that asking you for the truth will accomplish nothing, and I admit I'm a trifle disappointed. I thought you more honest than most."

A flush stung Silver's cheeks. "I'm honest with those I respect. You deserve only lies from me. I'll tell you nothing about Dominic."

"But when he finds you're gone from Mrs. Alford's nunnery, I'd say there's an excellent chance of him coming after you," he said softly. "I posted a letter to your former headmistress, telling her you'd decided to accompany me on a little pleasure cruise. If he's as loyal to you as you are to him, he should be waiting at the levee when we return to St. Louis."

"He won't even hear that I'm gone. There wouldn't be—" She stopped. "You'll be disappointed if you think you can use me to draw Dominic to you."

His gaze centered on her face. "You seem very certain." He shrugged. "No matter. Then you'll remain on the *Rose* until you tell me where he is."

"You can't keep me here."

"Oh, but I can. Shall I tell you how?" Nicholas's long, shapely hand reached out and smoothed her hair back from one temple, his touch as delicate as the brush of the wings of a butterfly. "There is no one to help you here. This boat belongs to me, and you'll find no one interested in any plea for aid. Mikhail and my friend Valentin are completely loyal to me. And the crew would lose very lucrative positions if they displeased me."

So she would be alone in her struggle. For a moment she felt a tiny *frisson* of apprehension. She dismissed it impatiently. Her struggles had always been faced alone, except when Rising Star had been there to support her. This was no different. "I don't need help. I'll still get away from you."

A flicker of admiration crossed his face. "No tears? No pleas? I can almost see why Mikhail has developed a fondness for you."

"I never cry." She met his gaze. "And you will never hear me plead."

"Oh, but I will." Passion flared in the darkness of his eyes. "And it will be my very great pleasure to grant those pleas."

The Delaneys, The Untamed Years:
COPPER FIRE

by Fayrene Preston

Minutes later Brianne closed the door to her room, then leaned back against it. Across the room, Sloan sat. He was so still he might have been dead—except for his eyes. They were blazing with a fiery, golden life. She should say something, she mused, but for the life of her, she couldn't think of anything. So she waited.

"Did you get your gentleman friend settled?" he asked in a voice that was very low and quite calm.

"I don't know him well enough to call him a friend. And yes, he's in his room."

"No doubt in one of Mrs. Potter's finest."

"He's on this floor," she admitted, thinking that she had never known anyone who could manage to convey so much displeasure without using a trace of emotion in his voice. "But he's at the other end of the hall."

"I must confess, I'm surprised."

"Oh?" She pushed away from the door and walked to the edge of the bed. "At what?"

"That you can still manage to stand upright with the problems of so many people weighing on your shoulders."

"Henrietta and Phineas are no burden."

He came up out of his chair and was standing in front of her before she had a chance to blink. "You little fool! Don't you know the jeopardy you put yourself in by stopping to help a strange man?"

"I couldn't just pass him by!"

Gripping her shoulders, he spoke from between clenched teeth. "Not only should you have passed him by, you should have ridden so wide a circle around him, he wouldn't have even known you were in the area!"

She wrenched out of his hold. "I wasn't going to leave someone alone out there who needed help!"

"No, of course you wouldn't! That would have been the sensible thing to do, wouldn't it?"

"Sloan! I was raised to take care of myself. I can put a bullet in the center of an ace of spades at a hundred paces."

"But can you put a bullet in a man's heart?"

"If I have to."

"I don't believe you."

Swiftly, Brianne moved to where her gear was piled and jerked up her rifle. Pointing it straight at his heart, she asked, "Do you want me to prove it?"

He smiled, and his voice softened. "You wouldn't even get that rifle cocked, redhead."

She believed him, and tossed the rifle down. "Get out, Sloan."

"When I'm good and ready."

Brianne exploded. "I don't understand you!"

Sloan didn't understand himself either. And he didn't understand her. She was standing within arm's reach of him, her hair streaming in wild glory down her back, her skin giving off the sweetly seducing fragrance he had first smelled when he had seen her rising from her bath. Only a thin sash held her robe around her, and delicate satin ribbons closed her gown over her breasts.

Angry at her for putting herself in danger, and angry at himself for being angry, he reached for her.

She didn't come to him easily. She pushed against him, fighting with all her might. But his strength was the greater, and so was his need.

His mouth crushed down on hers, his powerful arms pulled her tightly against him. Reason wasn't entirely lost, but what was left was fogged by a pounding desire. He stripped off her robe, then fell with her onto the bed.

Brianne felt the impact of the mattress against her back and was furious. She didn't want to feel the weight of his leg as it lay over hers. She didn't want to experience the rub of his tongue against her own. She didn't want to feel his hand covering her breast. She didn't! She didn't!

Sloan's fingers grasped a ribboned bow and pulled. So easy. He untied another, and another, until he could lay the edges of the gown back, baring her breasts. He tore his mouth away from her lips so that he could see her, and what he saw nearly took his breath away. No woman could be so perfectly formed, he thought. It had to be an illusion.

Brianne raised her fist and hit against Sloan's chest, but the blow had all the force of a puff of wind. When had she become so weak? she wondered. When had she become so hot?

"Stop," she said, in a voice that sounded more like an entreaty than an order. "Please . . ."

Gazing into her emerald-green eyes, Sloan saw that they had softened. He liked that look. "I don't want to stop, Brianne." A soft breath escaped her lips, and he tried to capture it with his mouth. "Say please again," he whispered against her lips.

Desire was a new sensation to Brianne. How easy it would be to give in to it; heat was exploding everywhere in her. Yet she couldn't surrender. It wasn't in her makeup.

She tried to twist away, but with one strong arm he brought her back. She rolled her head, trying to escape his mouth. "Stop it, Sloan. Now!" Her words were whispered, but he heard.

He raised his head again to look at her, but he kept his hand on her breast, as if he had no intention of letting her go. "I want you, Brianne."

"But I don't want you!"

He smiled. "I can make you want me, and I won't even have to work at it." To prove his point, he caressed her slowly, teasingly. She moaned. "See?" he murmured.

Brianne looked up at him and was immediately confused. How could Sloan's face remain so hard, even while he was seducing her, *even while he was smiling?*

Then, as if a flash of light had suddenly sought out and revealed the darkest place in her mind, she remembered why his smile seemed so familiar to her. She had seen that same smile on the only living thing that had ever hurt her—a wolf. He had looked at her with pale gold eyes and a teeth-baring smile right before he sank his teeth into her arm, tearing at her flesh.

The memory gave her back her strength. In the space of two heartbeats she rolled off the bed, lunged for the rifle, aimed it right at his heart, and thumbed back the hammer. "This is a Model 1873 Winchester .44/40," she said, "and it is now cocked, with a bullet in the chamber and fifteen more behind it." A forceful and cool assurance filled her voice.

With her face flushed with anger, her gown gaping open and exposing heaving breasts tipped by rigid nipples, Sloan thought he had never seen a more beautiful woman in his life. God, but he wanted her!

"Mrs. Porter is going to be awfully upset if she finds blood splattered all over this room," he said calmly.

"I'll buy this damn hotel if it comes to that! Now, get up, Sloan, and get out of here."

He sat up, slid to the edge of the bed, and stood up. Slowly, he walked toward her, stopping only when the barrel of the rifle was touching his chest. "You're an interesting lady, redhead. You're wealthy enough to buy a hotel, you have guts enough to shoot me, and you're beautiful enough to make me want you like I've never wanted another woman. I'll leave for now, but I'll be back. We're not through, you and I. Not nearly."

OFFICIAL DELANEYS, THE UNTAMED YEARS
MISSISSIPPI QUEEN RIVERBOAT CRUISE
SWEEPSTAKES RULES

1. NO PURCHASE NECESSARY. Enter by completing the Official Entry Form below (or print your name, address, date of birth and telephone number on a plain 3"x 5" card) and send to:

> Bantam Books
> Delaneys, THE UNTAMED YEARS Sweepstakes
> Dept. HBG
> 666 Fifth Avenue
> New York, NY 10103

2. One Grand Prize will be awarded. There will be no prize substitutions or cash equivalents permitted. Grand Prize is a 7-night riverboat cruise for two on the luxury steamboat, The Mississippi Queen. Double occupancy accommodations, meals and on-board entertainment included. Round trip airfare provided by Reliable Travel International, Inc. (Estimated retail value $5,500.00. Exact value depends on actual point of departure.)

3. All entries must be postmarked and received by Bantam Books no later than August 1, 1988. The winner, chosen by random drawing, will be announced and notified by November 30, 1988. Trip must be completed by December 31, 1989, and is subject to space availability determined by Delta Queen Steamboat Company, and airline space availability determined by Reliable Travel International. If the Grand Prize winner is under 21 years of age on August 1, 1988, he/she must be accompanied by a parent or guardian. Taxes on the prize are the sole responsibility of the winner. Odds of winning depend on the number of completed entries received. Enter as often as you wish, but each entry must be mailed separately. Bantam Books is not responsible for lost, misdirected or incomplete entries.

4. The sweepstakes is open to residents of the U.S. and Canada, except the Province of Quebec, and is void where prohibited by law. If the winner is a Canadian he/she will be required to correctly answer a skill question in order to receive the prize. All federal, state and local regulations apply. Employees of Reliable Travel International, The Delta Queen Steamboat Co., and Bantam, Doubleday, Dell Publishing Group, Inc., their subsidiary and affiliates, and their immediate families are ineligible to enter.

5. The winner may be required to submit an Affidavit of Eligibility and Promotional Release supplied by Bantam Books. The winner's name and likeness may be used for publicity purposes without additional compensation.

6. For an extra copy of the Official Rules and Entry Form, send a self-addressed stamped envelope (Washington and Vermont Residents need not affix postage) by June 15, 1988 to:

> Bantam Books
> Delaneys, THE UNTAMED YEARS Sweepstakes
> Dept. HBG
> 666 Fifth Avenue
> New York, NY 10103

- -

OFFICIAL ENTRY FORM
DELANEYS, THE UNTAMED YEARS
MISSISSIPPI QUEEN RIVERBOAT CRUISE SWEEPSTAKES

Name_____

Address_____

City_____ State_____ Zip Code_____

SW'10

THE DELANEY DYNASTY

where it all began . . .

Six daringly original novels written by three of the most successful romance writers today—Kay Hooper, Iris Johansen and Fayrene Preston.

THE SHAMROCK TRINITY

Heirs to a great dynasty, the Delaney brothers were united by blood, united by devotion to their rugged land and to the women they loved.

RAFE, THE MAVERICK by Kay Hooper
YORK, THE RENEGADE by Iris Johansen
BURKE, THE KINGPIN by Fayrene Preston

THE DELANEYS OF KILAROO

Three dazzling sisters, heirs to a rich and savage land, determined to fight for their birthright, destined to find wild and wonderful love . . .

ADELAIDE, THE ENCHANTRESS by
  Kay Hooper
MATILDA, THE ADVENTURESS by
  Iris Johansen
SYDNEY, THE TEMPTRESS by
  Fayrene Preston

THE DELANEYS . . . men and women whose loves and passions are so glorious it takes many great romance novels by three bestselling authors to tell their tempestuous stories.

Ask your bookseller for these Bantam books or use the handy coupon on the last page of this sampler to order.

The birth of the Delaney Dynasty

Iris Johansen sets the historical stage for the love stories of the colorful founders of the Delaney Dynasty that continue in trilogies from all three authors.

DON'T MISS THE ENTHRALLING

by Iris Johansen

☐ 26991 / $3.95

Scottish beauty Elspeth MacGregor travels to Hell's Bluff to hire Dominic Delaney to lead her to the magical lost city of Kantalan, but at first he refuses—the last thing he needs is to join a virginal scholar on a dangerous quest.

But Elspeth's fiery will coupled with her silky hair and milk-white skin prove irresistible, and Dominic acts—first with angry lust, then with a searing yet tender passion that brands her eternal soul and bonds them both to a heated and turbulent future.

Through wonders and tragedy, across the untamed splendors of Arizona and Mexico, Elspeth and Dominic draw closer to their dual destiny: to experience the dark mysteries and magnificent riches of Kantalan . . . and to fulfill the promise of lasting love and the birth of a bold family dynasty.

> "**SPLENDOR** is special—refreshing, riveting, fascinating.
> I loved it and hated to see it end."
> —*Johanna Lindsey*

- -